Pursued in Paris

ALSO BY SYDNEY JANE BAILY

The RAKES ON THE RUN Series
Last Dance in London
Pursued in Paris
Banished to Brighton
Gretna Green by Sunset

The DIAMONDS OF THE FIRST WATER Series
Clarity
Purity
Adam
Radiance
Brilliance

The RARE CONFECTIONERY Series
The Duchess of Chocolate
The Toffee Heiress
My Lady Marzipan

The DEFIANT HEARTS Series
An Improper Situation
An Irresistible Temptation
An Inescapable Attraction
An Inconceivable Deception
An Intriguing Proposition
An Impassioned Redemption

The BEASTLY LORDS Series
Lord Despair
Lord Anguish
Lord Vile
Lord Darkness
Lord Misery
Lord Wrath
Lord Corsair
Eleanor

RAKES ON THE RUN

SYDNEY JANE BAILY

cat whisker press
Massachusetts

Second Paperback Edition
ISBN 978-1-957421-28-5

Published by Cat Whisker Press

Cover: Victoria Cooper Art
Book Design: Cat Whisker Studio
Editor: Chloe Bearuski

DEDICATION

To Victor Baily
My dad's *first* little brother

I love you!

ACKNOWLEDGMENTS

Once again, thanks to Philip Ré, who listens to my story ideas and gives instant feedback, and to Toni Young, who reads a rough draft before I'm ready to let anyone else see it. Also, I'm grateful to Lana Birky and Zena Carroll for performing beta reads. And, as always, thanks to my beloved mom, Beryl Baily, who loves me unconditionally.

PROLOGUE

1814, Wiltshire, England

"Send her to France," ordered Serena's father. Lord Elmstead's tone would brook no argument.

From the other side of the slightly open door, she heard those words sealing her fate, and then her mother's anguished reply.

"But the danger, Edward."

"Far more dangerous here. She has been compromised by that half-wit. All of London is sniffing out the scandal, and if we don't get her away, they shan't let it drop."

"It was only a walk in Vauxhall Gardens," her mother persisted.

"In the dark, Hélène, away from the lanterns, alone with that rake of a man."

Serena sighed quietly. She'd shown extremely poor judgment, indeed, but the man's words had been so smooth and his smile so charming. *How could she know his true intent when no one warned her?*

In seconds, he'd become like that terrifying, multi-limbed sea monster, the squid, with one hand holding her against a tree, another attempting to reach under her gown, and somehow, a third stroking her cheek. Or so she recalled.

When his lips touched hers, she'd fled, not realizing her state of disarray nor that she had a leaf or two and a twig in her curls until she re-entered the Vauxhall pavilion at a trot, searching for her dear mother.

Immediately, people had pointed, and the whispers behind their colorful fans had begun. The following morning, *The Gazette* mentioned a ruined girl with her initials, and her father had been livid ever since, demanding his wife and daughter return to the country, interrupting Serena's first Season.

A week had passed since Serena along with her two younger brothers and her mother had returned to the family estate in Wiltshire, and her father had arrived from London the night before to say the *ton* was still chewing on the scandal, just waiting for Serena to return so they could pounce. And now, she knew his decree.

"It wasn't her first transgression," Lord Elmstead reminded his wife. "She is too flighty. She has behaved immaturely on more than one occasion and nearly came to ruin last month. She is gaining a reputation, Hélène. To protect her, we must get her out of the vultures' reach."

Serena bit her lip. Her father was right. She had treated the entire London season as a silly lark. After being presented at court, she'd been concerned only with dancing and dandies, champagne and kisses.

"With your parents, she can be an ordinary young woman, like you were." Then he quickly added, "Not that I ever thought you were anything but extraordinary." There was a pause while Serena knew her parents were sharing a loving kiss as they often did. Yet when her father continued, his stern stance hadn't changed.

"Paris has no Season to speak of. Instead of London's nobs and their shallow *bon ton*, there is merely *le bon genre* of which our daughter will most certainly not be a part. And there are far fewer scandal sheets."

"What if war breaks out again," her mother asked, "and Serena is trapped in France?"

"You're just coming up with excuses," her father said. "She is half-French and speaks like a native. She'll be perfectly safe with your parents. Besides, Bonaparte is securely in exile. How could war break out again?"

CHAPTER ONE

March 1815, Paris, France

Malcolm slipped through the streets of Paris in the dimming light of dusk, wishing he were back in London at White's or Boodle's with a glass of brandy in anticipation of a late night with a talented Cyprian.

Not that Paris didn't have its own outstanding courtesans, but he doubted he would be relaxing enough to enjoy the fair sex while on this mission for the Crown. It was a damn nuisance, all this cloak and dagger stuff, when Bonaparte had been taken care of once already. Only with either great incompetence or, more likely, the cooperation of his captors could the former emperor have escaped his exile on the Island of Elba.

In any case, Bonaparte was en route to Paris, which was putting a bit of a crimp in the coalition's celebratory air in Vienna, not to mention causing the new French king all manner of indigestion.

And Britain's Prince Regent was determined not to let his old foe return to power. If Malcolm could prevent such or, at least, bring a new Napoleonic rule to a swift end, then Prinny would be in his debt. Again.

And in the back of his mind was the hope this would be his last such adventure. At twenty-nine, he'd spent the better part of a decade serving the Crown, regardless of whether it was upon mad King George's head or his profligate son's. And by God, Malcolm had his own small empire to run, as the eldest son of the Viscount St. John.

He'd avoided the parson's noose so far, but his parents were increasingly demanding he fulfill his duty in that regard. This past Season, he'd even gone to a few insipid balls and now had two potential mates in mind, both eminently suitable with extremely pretty faces—Lady Dreadfully Dull, with her slender waist but off-putting vacant stare, indicating how little thought went on between her ears, and Lady Terribly Tedious, who could talk up a blue storm about anything and everyone, but had absolutely nothing interesting to say in the very many words she used. Still, she had full breasts to recommend her and was an earl's daughter.

Malcolm sighed. His joyful, single life as a raffish bachelor must come to an end, another reason he would bloody well rather be home to enjoy his last few months of freedom, depending on how long he could delay the process of choosing a wife. And Paris, as everyone agreed, was cramped and uncomfortable, not only its streets but also its buildings. The houses were miserable, the streets narrow, and there were no pavements in the so-called modern capital of the French Empire, thus one very often—

"Oof!" He ran directly into a small figure in a very large cloak, knocking the person down.

"*Je m'excuse,*" he said, offering his best apology as it had certainly been his fault, letting his thoughts drift when he ought to have them firmly on the mission at hand.

A torrent of angry French came from the figure, a woman's voice, so he instantly recalled his gentlemanly upbringing and helped her to her feet.

In doing so, her hood fell back, revealing a riotous mass of copper-colored tresses barely tamed in a chignon that was now half down across her right shoulder.

"*Êtes-vous blessé?*" he asked, hoping he hadn't injured her.

"*Non,*" she returned, quickly drawing up her hood and covering her head again.

For a moment, he thought her actions furtive, but there was a distinct chill in the March air, and he reminded himself he'd been sneaking around too long. Everyone seemed suspicious.

"*Après vous,*" he said with a gesture of his hand, indicating she should go along wherever she might be going, and he would bother her no more.

Nodding, although he could no longer see her face, to his surprise she went the very direction he'd been going, into the Galerie de Beaujolais arcade of the Palais-Royal, hurrying along past shops filled with jewelry and fine furniture, past billiard parlors, perfumeries, and sweet shops.

Perhaps she was a hard-working *grisette*, although it was too late for a shopgirl to be going to work.

Malcolm was struggling with the alternative, that she was a whore. For some reason, either her delicate beauty or the quick glimpse he'd had of her intelligent eyes, he hoped she wasn't one of the famed Palais-Royal prostitutes. On the other hand, that might mean he could meet up with her later.

Quick as a blink, she ducked into the doorway of the same restaurant that was his destination.

The devil! The lovely lass would think he was following her. He hesitated as the door of the Café de Chartres closed in his face. Waiting a mere five seconds, Malcolm pushed it open.

Nodding to the doorman, Malcom took a right into the establishment. The main floor was crowded, the tables filled with diners. And the female had already disappeared into the interior.

As on previous visits, he went to the back of the dining room to the familiar, black-painted staircase and ascended. Upstairs the fancy decorations, the statues and gilded objects, the extravagant floor tile, crystal, and china of the ground floor all vanished. Instead, there were plain wooden tables and comfortable chairs, at least in the rooms Malcolm had seen. As before, he was greeted by a nod and a wink and went past the armed man to the next room.

"Lord Branley, you have arrived at last," came the familiar and always cheerful voice of another of His Majesty's finest, Lord Herbert Randall.

"At last!" Malcolm quipped. "I received my orders less than thirty-six hours ago, and here I am, Randall. At your service as always."

The man laughed. "Not *my* service, surely. But what you do for Britain—what we all do—is well-appreciated. Now more than ever. If we're not careful, dark times are coming."

"Along with Bonaparte apparently," Malcolm agreed. "I hear he will be in the city before the month's end."

Randall nodded. "It would seem so." He glanced at the other men seated at the table. Directly to his left was General Scovell, one of Wellington's most effective intelligence officers and a codebreaker extraordinaire.

"General," Malcolm greeted him.

"Branley," the man returned with a nod. Then he stood. "I have to prepare for departure," he said, looking rueful. "I've been assigned as the Bourbon king's nanny."

Randall laughed and explained to Malcolm, "General Scovell is taking King Louis to a safe place, hopefully in England, along with members of the royal family."

There was no doubt then—they all believed the emperor would make it back to Paris.

Scovell left with a resigned shake of his head.

"Sit," Randall invited Malcolm.

He complied, noticing the map of the Continent laid out with markings and circles and some regions crossed out. Regardless of whether it was Napoleon's fault, his power caused the countries around him to wage war with him and sometimes with each other, destabilizing Europe. And now the great nations of Europe had formed the Seventh Coalition, deciding on their own that the French people did not want the emperor to reign over them once more.

Naturally, their own Prince Regent, like King George before him, wanted Bonaparte squashed before he grew so powerful he tried to launch an attack on British shores. Again!

Malcolm recognized the other man at the table, Jules Versanne, a French royalist. He had earned the trust of Bonaparte until his exile to Elba, nine months prior. Most of the men who'd worked secretly to overthrow the emperor and bring peace to the Continent had been exposed during the emperor's banishment, and now they were unable to perform the same duty a second time.

"Monsieur Versanne," Malcolm greeted the somber man, so different from the always sunny Lord Randall. "You look well."

The Frenchman's face turned bitter. "*Bah!* You lie as if I am a lover you are trying to woo into your bed," Versanne spoke in heavily accented English. "I do *not* look well at all, *Anglais*. And I feel even worse. Idiots!" he raised his voice. "The Fifth Infantry Regiment defected to our little emperor a few days ago and then the Seventh Infantry the following day. It's insupportable. As if we are starting over, and it is March 1814 instead of 1815. *Bah!*" He picked up the glass of wine before him and drank it down.

Malcolm locked gazes with Randall and raised an eyebrow.

"Monsieur Versanne brought word the Duke of Angoulême, heading up the royalist army, failed to stop Bonaparte in the southern Rhône River valley," Randall filled Malcolm in. "And now this latest intelligence bodes poorly for the coalition. So, gentlemen, the eagle is coming."

Malcolm felt a twist in his gut. He'd known it was inevitable, but the smallest part of him had held a spark of hope the French royalist armies could get the job done without the rest of the world having to get involved.

"Do you have a plan?" Malcolm asked Randall.

The man grinned. "Of course! We even have rumblings the Fox is in the mix helping out our side."

The French patriot, le Renard, practically a mythological figure! No one knew his identity, but he'd been working to provide intelligence and given a helpful nudge to daily events in one direction or another as far back as the Revolution two decades earlier.

"But there is no stopping Boney reaching the city," Randall continued. "We can only put people in place and wait for the emperor to get here."

"Him *and* his army," muttered the Frenchman.

"I cannot blame the army for defecting," Randall said. "Louis put his officers on half pay and disbanded most of the standing troops."

"It shall be harder to infiltrate this time," Malcolm pointed out. "Bonaparte will trust no one who wasn't exiled along with him or imprisoned by the king."

"Maybe Boney will accept new converts to his cause," Randall suggested. "His arrogance is such he'll believe those who now say they reject the Bourbon king. Let us face the facts, Louis did himself no favors this past year and alienated many who were hoping for a new start. Speaking of such, Talleyrand will not be forgiven by the emperor. He had best remain in Vienna."

Randall was correct about that. Talleyrand had managed to squeak through the dreadful Revolution without losing his own head. Then he rose to power with Napoleon before seeing how the wind was shifting. With the emperor's impending loss of power, Talleyrand helped King Louis claim the throne and restore stability. The man was either a traitor many times over or a skilled diplomat, or both.

"Whom does he serve now?" Malcolm asked idly.

Versanne shook his head. "Talleyrand serves France, as he should. Her interests above all. Like Fouché, who is talking out of both sides of his mouth, helping the king's brother and, by all accounts, already in communication with Bonaparte."

"What are they saying back in Britain?" asked Randall.

"Rather amusing actually," Malcolm told him. "The newspaper editors were caught with their pants down, still running pieces celebrating the end of Boney in the morning edition and then swallowing crow to write how he was coming back by the afternoon paper. I think word reached us just about the same time as Dover saw boats full of scared British swarming back across the Channel. So much for London's quality folk claiming the restaurants and culture of Paris."

The men chuckled.

"But sadly, our skilled Mr. Gillray can no longer portray the truth in his scathing drawings," Malcolm told him.

Randall cocked his head. "He didn't die, did he?"

"Nearly. Our favorite satirist is mad as a march hare," Malcolm declared. "Thus, no helpful caricatures from him. Having Gillray anger Boney was half the fun."

"The fun?" exclaimed Versanne. "You English are all mad, if you ask me. There is no fun in any of this."

Malcolm rolled his eyes. The Gallic nature of his associate was both too serious and too passionate as far as he was concerned. But Versanne was a solid gatherer of intelligence and absolutely indispensable.

"Luckily, we still have Mr. Cruikshank. Undoubtedly, his scornful wit shall be directed against all those who let Bonaparte return." Malcolm imagined neither the British nor the Russians nor the Prussians nor even the Bourbon royals would escape the pen of the popular caricaturist.

"Rightly so," Randall said. "This is a colossal debacle, and precisely when I was heading home, too. I've got responsibilities awaiting me in London. In any case, gentlemen, we need to wrap it up before the autumn. Prinny and Parliament refuse to sink a second fortune into fighting Boney. Thus, let us get to work. We no longer have our great

Admiral Nelson, but we have Wellington, by God, and he's going to kick some arse."

"And we have Scovell," Malcolm gestured his head toward the stairs, by which the clever English general had descended. He'd broken two of the codes used by Napoleon to communicate operations with his troops. "Smart to task him with protecting King Louis and taking him to safety if need be."

"Oh, there will be a need, *Anglais*," Versanne said quietly. "I have no doubt of that."

Randall stood up abruptly. "I'll go get more wine. Are you hungry, Branley? We're in the best restaurant in Paris, you might as well get a good meal."

And then the real work would begin. They would create a list—memorized but not written down—of all those who could be moved into position to gather intelligence, including those who might even still be embedded in the armed forces. With any luck, they'd switched sides in support of Boney for appearance's sake only.

After two hours, Malcolm was ready to go to his nearby lodging.

SERENA COULD FEEL THE heightened emotions of her fellow citizens. The anxiety in Paris was palpable. There were those who'd spent the past nine months during the emperor's exile convincing the royalists in power that they had never supported him despite all he'd done for the capital.

Not only bureaucrats and government officials, but also shopkeepers and café owners now wondered if they would be able to convince Bonaparte of their joy at his return and of their loyalty. Switching sides successfully was a dangerous attempt, like tiptoeing along the edge of a sword.

Fortunately, Serena didn't have that worry. Her grandparents sold their wine from the large storehouses at La Halle aux Vins, which in turn distributed it all over Paris. Napoleon had been their champion, as wine provided stability to the economy, as well as a soothing balm to the masses and the aristocrats alike. It was considered the third staple of any Parisian's life, along with bread and meat. Thus, Bonaparte had ordered the wine hall enlarged and improved, securing the wine-producers loyalty during the past decade.

Having concluded her business with the owner of the Café de Chartres, making sure she had the wine order to give her grand-père, Serena was seated at a table, enjoying a free plate of the chef's *spécialité* of the night, sole with truffle coulis. Friends had arrived, and she was in no hurry to return to the modest-sized apartment she shared with her grandparents, preferring their manor house in the Loire Valley, where their well-run vineyard and winery were located. In Saint-George-sur-Loire, it was easier to breathe, to feel the sun, to hear oneself think—and it simply smelled better. Nevertheless, it didn't have the energy and excitement of Paris!

Listening to Guillaume, Suzanne, Felicity, and Jean-Paul chatter on about Napoleon's impending triumphant return, Serena remained quiet with nothing to add or at least, nothing she could tell them nor say to anyone outside of her family, for that matter.

Her family. She frowned at the thought. Her parents had sent her into exile as surely as the heads of Europe had banished Bonaparte to Elba. She'd swiftly fit into her new life with the citizens of Paris and with her doting grandparents, who took a more lenient approach with their granddaughter. And while Serena had spent a quiet twentieth birthday at the family winery, it was Paris that she loved. Her freedom to come and go as she pleased, to sit with her friends both female and male, and to handle the wine orders for many of the restaurant and café owners was something she knew her father would be appalled to learn.

Naturally, she missed her parents, her brothers, and her London friends, not to mention the life she'd had before the final misstep at Vauxhall. She'd been on the path to triumph for the Season. Her presentation to the queen had gone well, and she'd even secured a ticket to Almack's to enjoy dancing with some of Britain's coveted young bucks. Moreover, she had a good number of invitations to private balls with the shiniest of the *bon ton.*

Yet here she sat, having traded her stifling, privileged life as a nobleman's daughter for the liberty that came with the less stratified society of post-Revolutionary Paris. Her clothing was indistinguishable from any female of the bourgeoisie. Moreover, she could bargain and barter with the best.

"You're very quiet, Mademoiselle Serena," Jean-Paul said in the fast, clipped Parisian tongue that she'd picked up as easily as breathing, having spoken French with her mother all her life. "Aren't you excited to see what will happen when Bonaparte returns? And what of our fat king?"

She sipped her wine. "Some say Bonaparte himself has grown a little soft while on Elba. His health might not be as it was a year ago."

Her friends looked shocked.

"Where did you learn such a thing?" Guillaume demanded, and his sister, Felicity, gave Serena a curious stare. Guillaume, who was a devoted newspaper reader, insisted, "I didn't read it anywhere."

Serena shrugged, wishing she'd kept her mouth closed. Her grandparents knew too much, and thus, so did she. She needed to be more careful. Her grand-père had told her how the wrong word in the wrong ear could spell disaster. Fingers might point, people could die.

And now she'd gone and disclosed something only those who traveled with the emperor and reported back to intelligence gatherers in the city could know.

"I didn't read it," she said, scraping her fork across her nearly empty plate to gather the last bit of mushroom and sauce. "I heard people talking in the *marché*, that's all. No one speaks of anything except Napoleon these days."

"She is right," Jean-Paul said. "His name is mentioned throughout the streets and even on the river, whether one is having one's clothes washed or washing one's body."

They all chuckled, thinking of the laundress's boats lined up near the floating baths. Both of these structures were as rife with gossip as any café. And the news was all the same—Bonaparte was coming!

Suddenly, Serena saw *him*, the handsome man from the street. Clearly English by his accent although he'd spoken to her in fluent French, he descended the back stairs, and she could easily see him in one of the large mirrors on the wall. His light-brown hair caught the candlelight as he scanned the restaurant, and she couldn't help turning. His eyes met hers, and Serena would swear recognition passed between them.

Perhaps he merely recalled how he'd knocked her over, but it seemed like something more. Something that made her insides quiver.

"Someone you know?" Guillaume asked, following her gaze. By then, the tall Englishman had turned away, moving swiftly through the dining room so his overcoat swung out behind him, and then he was gone.

"No," she replied. "Not at all."

CHAPTER TWO

Serena sat at the kitchen table with her grandparents. For a moment, no one was speaking, and that was only because they'd already been discussing events for the past half hour. With her grand-père, Henri Renault, smoking his favorite tobacco, her grand-mère, Adèle, knitting, and Serena snapping the ends off a bowlful of green beans, they were contemplating the future.

Marshal Ney, the famed commander working for King Louis XVIII, had defected with his six thousand men the day before. When Emperor Bonaparte returned to Paris, he would bring with him an army of well-trained soldiers. What had seemed impossible a month ago was happening.

Her grandparents didn't fear for themselves, but they had friends who'd openly supported the reinstatement of the Bourbon king. Some were leaving the city immediately, while some had already left.

"We shall finish selling Charles and Sophie's wine and send them the money," Henri insisted. "It will do them no good to send more barrels to the city in case Bonaparte discovers their wine was liked by the king."

"Not merely liked," Serena's grand-mère added. Their friends had sent wine to Louis XVIII as a tribute when he reclaimed his throne nine months earlier, and even taken it to the Palais des Tuileries. After that, the king asked for it by name.

Others, too, needed to flee or hide for being honored with such patronage.

"It is so unreasonable, isn't it?" Serena asked. "All this switching sides, having to pander to one or the other simply to make a living or keep one's head."

Adèle chuckled. "That is just the way of it, since forever."

"Why doesn't each new ruler recognize the people will still be the people? Wine must be drunk, bread must be eaten. Does it matter to the vintner or the baker, or the fruitseller or the cheesemaker for that matter who currently sits upon the throne?"

"You're right, of course," her grand-père said, "but they want to keep their heads."

"But they are no threat," Serena insisted, "be it to king or to emperor or to whomever comes next. Even if Charles and Sophie's wine was adored by Louis, what does it matter?"

Her grandparents looked at one another, and she felt instantly foolish.

"Some of them *are* indeed threatening to the latest ruler," Henri reminded her, "because they have pledged loyalty to one side or to a religion or to a family or even to one man. And thus, everyone is suspect."

Their family's allegiance was not in question, though, and Serena had never felt unsafe, even when she'd done exactly as her grand-père had asked. Like her grandparents' friends, she had taken wine directly to the Palais des Tuileries in the first months after Bonaparte had been pushed out of France. Her task had been simply to listen for any rumblings of discontent over the restoration of the Bourbon king.

"Am I going to the Tuileries again, Pépère?"

Her grandparents glanced at one another. "Yes, if that's where Bonaparte chooses to live," he said. "Unless you would rather not do so."

"I'll help however I can." It was as exciting as slipping down a dark path at Vauxhall or into an empty corridor at a private ball, both of which she'd done for an arranged meeting with a young man. Yet instead of for her own curiosity and enjoyment, this secretive task was for her grandparents and, thus, for France. Her heartbeat sped up, and she hoped she would glean important information.

Finishing the last of the runner beans, she rose to her feet.

"May I go see my friends?" Despite the growing anticipation of the emperor's inevitable return, Paris went on as before. In fact, even more people were staying out at night in the cafes. A curfew might be put upon them at any moment, so they would live while they could. Serena had learned it was the French way.

"Don't stay out too late," her grand-père said, standing up to hug her and kiss both her cheeks. Her grand-mère did the same. "And keep your ears open," he added.

Grabbing her cloak and gloves, she disappeared out of the apartment's front door and down the staircase into the central courtyard around which all the apartments were built. As usual, there were a few stray dogs, and also as usual, she had grabbed a little something for them, a small sack of leftover vegetables, chicken, and bread.

When the mongrels nearly knocked her over and were happily wolfing her tribute, after sneaking a quick pet of this one and a scratch behind the ears of that one, Serena strode past the concierge's small room and through the wooden doorway onto La Rue Coquillière.

Returning to the large shopping and dining area of the Palais-Royal, she went down a short flight of stone steps to the Café des Aveugles, located in the cellar of the Café Italien. The air was thick and warm, and more than a little musty, but Serena knew she would no longer notice it after a few minutes.

Directly inside the doorway where a lit candle rested high in a shiny tin sconce on either side, she halted to see if her friends were already there. As it had only recently opened at five o'clock, a mere hour earlier, there were still some vacant seats.

Upon each occupied table were a couple bottles of wine in various states of emptiness and a basket of crusty rolls or the remainder of crumbs. On Serena's left was the café's claim to fame, a good-sized orchestra, eight musicians that night, all of them blind.

Grisettes from shops all around the Palais, two of them her friends, Suzanne and Felicity, were chatting loudly, drinking, and tearing into the warm rolls. Before she could take a step toward their table, Serena was assaulted by several of the street vendors allowed inside to sell their small bouquets, cheap jewelry, and bags of sweets. She bought one of the latter for her grand-mère, then made her way to her friends.

"Don't ask me why I'm late," she said, but told them anyway, "I was preparing vegetables."

They often teased her mercilessly for being tardy.

"It's easy for you to get here," Serena reminded them as Suzanne poured her a glass of dark red wine. "You work ten steps away."

"We hurry here," Felicity said, "because we've stood on our feet all day and it's bliss to sit, even on these chairs."

"Sometimes, I stand all day, too," Serena reminded them, "when I am at the Halle aux Vins, and then I dash all over the city to collect orders."

Suzanne pressed a warm roll into Serena's hand. "Our poor wine princess!"

They all laughed. Serena understood her great luck in not being a shopgirl, working for pittance each day. Her friends' teasing remarks were never malicious. Her grandparents were well off, which her friends knew. But they would be surprised to learn her father was an English baron. And he would be apoplectic if he knew her daily activities and how she sat at night in a café without a chaperone. The previous year when she'd first arrived, it had seemed prudent to simply be a new citizen of Paris, to work hard, and to fit in.

After her missteps in London, the last thing Serena wanted was to draw attention to herself and stand out. That way lay ruin and ostracization as she'd so quickly discovered.

"What have you heard?" Felicity asked.

"What have you read?" Suzanne added.

"Not fair," Serena said, "tell me what you know first."

They spent the next half hour going over every detail, real or imagined by the newspapers, as to what was occurring, where Napoleon was at that moment, and when he might arrive. Much of it was unfavorable since, except for a very few presses, the emperor had shut the rest down while he reigned. During his exile, many had sprung up again like flowers, albeit with the permission of the king. Along with the pamphlets supplied to every coffeehouse and café, the daily newspapers provided enough fodder for an evening's discussion.

After another glass of wine, Felicity blurted, "Guillaume is sweet on you, Serena."

Startled by the confession, she opened her mouth, then closed it. If her friend hadn't been the young man's sister, then Serena would have been frank about her lack of interest. Even if she'd found Guillaume to her liking, she had no intention of remaining in France forever. She wanted to go back to England and hoped her father would relent in the near future.

After all, she had been out of sight, and hopefully out of mind, of the *ton* for almost a year already. Surely, she could slip back into her old life with no one caring.

Her mother wrote weekly to her own parents, including a few sheets to her daughter in her letters, and Serena hoped with each one she would be summoned home.

Besides, Guillaume was a little frightening in his intensity at times.

The café door opened, letting in a welcome draft of cool night air. The attractive Englishman who'd knocked her over two nights earlier appeared in the doorway. She felt herself becoming prickly while she waited for his gaze to land upon her as she knew it would. When it did, she experienced the same sensation as at the Café de Chartres, that of sharing a communication without saying a word. She half expected him to come over to her table.

He didn't. After staring at her, obviously with recognition, he might've given the slightest nod by way of greeting before joining a man wearing a red kerchief round his neck at a nearby table. She didn't know his companion's name but had seen him before, not only in the café but at the Halle aux Vins.

"There's a handsome devil," Suzanne said, following Serena's glance.

She felt her cheeks warm.

"Do you know him?" Felicity asked, sounding much like her brother. "Isn't he the same man from the Café de Chartres?"

"I don't know him," Serena insisted, "but I believe he was there, yes."

Suddenly, she didn't want to tell her friends how he'd knocked her over and helped her up. But if he was to be a new regular patron of the Palais-Royal, then life had just become a little more interesting.

He was handsome, indeed.

"You're looking over there again," Felicity said, sounding a little peeved, possibly on her brother's behalf.

"I'm only looking because you are both looking," Serena protested.

"And why not?" Suzanne asked. "Look at his shoulders and his fine head of hair."

"Hush!" Serena said, when her friend's voice grew louder. "Why don't we go elsewhere?"

"Nonsense," said Felicity. "I'm not leaving because some new monsieur has taken your fancy."

Serena sighed and poured herself another glass, hoping Felicity would not take offense at Serena's lack of interest in her friend's brother. They went back to chatting, and Suzanne told her everyone was buying red and blue fabric in anticipation of Bonaparte's return. They would make rosette badges for their hats and coats.

A crash at a nearby table grabbed her attention.

The red-kerchiefed man was standing, his chair on its side, and the Englishman rose slowly to his feet, glancing around uncomfortably. Silence blanketed the café for the span of about three heartbeats, and then conversation resumed. People having too much to drink and becoming boisterous was nothing new at the Café des Aveugles, where the working class had come since before the Revolution to discuss and debate, to smoke and to drink.

Nevertheless, the red-kerchiefed man was glowering, looking as if he intended to start a fight.

"Je m'excuse," she heard the Englishman utter, and Serena started to wonder if an apology was the only thing he could say correctly in French.

The other man let out a string of outraged oaths, gravely insulted and ready to do bodily injury the moment the Englishman stepped outside.

Unsure if he understood the kerchiefed man's intent to fight, Serena leaned over and tapped the table to get his attention.

The Englishman's rich brown eyes widened. Instinctively not wishing to speak in English in case he was hiding his nationality as many had done in France for the past two decades of war, which she herself was doing even then, she spoke in slow, clear French.

"He believes you have insulted him, monsieur, and wants you to go outside to be beaten."

"But yes, he did insult me," interrupted the other man, hands on his hips.

The Englishman looked confused and shook his head. "No," he replied in French. "I said you had a good solid head on your shoulders, *un tête de noeud*, yes?"

"What!" the other man exclaimed, growing red in the face as his anger increased until he matched the color of his kerchief.

Serena couldn't help smiling and her friends laughed outright.

"Monsieur," she spoke again to the Englishman. "I don't know what you're trying to say, but you're calling him a—" There was no choice but to slip into English. Dropping the level of her voice to a whisper while leaning closer, she said, "—a penis head."

Switching back to French at his shocked expression, she added, "It is very rude."

Her friends laughed again.

The handsome stranger immediately launched into a flurry of apologetic words, and, at last, the other man lowered his hands to his sides and nodded. Yet he didn't resume his seat. Instead, he turned and walked out, back rigid, obviously annoyed.

The Englishman looked deflated. Whatever his purpose with the other man, it had not gone well. He glanced over at her.

"*Merci*," he said. "Your English is very good."

She smiled and nodded. He had no idea.

"And since I am in your debt, not to mention what occurred last night," he continued, "may I buy you a bottle of wine?"

She felt her friends' stares, as they wondered to what he was referring.

"That's not necessary, monsieur," she said. "We have plenty of wine. Thank you."

"I insist. I'll send it over. Again, I apologize for yesterday, and I thank you for your help this evening. I bid you good night. Mademoiselles," he said including all of them as he offered a shallow bow before walking away.

Serena and her friends followed his departure with their eyes, noticing him snag a waiter, give him some coins, and nod toward their table.

Then her friends turned their curious stares upon her.

"It was nothing," she insisted.

"You said you didn't know him," Felicity said, accusingly.

"I don't. He walked into me in the street and knocked me over. That's all."

She didn't like Felicity's reproving look.

"That's all," Serena repeated, wondering why she felt she owed an explanation. Probably because the disaster at Vauxhall still haunted her. While some manners and etiquette were different here in Paris than back home, she didn't want to gain an unwarranted reputation as someone who knew strange men, particularly not Englishmen! More than that, in the current climate of unrest, she wished to appear as an ordinary citizen and avoid incurring Felicity or Guillaume's suspicion.

Nevertheless, the English monsieur had a tempting smile and lovely brown eyes that made her wish she'd been on the Vauxhall path with him that fateful night in London. She wouldn't have run away at his touch or his kiss.

CHAPTER THREE

What a ridiculous stroke of bad luck! Malcolm couldn't believe he'd called his contact a prick-head. However, as he entered the vast round building of the Halle aux Vins two days later, he was determined to make amends. Besides, all his cards had turned up aces anyway, considering he'd spoken with the fiery-haired mademoiselle once again. Her stunning green eyes and sweet lips already haunted his dreams and had been worth ruining his first meeting.

Hopefully, Monsieur Christoff would have cooled down in the meanwhile.

Strolling through the various vendors, Malcolm followed instructions on where the correct stall was located. The smell of so much wine in one place was cloying, but this was where Christoff worked for Cerise Winery, and it was now the only way to contact him.

Spotting him, although the man no longer wore the red kerchief that had been his identifier, Malcolm strode toward the table surrounded by barrels with the Cerise brand scorched into each one. He tried to plaster a conciliatory expression on his face, but being extremely tall, he often appeared as though he was looking down on people in a supercilious way, when he intended no such thing.

Besides, a misunderstanding due to language shouldn't be of any importance compared to what they were trying to achieve. Christoff ought to realize that, but these Gauls had high passions and hot tempers, and they could hold a grudge like no other. Of utmost concern to all the Parisians should be what Bonaparte might do to anyone who'd welcomed the return of the Bourbon king.

There were grudges and then there were grudges!

One of the reasons the generals who'd pledged allegiance to King Louis XVIII were now embracing Bonaparte's cause was undoubtedly a desire to save their own skins. But if they survived Napoleon, after Malcolm helped get rid of the emperor as he hoped to do, then these same men would have to survive the purge that followed the king's second restoration. Politics was a nasty business.

"Monsieur Christoff," he greeted him. "I hope you are well. I bring you a gift." On Randall's recommendation, he'd bought a container of expensive tobacco, which he now withdrew from his pocket and handed over.

The man made a face that might have been a forgiving smile but which looked like a grimace. Regardless, Christoff hadn't punched him in the face, so perhaps Malcolm was forgiven.

"Are you still willing to help the cause?" Malcolm asked without preamble.

The man gestured for Malcolm to take a stool, then he pulled the stopper from and already open bottle and poured them each a glass.

If Christoff were a fellow Englishman, Malcolm would ask in jest if the wine were poisoned in retribution for the egregious yet unintended insult, but that wouldn't go over well with the Frenchman.

They clinked glasses and took a good swallow. Cerise was a fruity, jewel-toned wine, and Malcolm knew Bonaparte had enjoyed it in the past, which was why Randall had targeted Christoff.

"Will you take your wine to the emperor when he arrives?" he asked. Malcolm wanted him to supply wine to Boney, and each time he did, to try to learn more of his plans. Specifically, they hoped to learn whether the emperor intended to be the aggressor, sending troops out to France's borders and beyond, or if he would set up only a line of defense against the coalition.

Monsieur Christoff considered. "I have thought it over." He drank down the wine and set his cup down. "What is your purpose? If Bonaparte can escape an island, rebuild an army, and return triumphant—all without firing a shot against another Frenchman—then he should lead my country, no? Who is better? Not our fat king."

Malcolm had been afraid of this. Many of Christoff's fellow Parisians felt the same way. But allowing Bonaparte to remain would mean the fragile peace those in Vienna had spent nine months constructing would shatter. The entire European continent would be plunged into war before Christmas. The allies needed to secure France and then continue to work on stabilizing Russia, Prussia, and Austria.

Or someone did, at any rate. Yet not Malcolm. He would be done. Hopefully sooner rather than later. And when Boney was defeated again, Malcolm would be back on English soil before the ink was dry on the emperor's next banishment decree. And then, he would knuckle under and submit to his obligation to find a Lady Branley.

To Christoff, he said, "A week ago, you gave my associate your word. Nothing has changed. France is not an empire, and it doesn't need an emperor, a greedy one at that."

Christoff crossed his arms. "I don't think the British have the right—nor the power when it comes to it—to decide for France. We shall work it out ourselves."

Well, shit! Malcolm set the glass down. It had been his experience when an ally became a foe, it was best to put distance between oneself and him. Especially if one had called the man a prick-head!

Rising to his feet, he turned to find a number of men standing nearby, watching, listening, most with arms crossed, all of them wearing hostile expressions. While not quite surrounded, Malcolm was certainly outnumbered. Four to one.

Randall needed to be a tad more discerning in discovering partners for this battle with Boney. And Malcolm would tell him so—if he survived the vintners' marketplace and made it back to the relative safety of the upstairs room of the Café de Chartres.

With calm intent, he walked directly toward the closest of the three men, despite there not being room for him to squeeze between them. At the last moment, when he was nearly within their arms' reach, he swerved to the left, pushing between two others, using his height as a vantage point from which to shove them hard to the side. Then amid barrels stacked three high, he tried his best to disappear.

They yelled behind him, and he moved faster, hardly pausing to duck for cover until he got far enough away that they wouldn't be able to see where he went. And then he saw her—his copper-haired goddess!

As quick as a rabbit and as straight as the crow flies, he hastened toward her. She was marking sheets of paper, perhaps inspecting orders, and dressed in a pale green gown. Despite the situation, he was certain her dress went perfectly with her eyes.

"I need a place to hide," he said. Without waiting for her response, he dodged behind her worktable to the neat barrels behind her and ducked out of sight.

If she gave him up, so be it. He had a feeling she wouldn't let him be caught, perhaps a foolish hope based upon nothing more than how he thought her too lovely for words.

Footsteps and shouts were close behind him.

"Did you see a tall, brown-haired man go by?" someone asked her a few seconds later.

"Yes, of course," she responded, and his heart skipped a beat. "He ran that way, toward the exit."

The footfalls hurried away, a number of them—hopefully *all* of them—but he was going to wait in any case.

For a few moments, nothing happened. Someone else came close, and they discussed the excitement of a chase in the Halle aux Vins. Then another person came by and asked how many barrels to take to each of three restaurants on the Champs-Élysées. And then, again, silence.

Malcolm's heartbeat had slowed, and he was crouched inside a small prison of wine casks, his thighs burning from the position he was in. But he hadn't been caught, nor betrayed by the woman, so he didn't give a damn.

After another few minutes, she came close.

"That *is* you, is it not?"

What did she mean? Of course it was him, but if she hadn't clearly recognized him, it might be better not to remind her, and thus, he said nothing in response.

"You are the man from the café, *oui?* I think you should stay right where you are for a while, at least, maybe until we close and go home for the night. Your friend, Monsieur '*tête de noeud*' looks very cross walking around, trying to sniff you out like a dog."

Malcolm sighed. The Crown should have sent his friend Denbigh. The man had a better command of the French idioms. Nevertheless, taking her point that it was unsafe to come out, he tried to shift his weight and sit on his bottom.

There wasn't room and the barrels at his back seemed to wobble. If they toppled onto him, he'd be done for.

"Careful, do not move," she warned, in her fast Parisian French.

Malcolm thought it would be nice to hear her speak her perfect English again, saying something other than "penis-head." Perhaps over a meal, perhaps stretched out on a soft bed where the only words necessary were whispers of each other's names.

He managed to fall forward onto his knees and give his burning thigh muscles a break.

IMPOSSIBLY, SERENA had an attractive stranger hiding behind her grandparents' barrels of wine. She ought to be alarmed. Instead, she was thoroughly entertained. The Renault delivery team, two men whom her grand-père had known since they were boys, continued to come and go for the remainder of the day. She directed them to take barrels that were well away from where the Englishman crouched.

When it was dusk, the hall emptied, but still the man who'd worn the kerchief at the Café was loitering by the stall of the Cerise vintners. Although not the owner, she thought he might be the manager of sales. In any case, he seemed in no hurry to depart.

"Hey, Mademoiselle Serena, we have finished for the day," said Michel, one of their delivery men. The other, Jacques, already stood by the far exit. "Time for a good meal. My Marie said lamb tonight. Do you want me to walk you home first?"

"No, thank you, Michel. I'll go soon."

He touched his cap and left. Another ten minutes passed. She wondered if her hidden Englishman had fallen asleep. Finally, when she could not pretend to straighten her papers one more time, the man from the Cerise winery walked past and out the door. Immediately, she hurried to the stacked barrels and peered between them. She could see no one until she realized, he was on the ground.

"Are you well?" she asked, bending low.

A brown eye appeared at the crack. *It was a beautiful eye,* she thought. Then she heard his fingers scraping and scrabbling at the barrels as he drew himself up to standing with an audible groan.

A strange sound that made her insides tingle.

"I think I'm crippled," he declared in English.

She knew it wasn't the least amusing, but it made her smile nonetheless. Walking around the stack, she found the narrow opening through which he'd squeezed his muscular body. Out, he came.

"*Ow,*" he said, hopping around. "For Christ's sake, *ow!*"

She said nothing as he did a little dance restoring the circulation to his limbs. She didn't tell him he would have been better if he'd remained standing the whole time. Instead, she poured him a restorative glass of wine, and when he finally grew still, she handed it to him.

He drank it down in two long gulps.

"Thank you." His tone was a little husky, and again, she felt a tingling response.

"I think you should stay away from that man who manages the Cerise wine shipments," she suggested.

Immediately, he grinned, and the tingling became a fiery shiver.

"You're right, mademoiselle. May I know your name?"

"Renault," she gave her grandparents' surname, as that was how she was known in Paris.

"I appreciate the place to hide and the wine, Mademoiselle Renault."

"And may I know yours?"

He hesitated, before saying, "Branley."

"Shall we go, Monsieur Branley?" she asked.

"Where?" he looked curious.

She had the distinct impression he imagined she was inviting him to go somewhere private for a tryst. With his good looks, that was undoubtedly a regular occurrence.

"Away from here, monsieur," she explained. "They will lock the doors soon." Serena gestured toward the entrance.

"Oh, yes, I see." He set the empty glass down as they walked past her stall's table. Glancing back, noticing the name on the barrels, he said, "Your family owns the winery."

"Yes."

As they stepped into the dusky light of the Quai St. Bernard, Serena looked right while Monsieur Branley looked left.

"He's there!" she said, not knowing the *tête de noeud*'s name, but he was leaning against a tree, looking at the Seine while smoking and chatting with two other men.

Her companion's head swiveled round.

Without speaking, Monsieur Branley grabbed her hand and headed in the opposite direction.

She didn't think they were spotted, since there was no outcry, but they ran around the corner of the building onto the Rue des Fossés Saint-Bernard before they began to stroll at a calmer pace up the boulevard away from the river.

How extraordinary! Suddenly, she was part of a caper, an adventure, something far more exciting than ballroom intrigue.

After a few minutes' silent walk, Monsieur Branley asked, "Are you crossing to the Right Bank?"

"Yes," she said. "I usually cross at the Petit Pont on this side."

"Very well," he said. "That's where we'll go."

They turned right and right again toward the little bridge from the Left Bank to the small island in the Seine from which the Cathédrale Notre-Dame rose majestically. Serena felt giddy, keeping her hand tucked in the crook of his arm. The boredom and routine of her daily life had been replaced practically overnight by the presence of Monsieur Branley. For everyone else, the current upheaval was because of Napoleon's return, but she considered the emperor to be of far less significance than the tall, dashing man striding alongside her.

They crossed onto the Île de la Cité, both of their heads naturally turning toward the cathedral. No matter how many times she saw it, Serena couldn't help but gape at its magnificence and beauty.

"It's breathtaking," Monsieur Branley voiced her thoughts.

She merely nodded, saying nothing until they crossed off the small island on the other side via the Pont Notre-Dame, the bridge taking them to the Right Bank. Then she needed some answers.

"Why do you keep going to see that man, the one who wore the red kerchief, only to make him mad and then run from him?"

Instead of taking her question seriously, Monsieur Branley laughed.

"I suppose it looks like the actions of a madman." Then he paused. Instead of answering, he asked, "Which way are you going now?"

She would never lead him back to her grandparents' apartment in the fourth arrondissement, but they could go close by.

"To the Palais-Royal," she said.

"Again?" he asked.

She nodded.

Then Monsieur Branley shrugged. "It is very different here than back home."

She startled when he said the last word, thinking he knew she was English.

"The females in London," he continued, "live in a far more restricted way than you Parisian ladies. I doubt one would have let me hide behind her in the wine market or walk with me such a distance or go to a café without a chaperone."

She offered him a wry smile. She knew all too well how constrained her life would be if she were back in England among the *ton*.

"I believe you are right. And I enjoy my freedom." Serena realized at that moment, however, she was behaving exactly as her father had feared, and not at all properly. She sighed. Keeping up the appearance of propriety was more difficult than actually being proper, for she hadn't done anything untoward since arriving in Paris.

"I thought you were a *grisette* or a—" Monsieur Branley suddenly swallowed whatever he'd been about to say.

When he broke off so abruptly, she had to ask, "You thought I was what exactly?"

"My apologies." He looked chagrinned. "I nearly said something far too familiar."

"Go on," she prompted.

"It's simply that among certain circles, women without chaperones are either in the working class or they are ladies of leisure."

Ladies of leisure! Even in his crude French translation, she knew he meant a harlot. *What cheek! What gall!* She ought to feel her father's fury, not only at Monsieur Branley's impertinent assumption but also at herself for allowing their conversation to stray to such an unseemly topic.

In truth, though, she couldn't feel even a modicum of outrage. It was a flaw in her nature, she decided, a wayward trait that might land her with the label of a jade or a light-heeled wench if she wasn't careful.

Trying to sound grave, she asked, "You didn't answer my question regarding what precisely you are doing here?"

He sighed. "Mademoiselle Renault, are you aware Emperor Bonaparte is returning?"

She nearly laughed. "I am not a nitwit. It is all anyone is talking about."

"Do you have thoughts on the matter?" he persisted.

Serena hesitated. Obviously as an Englishman, he would be wary of the emperor's return. He probably had supported King Louis's reclaiming of the throne the previous year.

She thought carefully about her response. "I only want for my fellow Parisians to live in peace."

"Bonaparte is not bringing peace, I assure you," Monsieur Branley shot back.

"Why do you say that?" she asked.

"Because the rest of Europe, as well as Britain, do not want him here. Thus, war will inevitably break out as soon as he declares himself ruler again."

She shivered, knowing it to be the truth. Her grandparents had said as much.

"*Je m'excuse,*" he said, "I don't wish to frighten you. I doubt the fighting will be in Paris. At least not the main battles anyway. Everyone respects the city as a jewel of historic importance, even if it is cramped and filthy," he added under his breath, although she heard him.

"You are here from Britain to do something about Bonaparte," she surmised.

He glanced at her yet didn't confirm her guess.

"And the man from whom you keep running?" she prompted again. If there was danger at the Halle aux Vins, Serena wanted to know about it.

"I wouldn't have run earlier if we weren't in a busy market and if he didn't have three fellow citizens who looked ready to anoint me with the oil of gladness."

He'd switched into English, but she still hadn't a clue what he meant.

At her bewattled expression, he spoke in French. "To give me a robust beating."

"But just now," she pointed out, "we ran again."

"Just now, *you* were with me, and I wouldn't have him see us together for all the world. After all, you came to my aid and translated at the Café des Aveugles. Seeing us in close proximity twice might lead him to think you know something about my actions or his." He sent her a small smile, enough to warm her toes.

"Either way," he added, "I don't want you involved. But in case you fear for your safety, I am armed." He patted his pocket.

She wondered what he would think if he learned she carried a pistol, too. When her parents had brought her to France, her father had given her a pretty but deadly silver muff pistol, although she usually carried it, as she did that day, in a leather holster her grand-père had made, strapped just above her left boot.

"If it had come to it, I would not have let him or his men kill me," Monsieur Branley added matter-of-factly. "Although as I said, I would have greatly disrelished drawing my gun and opening fire in the Halle aux Vins. It would have drawn far too much attention."

She was wondering if she should tell her grandparents any of this, or if they would decide she was enjoying a bit too much freedom. Possibly, with involving herself in the actions of a British spy, she was going too far.

"I say, Mademoiselle Renault, do you always walk this far?"

"Not at all." Actually, she was rather weary after a long day, and her feet were tired. "Normally, I would signal a *fiacre*—a taxi, you understand?—but I thought *you* wanted to walk."

He laughed. "Thank God! While it was nice to stretch my legs, I'd prefer not to still be walking at midnight."

With that, he waved down a single-horsed carriage and helped her into the back before climbing in beside her.

"Café de Chartres at the Palais Royal, monsieur," he told the driver.

At that moment, as the English stranger took the seat beside her, their shoulders and hips pressed side-by-side, Serena knew she was definitely pushing the boundaries of the independence granted by her grandparents. She was riding alone with a man she barely knew, a rather spirited one with a gun in his pocket.

Moreover, this particular man had caused some especially interesting feelings to swirl inside her. Perhaps he was even more dangerous than a Vauxhall rake.

CHAPTER FOUR

When Malcolm helped his new acquaintance and rescuer down from the hired taxi, he kept hold of Mademoiselle Renault's hand, causing her to glance up at him. Her verdant gaze was mesmerizing, and her lips seemed the perfect shade of rose. More than one time on the quick ride across Paris, he had the urge to kiss her.

An absurd and inappropriate notion, to be sure, albeit one he'd acted upon numerous times when in London, while rushing between Prinny's flamboyant Oriental drawing room at Carlton House and some well-attended ball. If he was in close quarters with a beautiful woman and had the desire to kiss her, it would be foolish not to.

If the lady was willing, why not steal a kiss?

But this mademoiselle would not know of the games played by the *ton*. A kiss could be a prelude to something far saltier, or it could be nothing more than a momentary remedy for ennui, enjoyed by both parties.

"Are you going into one of the cafés?" he asked her.

"No, monsieur. I am going home." And she carefully withdrew her hand from his.

That surprised him. *Why hadn't she let him escort her to her residence?* He had to squash down the notion her actions were suspicious, and she had something to hide. Probably nothing more than an overly protective mother, or less likely, a jealous husband, both of whom he'd dealt with before. There was a reason rakes turned to willing Cyprians, to avoid trouble.

Then he surprised himself. "I hope to see you again."

Her lovely green eyes widened. "Will you be in Paris for very long?"

He noted she didn't ask him *what* he was doing there precisely.

"As long as it takes," he said. "And you spend your days at the Halle aux Vins and then come here to the Palais-Royal to meet your friends?"

"Often, yes. And you spend your days angering people and then come here to meet . . . whom?" she asked.

He grinned. "I, too, meet friends here."

"Then we may, indeed, see each other again," she concluded with a flirtatious smile making him fervently hope that was true.

"*Bonsoir, monsieur,*" she said.

She must know he was watching her every move as she strolled away with a slight yet utterly enticing sway to her hips that women must instinctively know how to do. Her movements assured his continued stare until she disappeared down one of the columned arcades.

Sighing, he dashed into the Café de Chartres and up the back stairs, past the armed guard to find Randall, who was not his usual smiling self.

In fact, the Englishman looked uncharacteristically sour. Perhaps he had heard word of Christoff's defection.

"Prick-head? Really?" Randall demanded.

Apparently, he'd only heard the beginning. Malcolm shook his head.

"It was an unintentional error, I assure you. I was trying to say something about him having a good head on his shoulders. But it wouldn't have mattered. He turned on me at the Halle aux Vins today. I barely escaped without a beating."

"How many?" Randall demanded.

"Four men. Interestingly, they weren't joined by a mob of vintners and workers. I don't think the entire wine market is going to take up arms for Bonaparte."

Randall shrugged. "They don't need to. He's amassed himself quite an army. Our spies tell us everywhere he goes since landing at Golfe-Juan, Boney spouts his poppycock about free elections, reforming the government, peace, prosperity, and more liberty for the citizens of France. He stirs the French people with his discourse, and then they join him. Who can blame them?"

"*Vive l'Empereur!*" Malcolm quipped and poured himself a glass of burgundy from the bottle in front of him before topping up Randall's.

"Did you see some jester's idea of a joke at the Place Vendôme?" Randall asked

Malcolm shook his head.

His associate rolled his eyes. "I kid you not, Branley. A message was hung across the Vendôme column. It read, 'From Napoleon to Louis XVIII, my dear brother, it is not necessary to send me more troops, I already have enough of them!'"

Malcolm barked out a laugh and slapped the table. "That's quite clever."

Randall cracked a crooked smile in agreement.

"Has Louis gone?" Malcolm asked.

"Yes, and the crown jewels, too, if reports are true. The king left at midnight with General Scovell," Randall said. "They were heading for Calais with hopes of passage to England, and the rest of the royal family with them. Royalists and anyone who doesn't think they can successfully switch sides have also fled the city."

"Louis should have gone south instead, days ago," Malcolm said, "and fought Bonaparte. Perhaps with a king at the head of the army—"

"Unlikely to have done any good," Randall interrupted. "He was never inspirational that way. If the king had been on the battlefield, he might have got himself killed. If not by Bonaparte, then by one of his fanatical grenadiers. Then what would we do when we are rid of the emperor a second time? Who would we put upon the throne?"

"Bonaparte said he thought beheading the last king was a mistake," Malcolm reminded him, not believing even Bonaparte would execute a member of the Bourbon royal family.

"It doesn't matter. Louis had a convenient case of gout, and now he's fled."

They heard shouts of *"Vive l'Empereur!"*

"It would seem Boney has arrived." Randall spoke calmly, but they both rose to their feet and dashed down the stairs to join the flood of citizens pouring out of every café and shop within hearing distance of the Tuileries Palace a few blocks away.

Racing down the Rue St. Honoré, they pushed their way through the throng of people, expecting to see a hostile army surrounding the palace, instead, only plain carriages met their eyes, along with military officers they both knew only too well.

Colonel Léon-Michel Routier chatted with fellow officers. He looked stunned to see the carriages appear without any escort at the wicket-gate by the river. The citizens already seemed to know what was happening, still chanting *"Vive l'Empereur"* even before he showed himself.

When Napoleon stepped out of one of the carriages, a great cheer arose. Mayhem ensued, but Malcolm detected not a whit of hostility toward the ruler who'd led them through so many years of war. Instead, men hugged him until he seemed almost suffocated with the loyalty and admiration.

"It's like magic," Malcolm said to Randall, not concealing the wonder in his tone. "Eighteen days on French soil, over 560 miles traveled, and without spilling a drop of blood, here he is, back at the palace as though he never left."

"He'll be sitting down to the king's dinner tonight, I'll wager," Randall added.

Malcolm couldn't help taking in the joy of the people around him. His thoughts, some of them doubtful as to their mission, must have shown upon his face. For Randall suddenly grabbed his arm and steered him away.

"Don't go getting all philosophical on me, Branley. We have a sworn duty, do not forget."

"I haven't." They walked back toward the restaurant. "In a case such as this, however, it's hard not to give a moment's consideration as to whether we're on the wrong side of history. Many would say if he's the one the people want, then let him rule. Many will say it, no matter how this turns out. The Seventh Coalition might be wise to put down our swords and pistols because no one is trying to fight us."

"Not yet," Randall said. "Give Bonaparte a chance to get settled, and then you'll see how he starts to make plans to grow the borders of France again." He sighed audibly. "If the man had simply stuck with doing good things for his people like providing free water and all the new city fountains and his so-called *Code Napoléon*. Alas, he had to go and make himself an emperor," he mused.

"Don't forget the education system, the Banque de France, and the Légion d'Honneur," Malcolm said. "Do you think King Louis would have done any of that, or even managed to build *one* bridge, never mind four? And the Arc de—"

"Stop it." They had gained the second floor of the Café de Chartres once again. Randall shook his head. "You're speaking of Bonaparte like a schoolgirl in love."

"I'm speaking like a man who's not sure we have the right to determine another country's ruler."

"I agree, but even if we folded our cards and went back to Prinny today declaring Napoleon to be as peaceful as a puppy, no threat to England whatsoever, which we cannot guarantee. Even if we did that, the rest of the Continent is determined to reinstate the Bourbon king. I was in Vienna a very short time ago. The views of the Austrians, the Russians, and the Prussian's have not changed."

"I know," Malcolm said grudgingly. He poured himself another glass of wine and one for Randall.

It seemed a piss-poor business to him, and he would rather be wrapping his arms around a beautiful woman—Mademoiselle Renault came instantly to mind—than plotting to take down a beloved emperor whom he could not help but view with grudging respect and even admiration.

SERENA'S GRANDPARENTS WERE CALM, but an air of purpose hung over them. Things were moving more quickly than they'd expected, including seeing the word *royaume* being changed everywhere to *empire* once more.

The following day, she found herself heading to the Palais des Tuileries, along with Parisians trying to renew their connections with the emperor. He had already left before she set foot in France the previous year.

The excitement was profound and almost tangible. Serena couldn't help feeling it, like catching a brisk breeze on a warm day and shivering as it whispered over one's skin.

With other vendors, she waited in the crowded cellar, holding only one bottle while Michel carried a cask. There were other vintners, as well as bakers, grocers, and sweet-makers, all vying for the chance to pay tribute and earn a place on Napoleon's dining table. Even more lucrative would be securing a contract to supply his troops, not only while housed in Paris but on the march. For everyone seemed to believe another military campaign was imminent, and the foot soldiers and cavalry would need to be fed.

Before she could see the emperor, her goods were examined and tasted, and then she was escorted upstairs into a grand reception room with a vaulted ceiling from which hung a crystal chandelier. Although it wasn't lit at that time of day, two massive candelabras were fully aflame, each standing on its own golden pedestal with a mirror stretching to the ceiling between them. In front of this stood Emperor Bonaparte on a gold-and-white carpet spread across the tiled floor.

Vendors moved in an orderly fashion, shuffling forward when called upon, and Serena, along with Michel, waited her turn until she was brought before Napoleon. Her grand-père had said it would be most helpful if she could secure a position in the palace for the ongoing delivery of Renault wine. All she needed was Bonaparte's favor, and if granted, she could come and go almost at will, easily able to eavesdrop for critical information.

As an Imperial Guard beckoned her forward, she dropped into a curtsy before the man who many were calling a miracle. Not tall in stature, still, Bonaparte was an inch or two taller than her and apparently fit, despite rumors of him having grown portly.

"Tell me your name, mademoiselle."

Those were the first words she heard from him, and she nearly answered him with the words "Miss Serena Elmstead."

Even if she'd said that, he would believe her to be nothing more than a successful merchant's granddaughter. Her clothing was clean and of good quality, a calico gown with a dark-green spencer over the top, every bit the well-to-do Parisian.

"Mademoiselle Renault," she said, her voice cracking slightly. *Gracious!* This was like no other lark she'd ever participated in. Not terribly dangerous at this stage, but with the existing climate of conspiracy and shifting allegiances, it could become so in an instant.

"I know you," the emperor said, and Serena felt her heart pound. *What did he know? Her true identity as an English woman?* "You are Joan of Arc, aren't you?" he asked. "Or maybe Mary Magdalene?"

She shook her head, unsure what he meant.

"Under your bonnet," he said. "I can see your crowning glory, like sun-burnished rubies."

Dipping her head in acknowledgment, Serena felt her cheeks grow warm.

"I bring you my family's wine, Your Imperial Majesty."

"Wonderful," he said and clapped his hands. "Two glasses," he said to the man who stepped forward.

Before she knew it, she was sipping wine with the ruler of France.

He smacked his lips. "I hope you brought more than this one bottle."

"Yes, Your Majesty." She gestured behind her to Michel holding the cask.

"Set it down," Bonaparte ordered, and he did. "Thank you, Mademoiselle Renault. I will make sure your wine is on the list to be served at my table."

"My family is grateful," Serena said and curtsied again, before backing up a few steps and turning to go.

"Mademoiselle," the emperor called to her, even as the next vendor was stepping forward seeking patronage. "Please feel free to return to my palace and personally bring me more wine whenever you can."

Again, she thanked him, hardly able to believe her good fortune. Nodding to Michel, they departed the reception room and made their way downstairs to the servants' exit.

Outside the double doors, still in the crush of other hopefuls, they grabbed each other's hands, forming a small circle, and stared at one another with large smiles.

"Bravo," said Michel.

"It was the wine," she said, "not me."

"Do you think Bonaparte would have invited Jacques to return 'whenever he can,'" Michel asked, "or me?" He hooked a thumb at his own burly chest. Then he broke out in loud guffaws.

Shrugging at his silliness, Serena turned to leave, and her gaze landed upon Monsieur Branley. Against all reason and commons sense, the Englishman was dressed as a French baker and holding a basket of loaves.

Dear God! Did he not understand the risk?

"I'll see you later," she told her grandfather's delivery man. "I've noticed a friend with whom I wish to speak. Please tell Pépère how well it went, yes?"

When Michel had left, she bit her lip. Monsieur Branley was shuffling ever closer to the door that would gain him entrance to the emperor. *What if he were going to try something drastic?* He'd confessed to being armed before. Perhaps he was unhinged and had a gun in his basket, hidden under the bread.

Approaching closer, she noticed how he glanced around in a continuous motion, surveying those around him. When he saw her, he flinched.

"I didn't mean to startle you," she said, as his eyes narrowed at her.

"You didn't," he said, "but I thought you had left already. What are you doing here?"

"I offered Renault wine to the emperor. The question is, what on earth are you doing here?"

He glanced at his basket, and his cheeks took on a ruddy stain. After all, she knew despite his loose cloth cap, his apron, and his baggy coat over it that he was most assuredly not a baker.

"I am helping out a friend," he said finally. "I must get the emperor to accept this bread . . . and me," he added.

"A friend?" she asked doubtfully.

"He is sick, but he can bake very well," Monsieur Branley added quickly.

"Which bakery?"

"Boulangerie Marineau," he said without hesitation.

"It is not a small bakery," she pointed out. "Didn't they have someone else to represent them?"

"They are *all* sick," he said defiantly.

"That may be, but you cannot go in there."

"I can and I will," he told her calmly, although he lifted his chin to a stubborn angle.

Since he was so tall, this only put his eyes farther from hers, and she wanted to stare into them until he understood the risk. For whatever reason, it terrified her that he was performing such a perilous masquerade.

Serena hated to break it to him in case he really didn't know and was insulted, but her words might save his life.

"You do not have the worst accent I've ever heard," she said, "but it certainly marks you as an Englishman. Here in Paris, we say, *'Tu parles Français comme une vache Espagnole.'*"

"I speak French like a Spanish cow?" he repeated with his poor accent.

'Oui, monsieur. And the emperor will not be pleased to be approached by an English baker pretending to be Monsieur Marineau."

Monsieur Branley nodded, as if he'd already accepted that fact.

"I'm fully aware of the shortcomings of my accent. But I assure you, I've managed not to be executed because of it, so far. If this were Prussia or even Russia, mademoiselle, I would be the one helping you."

Did he really speak those other languages so fluently? Before she could ask, he said, "Will you help me?"

Serena hadn't expected such a request. "What do you mean?"

"I must get access to the palace. It is vital."

At this juncture, he made sure to lock his gaze with hers. They stared into one another's eyes, and Serena knew she couldn't refuse him. With an inkling they were on the same side, she nodded.

"I shall pretend to be mute," he offered, "and you must speak for me."

She, as English as a rainy summer day, would pretend to be French while speaking for the mute Englishman playing the part of a Parisian *boulanger*. It was like a comedic farce at the theatre.

When she hesitated, he put on a beseeching expression. "Please, Mademoiselle Renault, accompany me back into the reception chamber. Tell Bonaparte you took pity on me when you realized I couldn't speak."

She thought about her family and their safety.

"I will not go so far as to tell anyone I believe you are Monsieur Marineau," she said finally, "but I will speak for you simply to offer the bread from the Boulangerie Marineau. If the bread isn't good, that is too bad for you."

His smile grew, and her stomach twinged pleasantly.

"And I suggest you slouch a little," she advised, as they stepped through the doorway together. "Try to be shorter."

She hoped she wouldn't regret her quick decision.

CHAPTER FIVE

Malcolm could hardly credit his good fortune. Seeing Mademoiselle Renault had shocked him momentarily, especially as she knew he thought Bonaparte a threat to peace on the European continent. Moreover, despite his tale, she probably guessed he was there on the Crown's business.

Yet she'd agreed to help him when she could easily have turned him in. While he had no way of knowing whether the young Parisian female supported the emperor or the king, Malcolm believed she meant him no harm. And that was as good an ally as he could currently hope for.

"He is a mute," she said to anyone who asked why she was no longer holding wine but accompanying a tall baker.

"Stoop a little," he heard her mutter.

Soon, Malcolm found himself face to face with Boney.

He was not impressive in the fashion of a king, no powdered wig or ermine robes while meeting his subjects. Malcolm supposed that was one reason the people liked him, believing he was one of them. Yet that was a carefully crafted ruse.

His ambitious and aggressive military nature was apparent in his green and white uniform, that of a colonel of the *chasseurs à cheval* of the Imperial Guard. Piped with red, his jacket was accessorized with gold, embroidered hunting-horns and adorned with eagle crowned buttons. Napoleon enjoyed all the trappings of an emperor and lived a lifestyle far above any ordinary citizen of Paris, yet in the guise of nothing more than a distinguished soldier.

At Mademoiselle's Renault's behest, Bonaparte took a loaf from the basket Malcolm held out to him and brought it to his nose.

"Smells delicious," the emperor said, before tearing off a piece to taste. "Not as good as your wine, but it is very good bread." He spoke to Mademoiselle Renault, even though Malcolm had said nothing about being deaf. It was almost as though he didn't exist next to the beautiful fiery-haired woman. And that was perfectly fine.

"*Mm,*" Malcolm said, and they both looked at him. Adjusting his cap which had slipped, he set the basket at the emperor's feet, crouched down, and fished out a paper sack.

When she appeared alarmed, so did Boney, and Malcolm realized Mademoiselle Renault probably thought he'd brought a pistol. Quickly, before he was grabbed and put in chains, Malcolm ripped open the sack to expose a piece of perfectly baked *pâte feuilletée* with slivers of almonds on top.

"What is this?" Bonaparte asked, and Malcolm shoved it closer.

The emperor accepted it, sniffed it, and then took a bite. He closed his eyes as the buttery pastry melted upon his tongue.

"*C'est incroyable. Trés delicieux,*" he added. "This actually might be as good as your wine, mademoiselle." And he stuffed the rest into his mouth without offering anyone a bite.

"You must return with your bread from Boulangerie Marineau," Napoleon told him, "but only if you bring more of these pastries."

Malcolm bowed low. In a very few minutes, they were outside, walking beside the Seine in the sunshine.

Mademoiselle Renault had remained silent since their departure from the Tuileries. Now, she spoke.

"That was a stupid thing for you to try by yourself."

He appreciated her honesty. "I was not supposed to play the part of a baker." Malcolm wasn't going to disclose how Versanne had not shown up. There must be a good reason for it, albeit one he wouldn't like. Perhaps, the Frenchman had been compromised and could no longer walk the streets without someone pointing him out as a royalist.

"My friend," Malcolm said carefully, "should have been here. He is French through and through, I assure you."

"Monsieur Marineau?" she asked, sounding doubtful.

He ignored her question because he hated lying when unnecessary. "We knew today was the day to make these connections with the palace, and I thought I would try on his behalf." He couldn't tell her anything more.

"What would you have done if I hadn't been there?" she asked.

That was a good question.

"Believe it or not, I would still have pretended to be mute. I would have done exactly the same. Although without your charm, I doubt the emperor would have even tasted the bread, let alone the pastry. I am again in your debt."

She nodded. She had a quiet maturity about her beyond her years, and an admirable confidence.

"It seems we are somewhat aligned in our purposes," he ventured, for if she was entirely in favor of the emperor's return, she wouldn't have risked helping Malcolm to get close.

"Perhaps," she said. "Or maybe I just didn't want to see you taken into custody."

That made him smile. "Why, mademoiselle? Have you developed a *tendre* for me?"

Her steps faltered briefly, and he regretted embarrassing her, especially after she'd been so helpful.

"*Je m'excuse,*" he said at once.

That made her smile at last. "We are back to where we started," she pointed out.

"Let us start over," he suggested, feeling like a buck in Mayfair. "Will you tell me your first name?"

She narrowed her eyes at him over the personal question. *Would she tell him?* He hoped so since he'd guessed every possible name when thinking of her, and none of them seemed to suit.

"Serena," she said softly.

He nearly laughed.

"Why are you smiling?" she asked, her green eyes flashing at him.

"Don't take offense. It's a lovely name. But none of our encounters have been in the least bit serene. Have they?"

He watched her pause and consider, before her own lovely visage broke out into a charming grin. "I suppose you are right. I didn't think about it, but I have never lived up to my name."

"Regardless, it is a very pretty one. There will be celebrations every night this week to welcome Bonaparte's return, maybe even longer. May I escort you to a dance?"

After another hesitation, she nodded.

"Then I need to know where you live."

This time she dithered longer, and he felt the prickling of suspicion. But then she sighed.

"I suppose I will have to tell my grandparents about you, monsieur. If my grand-père says it is permissible, then I will go with you. I warn you, however, Englishmen are *not* his favorite people."

She lived with her grandparents! Considering he gathered information for a living, he'd been woefully inept at learning more about this young woman who'd sparked his interest. Of course, an Englishman wouldn't be any Frenchman's choice, first or last.

"Where are your parents?" he asked.

"They sent me to live with my grandparents," she responded, which didn't answer his question, but he sensed that was all he would learn about them, until he earned her trust.

"You must now tell me *your* Christian name," she demanded saucily. "And where does your family reside?"

She knew he was English already, but nothing else. In truth, he could tell her everything about his family since they would never meet.

"My name is Malcolm, and my home is in Berkshire." Or at least his family's estate was. He preferred his London house, and his parents, Lord and Lady St. John, also had a Mayfair address for part of the year. "You probably haven't even heard of it."

"Of course I have," she said, then clamped her mouth shut, leaving him curious.

Perhaps he'd insulted her intelligence. "I only meant Berkshire is not London or Bath or even Brighton," he said. "Nowhere I would expect a Parisian to go upon visiting England."

"True," she agreed. "I have heard of it nonetheless. Windsor Castle is there, is it not?"

"Yes. You are quite correct."

They had strolled the riverside walk from the Quai de La Galerie du Museum all the way along to the Quai de L'École before she stopped by the Pont Neuf and spoke again.

"It seems as though Paris has only just seen the backs of the foreigners who camped here after the emperor's exile. The Prussians and Austrians, the Russians and the British." She glanced at him, as if to say, *yet here you are again.*

Malcolm wished to God he hadn't been called to return under these circumstances. As far as he knew only British intelligence officers were currently roaming the city, coordinating with the royalists. But she was right that agents from other countries would soon follow. Malcolm only hoped they could get Boney out of Paris and ensure no serious fighting occurred in the city.

"No one here wants another war," she added.

"Including me," he agreed.

Nodding, she gestured to the left. "I must go this way to get home."

He was as excited at the notion of seeing her again as he was having successfully guaranteed his welcome at the Tuileries Palace.

"May I accompany you so I know where to collect you? There is a ball in two nights at the Palais du Luxembourg. I promise I will obtain tickets."

"You can find me at 29 Rue Coquillière. It is just off the Place des Victoires."

"In two nights," he promised. "Eight o'clock."

She tilted her head, considering him. "You will not come wearing an apron, will you?"

Her humor lifted his spirits. If he had to be far from home, at the beginning of a new conflict, better to be in the company of a charming Parisian girl than with crotchety Versanne.

"A CHAPERONE? BUT MÉMÈRE—"

"Don't *but* me, Serena. I know my duty to my only granddaughter."

Serena didn't like to point out the obvious in case she lost any of her precious freedoms, but she couldn't help reminding her beloved grandparent, "You allow me to go out alone every day."

The older lady shook her head. "When you are at the Halle aux Vins, Jacques and Michel look out for you, as do all the other vintners whom your grand-père has known for years. Some are old enough to have watched over your mother, too."

"You also let me go to cafés with my friends, and they are not all female," Serena said stubbornly.

"You've been honest with me, yes?" her grand-mère asked. "Always at least one girl sits with you if you are in the company of a young man. Tonight is different. Your mother met an Englishman and had you nine months later."

Serena snapped her mouth closed. Her grand-mère had never put it like that before. She knew her grandparents would have wished for their daughter to marry a Frenchman and stay closer to home, especially with the years of war making it difficult to travel between the two countries. But there had never been a hint of scandal regarding her mother and her father, Baron Elmstead.

"My parents married," Serena said quietly.

"In the nick of time," her green-eyed grand-mère shot back. "There is a reason they married here in Paris and not in a grand ceremony back in England, but your grand-père wishes you were going out tonight with a nice Parisian boy."

"Why did you never speak of this before?" Serena asked.

Her grand-mère shrugged. "This is the first time I've seen a sparkle in your eyes. I'm glad for you, but possibly it indicates trouble. While I know you are safe in the wine market and in a café with your friends, going to a party with a man unknown to our family—why, he may be *un homme libertin*, yes?"

"A libertine!" Serena considered Malcolm Branley's behavior. He certainly had dash-fire.

"Besides," her grand-mère continued, "you are a baron's daughter, and you must behave like a lady. Those officers and government workers and all the *haute bourgeoisie* will be in high excitement tonight, some perhaps agitated, some may drink too much."

"I will take my pistol."

"No," the older lady said. "Not in your fine gown and not to a party at which the emperor may attend. You must be protected by a chaperone." Her grand-mère gave her a stern look. "Not everything works out as well as it did for your mother."

And her parents had undoubtedly given her grandparents an indication of Serena's somewhat puerile behavior during the London Season, but she liked to believe she'd matured in many ways since Vauxhall. While life was to be lived as fully as possible, it wasn't to be squandered or wasted, at least not on unworthy rakes.

Then her grand-mère gently caressed the back of Serena's hand in a way she'd always found loving and comforting.

"Maybe now, dear one, you will understand a little why your father was so angry with you for the risk you took in London. Not all men take responsibility for their actions, and some will say anything to tempt a woman's heart."

"I understand," Serena said, feeling grateful her grandparents were looking out for her. Knowing some of Mémère's friends, she considered who might have been chosen to attend a party with her and Monsieur Branley.

"Very well, but please not—"

"Madame Fournier, *bien sûr!*"

"Of course," Serena echoed. *Bien sûr.* Her grand-mère had chosen the most prying, hawk-eyed woman she knew. Also, in Serena's experience, a woman with tongue enough for two sets of teeth, constantly jabbering away and prone to bouts of indigestion.

"She will be here before you make it downstairs." The older woman kissed Serena's cheek. "You look lovely, just like your mother. I'll go pour the wine and make sure your grand-père isn't going to say anything insulting to your Englishman."

When her grandparents had learned Malcolm Branley's nationality, they'd agreed it was for the best if her escort remained in the dark about her own.

Her Englishman!

Serena shivered. Excited anticipation had been her companion all day long, and now, as she put the finishing touches to her hair, she could hardly contain herself. She hadn't dressed up and gone out for over a year. Moreover, she hadn't wanted to keep company with the opposite sex, mostly because none of the young men in Paris had sparked her interest. While a few had caught her eye, their attitude had been unappealing. Some behaved too familiarly with her. Some seemed like brothers. Some, like Guillaume, were angry all the time and far too bossy with all the females.

Monsieur Branley made her insides feel warm and tingly, and that had never happened before.

"Serena, your guest is here," came her grand-père's deep voice from the bottom of the stairs.

She startled despite having been watching the clock on the mantle over her hearth. It wouldn't do to go charging down the stairs like an eager colt.

Instead, she called out, "Coming."

Taking a last glance in the small square looking glass resting on top of her chest of drawers, she found her reflection to be favorable. A silk gown in her favorite shade of vibrant green with delicate flowers embroidered on the skirt, it was one of the few evening gowns she'd brought from home.

A silver chain holding a jade pendant from her grand-mère lay against her chest. She accompanied this with silver ear-bobs she'd bought at the shop where Suzanne worked in the Palais-Royal.

In her hair, a silver comb held up carefully crafted curls at the back. The last time she'd got ready for an evening, she'd had her mother's maid to help her and had worn emeralds and gold instead, but her grand-mère had done a spectacular job.

Grabbing a soft shawl, Serena descended to find Monsieur Branley in the sitting room with her grandparents, already drinking fine Renault wine.

And perhaps taking her chaperone duties too literally, Madame Fournier was seated on the divan *between* her grandparents.

However, Serena's gaze landed and remained on Monsieur Branley.

Setting his glass down, he rose to his feet when she entered, as did her grand-père.

"Mademoiselle Renault, you look well," her escort said, and his gaze flickered up and down with particular appreciation.

Serena hadn't imagined Malcolm Branley could look more handsome than he already did, but his present appearance nearly knocked her off her feet as assuredly as he had done physically the night they'd met.

Looking polished for the evening, he wore the black coat and cream breeches of a gentleman, with tall black boots and a proper hat, nothing like the cloth cap of a baker. And his thick brown hair was brushed back most becomingly.

The flickering warmth became a sizzling heat inside her, and she was thrilled at the thought of being in his arms for a dance. Or maybe two.

"Will you have some wine?" he asked, which struck her as amusing since it was her home and her grandparents' wine, but she nodded all the same.

He turned to the table where the carafe and glasses were, but her grand-père was already pouring. When they all had a glass again, it was her sparkling-eyed grand-mère who made the toast.

"To a wonderful night for you young people."

Her grand-père glowered. "To a peaceful, prosperous time for our kingdom."

Serena was surprised he had mentioned such a thing, since France was already being called an empire again. Her escort for the evening hesitated, but then he raised his glass to his lips with a nod of agreement.

"The wine is delicious. I can see why it is so popular at the cafés and restaurants of the Palais-Royal and at the Tuileries Palace."

Her grand-père cleared his throat. "Sometimes, it is necessary to have the favor of the latter in order to be able to continue doing business with the former."

"Of course," Monsieur Branley agreed, and nothing more.

Serena wrinkled her nose. Her grand-père made it sound as though the Renaults were entirely mercenary and had no firm belief, as if it didn't matter whether there was a Bourbon king or a self-appointed emperor as long as they could continue to sell their wine. She knew this wasn't the case at all.

The two men stared at one another for a moment. Then her grand-mère said, "Your French is good, monsieur."

"My vocabulary is, I suppose, although as your granddaughter has reminded me, my accent is not particularly fine. Something along the lines of a Spanish cow, I believe."

"Mon Dieu!" her grand-mère exclaimed. "You didn't?"

Serena's cheeks turned pink at her reproachful look, as if she'd come downstairs and insulted their guest on the spot. Even Madame Fournier made a clucking sound. Yet her grand-père nodded in agreement, although he never tried to speak a word of English himself.

Serena could do nothing more than offer a smile of apology. She hadn't meant to be rude at the time, only cautious.

"Obviously, monsieur, you do not live here permanently," her grand-père said, giving Serena a meaningful nod. *Don't get too attached,* he was reminding her.

That struck her as ironic considering she hoped with each of her mother's letters that she would be invited home. Instead, it was always stories of how trying her teen-aged brothers were, even though Serena knew her mother was comforted by having them under foot to keep her busy.

What's more, with Monsieur Branley in Paris, she felt perfectly satisfied to stay put for the time being.

Her escort paused again. *Would he divulge more than he had before?*

"That is true. My permanent home is in Britain."

"And you are here for work or for pleasure?" her grand-père persisted.

Rolling her eyes at Pépère's interrogation, she decided to put a stop to it before she lost her chance to go to a fête at the Palais du Luxembourg. She would hate to have to return to her room and remove her finery.

"Regardless of whether Monsieur Branley is in France for work, tonight, it is supposed to be for fun, *n'est-ce-pas?*" She turned to him. "Shall we go?"

"I am honored to escort you, mademoiselle."

Madame Fournier cleared her throat.

"And madame, as well," he amended.

Soon, they were squeezed into a *fiacre*, riding down the Rue du Louvre toward the Pont Neuf, taking the bridge over the Seine and down toward the old royal palace on the Rue de Vaugirard. While she'd strolled its beautiful gardens, Serena had never been inside the Palais du Luxembourg where the emperor had once lived before turning it into a building for the legislature.

Perhaps to show his solidarity with the common people and with the Parisian senate, Napoleon had decided to hold one of his celebrations there. On the same night, others would rejoice at the nearby Odéon theatre, while still more Parisians would be across the Seine at the Comédie-Française.

"It looks beautiful, doesn't it?" Madame Fournier was the first to speak when they came upon the well-lit pale, stone building.

Since the gardens were for daytime viewing, Serena had never been there at night and never seen how the old palace appeared with lanterns shining through the windows. The entire façade was shimmering.

"It does," she agreed.

Monsieur Branley helped both of them down, and then as naturally as a gentleman at Mayfair, he took Serena's hand, placing it in the crook of his arm, letting her chaperone fall into step behind. Her father would approve of his manners so far.

Once inside, they climbed the immense staircase, the Escalier d'Honneur, to the second floor. Everywhere were vases of fresh flowers from the surrounding countryside, giving the interior a splendid scent as rich and fragrant as the bouquet of a French perfume.

In the long hall where everyone had gathered, her gaze was instantly captured by the domed, painted ceilings, as fine as any artwork she'd ever seen. An enormous central chandelier glowed with enough candles to light the entire spacious chamber, although wall sconces were also lit, reflecting a room that was gilded from top to bottom.

"Gracious!" said Madame Fournier, her mouth open.

"Do you like to dance?" Monsieur Branley asked Serena, as musicians were already playing somewhere at the far end, beyond the crowd of guests.

"Very much," she said. "Although I haven't danced recently."

"Nor I," he agreed. "We shall enjoy recalling our steps together."

Everything was very much like the private balls she'd attended in London. People in their finery stood around the edges of the room, the musicians were at one end, and the dancing was in the middle, beginning with a quadrille.

Leaving Madame Fournier by the floor-to-ceiling windows, Serena let Monsieur Branley sweep her onto the dance floor. In the middle of the crowd of other dancers, he gave her his winsome smile.

"Finally alone," he quipped, referring to her chaperone.

She laughed, and at that moment, had to do a quick spin with another man before she returned to him. That would be the way of it all night, Serena feared, with only the briefest chance for anything more than a few words.

However, to her delight, the next dance was a waltz, not the quick *sauteuse*, either. It was a slow, romantic waltz, and Monsieur Branley did not turn her over to another partner. Since it was demanded by the dance, he held her closely without censure, even from her chaperone.

The warmth of his palm in the small of her back seemed a most intimate touch, and their clasped hands, even with gloves on, was thrilling. Letting him lead her through the exciting steps, Serena felt as if her slippered feet barely touched the polished floor.

He looked down at her. "I'm glad we've had this opportunity."

"As am I," she agreed, letting her gaze drift to his attractive lips which curved into a grin.

"You have an expressive face, mademoiselle. I can almost tell what thoughts are flittering behind your emerald eyes."

Hopefully not, she thought. For her mind was taking her places she shouldn't want to go. Not with him. Not alone.

She merely smiled back at him. And too soon, their waltz ended.

Serena had nearly forgotten how much she enjoyed attending a ball. As it turned out, it was nothing like a Mayfair ball in a private house. There at the old palace, people of various classes mingled, and wine flowed rather than the usual lemonade or restricted amount of champagne.

People were growing merrier and louder by the minute.

"*Vive l'Empereur!*" rang out occasionally, the intervals between the cheer growing shorter and the voices becoming more strident.

Even the dancing seemed increasingly frenzied, and as the evening wore on, more people were misstepping and bumping into one another. In mid-dance, a partner lifted her off her feet, making her shriek. As he set her back down, he tried to kiss her.

"Take your hands off the lady," came Monsieur Branley's commanding tone.

CHAPTER SIX

Malcolm Branley looked furious, apparently summoning more emotion than Serena could. Although not in fear for her safety since she was in a crowded room, she was relieved when he rescued her from her boorish partner.

As the man stepped back and stumbled over his own feet, Monsieur Branley took her arm and steered her off the dance floor.

Madame Fournier showed up a second later. "Thank you, monsieur," the older lady gushed. "What a disgrace! I was going to clobber him with my wine glass if I'd reached him first."

Serena opened her mouth to thank him as well, but he seemed ready to put the unpleasant scene behind them.

"I believe they've provided a feast outside," he said. "I'm sure our fellow guests will benefit from some food in their stomach after so much wine. I know I will appreciate a good meal."

Before the first line of small trees and shrubs, which provided a screen for the House of Peers during the day and divided the Palais du Luxembourg from the rest of the expansive gardens, tables had been set up under tents. They found chefs from the best restaurants in Paris, including the Café de Chartres, which Serena only knew because she'd seen him "in the back of the house," as she had heard the kitchen called.

Upon each receiving a plate, the three of them walked along the line of tables, taking some of this and some of that from the platters and bowls laden with tempting morsels. Then they found seats farther into the garden.

"Cleverly done," Monsieur Branley remarked, referring to the types of food they'd been offered, none needing a knife, easily eaten with the hand.

"Hors d'oeuvres," she told him, as they sampled pigeon-filled pastry tarts, small pieces of toasted bread topped either with ham or with savory mackerel and herbs, and egg-pastry balls filled with soft baked cheese. Naturally, there were selections of fresh fruit and various cheeses, as well.

Under Madame Fournier's persistent questions, Serena's escort talked about his Berkshire home, his London house in Piccadilly, a younger brother and sister, and a fondness for riding in Hyde Park. It was obvious that her chaperone was interrogating him like a matchmaker.

And while doing so, Madame Fournier sat close beside her, keeping an ear to Monsieur Branley and watchful eyes on the rowdy revelers.

In return, Serena told him only of her life with her grandparents. She said nothing about her parents or having two younger brothers of her own, as that would only beget questions as to where they were.

"I've never been to a vineyard," Monsieur Branley said, after Serena described her grandparents' estate in the middle of the Loire Valley, renowned for its good grape soil and climate.

"If it were not so far," she said, "I would take you for a tour." Even if they took Madame Fournier, Serena doubted her grandparents would let her spend a night with a single man under the same roof.

Abruptly, that good woman jumped up, setting her plate behind her on her chair and causing Monsieur Branley also to rise quickly to his feet.

"The ladies' retiring room," Madame Fournier announced, staring hard at Serena.

Madame's indigestion had obviously struck. Realizing she was required to go with her chaperone whether or not she wished to, Serena set her empty plate down before giving Monsieur Branley a small smile.

"If you'll excuse us." She couldn't resist raising her eyebrows at being put on a leash.

"Of course," he said, before winking in return.

It made her insides flutter again. Something about this man had her decidedly ensnared.

Leaving the makeshift ballroom, they found a small *garde robe* that had been turned into a ladies' retiring room, and an even smaller *cabinet de toilette*, far too small for the number of guests who needed to use it at any given moment. Rushing from torn hems to fallen coiffure to bodices drenched in spilled wine, even assisting with a chamber pot behind a screen, the attendants helped the crush of ladies with their every need, except the ability to breathe in the stuffy environment.

Serena edged closer and closer to the door until finally, Madame Fournier indicated her readiness to return to the party. Stepping back into the throng, Serena thought full stomachs had done little to calm the party guests. If anything, their emotions seemed inflamed by the rich canapés they'd consumed.

"The next dance, mademoiselle," a young man said, not waiting for an answer, nor consulting her chaperone. However, instead of being content on the dance floor, he twirled her to the far end of the room and, with a firm hold of her hand, pulled her outside.

Not unduly alarmed at first, knowing Madame Fournier had seen the man's face and that Monsieur Branley was somewhere nearby, Serena protested only mildly. She had engaged in precisely this sort of improper behavior during the Season, and knew a kiss was the prize her admirer sought.

Unlike her prior indiscretions, though, she felt no compunction to let him give her even the smallest peck. The only lips she found herself craving were the tall Englishman's.

As her admirer drew her from the well-lit patio where the tables were still set up, Serena felt a frisson of apprehension shiver down her spine. She wished she'd worn her pistol under her gauzy skirts after all, even if it had shown when she danced. Merely waving it toward a man would make him turn tail and run.

"Release me, monsieur. I must return to my chaperone," she told him firmly.

"Please, just a kiss," he begged, despite his behavior being more aggressive than beseeching. "Our glorious emperor has come back to us!"

She could not comprehend how Bonaparte's return to France was a reason for her to kiss anyone or for this man to behave badly.

As best she could, Serena dug in her heels, despite her soles being soft for dancing. Unfortunately, the slippery grass gave her no grip, and she found herself in a similar situation to Vauxhall, except this time, a tall hedgerow grew behind her instead of a leafy tree. The eager young man gripped both her wrists as she raised her fisted hands to pummel him, but at least he'd stopped trying to get her farther behind the shrub-line.

Drawing her against him, he trapped her arms. However, as he leaned down to kiss her, she drew her knee up sharply and slammed it against the bulge between his thighs.

No pistol needed, she thought to herself as he released her at once, doubling over and swearing blue oaths. If her father was correct, such language could blister her ears, but she believed he would be proud of her swift action.

Turning from her would-be kisser, she spied Monsieur Branley charging toward them.

"Happily," she told him when he got closer, "I have convinced the gentleman to leave me alone."

Her handsome escort glanced from the crouching man to her satisfied smile, and then he shrugged.

"It appears you have." But he couldn't resist giving the man a shove from behind that sent him flying into the prickly hedge.

Another flurry of oaths arose and then receded into the background as they walked away along the paved walkway toward the well-known Medici Fountain.

"Where is your chaperone?" Monsieur Branley asked.

Serena hesitated since they were obviously going in the opposite direction to the other guests, farther from the lights of the Palais du Luxembourg and toward the dark and sprawling gardens she'd been trying to avoid.

Out of the frying pan and into the fire, she thought. Except this fire had a matching flame flickering inside of her, and she felt no wish to avoid being alone with him.

Perhaps her escort *was* a libertine, as her grand-mère suggested.

"I lost Madame Fournier on the edge of the dance floor," she confessed.

But he didn't turn back as he should. And suddenly, the evening had become far more interesting. Even more so when they circled past a reflecting pond and reached the fountain's secluded grotto, a Tuscan portico lushly surrounded with fragrant spring cherry blossoms.

Without comment, her Englishman led her inside, and the rest of the world fell away beyond the flowered curtain. Finding herself in the unthinkable situation of utter isolation with Monsieur Branley—*Malcolm,* as she recalled from the night he introduced himself—Serena's heart seemed to be trying to escape her chest.

For a moment, they stood face to face, and he took hold of both her hands. Her insides did a singularly unusual flip. Finally, he spoke.

"When I saw that idiot pawing at you, I felt the strangest sensation."

"Really?" she asked before licking her suddenly dry lips.

"The first one wasn't so strange, I suppose," he admitted, releasing one of her hands and taking a lock of her hair between his fingers, seeming to caress it. "I felt murderous."

"Oh my!" Serena was glad she'd handled the matter without bloodshed.

"But the second was a wish to trade places with the man."

When her eyes widened, he added, "Not *after* you'd rightfully kneed him in the . . . *um* . . . giblets."

She laughed at the funny word, said in English since he probably didn't know the French equivalent.

"His twig and berries," she teased, and he looked shocked at her language, or maybe surprised because she had also spoken in English. She had shocked herself, frankly, by referring to a man's private parts. The wine and excitement were making her giddy and outlandish.

"I had the oddest notion," he added, "both of wanting to protect you and ravish you at the same time."

"Oh," she said again, instantly sobering and returning to French. "Are you a rake?"

"Am I a—?" He looked as if he wanted to laugh, but instead he said, "No one has ever asked me outright, although I confess I've been called such."

Her hopes sank. If he was truly a rake, then she'd fallen into the same circumstance as in London.

"And have you been called one for good cause or unjustly?" she asked.

The last of his smile left his face. "Why don't you find out for yourself?"

Leaning down, tugging her closer by the skein of hair still between his fingertips, his gaze held hers until she had to close her eyes right before his lips touched hers.

A spark, a sizzle, a jolt of pure vigor! Mercy!

Malcolm's firm mouth closed over hers and in the next instant, his hands were splayed across her back. Unlike a few minutes earlier, with the stranger, she felt neither danger nor disrelish, no inclination to push him away and run. *Quite the opposite!*

Placing her hands on his chest, Serena couldn't help sliding her fingers up past his snowy cravat before she laced them behind his neck. Nor did she resist her own desire to raise on tiptoe and get closer.

As he angled his head and their lips fused more firmly, she sighed. A warm and urgent throbbing had begun low in her body, making her wish almost desperately to tilt her hips toward him. While resisting the urge, she instead pressed herself closer, resting her thighs against his long legs.

Realizing her intent, Malcolm held her more tightly, deepening the kiss by sucking her lower lip into his mouth.

Shamelessly, she crushed her now-sensitive breasts against his coat front, aroused by the feel of him, hard against her softness. When he lifted his mouth momentarily, she drank in his subtle bergamot and carnation scent with each gasp for air before he reclaimed her lips. And then all she knew was the taste of him, salty from their meal and sweet from the wine.

Surely, she would ignite in flames.

This was desire!

"Serena? *Où êtes-vous?*"

Madame Fournier was searching for her, the cooling night air amplifying her voice across the small canal of water that stretched away from the secluded grotto by the fountain.

Untangling her fingers from Malcolm's hair, Serena pushed away from him. *How thoughtless of her!* The poor woman was probably beside herself with worry. But the kiss had been perfectly wonderful, and she could confess to not an ounce of regret.

"Your chaperone is nearby," Malcolm said, but when she moved to reveal herself, to step out from the portico, he stopped her, blocking her with his body. "You mustn't be seen," he reminded her, "not with me."

"How will I get back to the other guests?" she asked. The correct action wasn't to run headlong back to the party. She knew that from experience, especially if Madame Fournier witnessed her leave the fountain's confines.

"Stay here, back in the darkness. I shall be very quick. I'll find her and together, we'll search for you, and you shall appear perfectly innocent, enjoying a breath of air. Why don't you start humming in a minute so we can find you?"

"Humming?" she repeated.

"Whistling a tune, perhaps?" he suggested.

"I can't whistle."

In the dim light, she could see him roll his eyes. "Then sing, cough, or sneeze, mademoiselle. Anything to make a little noise so it isn't obvious I found you because I knew where I left you."

"Very well. But hurry."

"I will," he promised. Yet he hesitated, turned, and dropped another kiss upon her lips, so swiftly, she couldn't react.

"Yes," he said, "I am a rake."

He disappeared into the dark garden.

MALCOLM RAN LIKE A rabbit with a fox on its heels, around one side of the shrubbery and up the other side until he reached the area where people were still eating and talking outside. There was Madame Fournier, looking perplexed. He circled around before approaching her.

"Madame," he said, making sure it appeared as though he'd come from indoors. "I wondered where you and your charge had got to." He had a smile on his face, which he turned into a frown a moment later. "But where is she? Is she not with you?"

"Oh, monsieur, I half hoped, half dreaded she was with you. I will never forgive myself if something has happened to her. We came out of the retiring room, and she went immediately onto the dance floor, then I lost her in the crowd."

"Let's find her together," he suggested.

The chaperone turned toward the back doors of the old palace.

"I think we should search the gardens," he said, "since we are already out here."

In a very few minutes, Malcolm steered Madame Fournier toward the small canal of water. As they approached the fountain, he could hear alternately humming and coughing. He nearly laughed outright.

"Serena?" Madame Fournier called out, rushing forward.

Malcolm let the chaperone go in and discover her. His only worry had been some other buck would find her first, but luckily, she was still alone.

When they came out, Madame Fournier appeared annoyed but relieved.

"I think it best if we depart. The crowd is not behaving as finely as one could wish. I saw some untoward behavior when I was searching for Mademoiselle Renault," she said.

With the amount of wine flowing, Malcolm had no doubt she'd had an eyeful of amorous congress in the hallways, and she'd nearly seen more at the Medici Fountain, too.

In any case, having claimed the kiss he'd been hungering for since meeting Serena Renault, with little chance of sharing any further intimacies that night, he might as well concede the field and take the ladies home.

As they reentered the building, a wave of new excitement rippled through the party-goers and washed over them. Continuing through the old palace, they were nearly at the main entrance when chants of *"Vive l'Empereur!"* erupted.

The front doors were thrown open as Bonaparte crested the outer landing with officers flanking him on either side and Imperial Guards coming behind. The emperor looked triumphant wearing another of his uniforms, different from the light cavalry he'd worn at the Tuileries. In a grenadier's royal blue coat with its simple blue collar and pure white square-cut lapels, he waved to acknowledge the cheers while showing off his brilliant scarlet cuffs that matched the coat's lining.

As Napoleon strode forward, his coattails flapped behind, also showing flashes of scarlet facing. The candlelight caught the emperor's gilt buttons, each embellished with a crowned eagle, and the splendid gold epaulets danced as he walked. And of course, he wore a black felt bicorne without trim or plume, only a simple cockade, secured by a black braid. He looked to be glowing with the festive energy of the crowd who rushed to greet him.

Malcolm thought the whole display to be an effective show of power. Anyone who could see Boney's arrival cheered before a hush fell over the party guests, hoping to hear the emperor speak.

Malcolm saw Napoleon's eyes alight upon Mademoiselle Renault. *And why not?* She was easily the most beautiful woman in the palace, standing out due to the flaming color of her hair. Moreover, she happened to be directly in the man's path.

"The Renault vintner!" Bonaparte exclaimed.

Malcolm's blood chilled. If the emperor remembered her so easily, he would assuredly recall the mute baker for whom she'd spoken. And Malcolm no longer resembled such, nor could he pretend to be mute, especially not in front of Madame Fournier. Moreover, if he was discovered to be a fraud, it could put the Renault family in danger, as well.

As Mademoiselle Renault and her chaperone dropped into curtsies, Malcolm bowed low and stayed down, backing up a step and then another. Soon, he was behind a wall of people, crowding forward to see their hero.

Cursing his luck, he could do no more than watch as Mademoiselle Renault chatted with Bonaparte, introduced her chaperone, and then turned to where her escort should be standing beside her.

Smart lady, she barely hesitated, probably realizing why he'd departed. However, to his horror, Madame Fournier, in a loud voice exclaimed, "Where is Monsieur Branley?"

Turning, the older woman was trying to see where he'd gone. Malcolm was forced to disappear farther into the crowd until he was practically trotting, head low, down the corridor toward the Senate chamber. Knocking his shin against a low display table in his haste, he finally found an inconspicuous spot behind a marble pedestal with a tall vase and flowers.

What a debacle! He could hardly fulfill his duty to escort Mademoiselle Renault home if he had to hide behind a plant. He couldn't even keep an eye on her. For all Malcolm knew, the emperor might request the lady's presence at his side for the rest of the evening since Napoleon's wife, Empress Marie-Louise, had declined the invitation to go into exile. Instead, she was living comfortably with her lover in Austria. Whether she would return with Bonaparte's son and take up her duties beside her husband was as yet unknown.

Seething, Malcolm waited until the noise in the antechamber died down. Either the emperor had left the party to make a showing at one of the other events celebrating his return or he'd gone into the gardens to what remained of the feast.

Cautiously, he made his way toward the entrance. It was conspicuously empty. Beyond the large doors in the ballroom, he could hear the crowd outside, but whether Napoleon was out there along with Mademoiselle Renault, he had no way of knowing.

Dammit! He was an Englishman and a nobleman. Cowering was not his way. Stalking through the all-but vacant ballroom, he had his fingers on the door handle when a hand grasped his shoulder and spun him around.

CHAPTER SEVEN

"**R**andall!"

"Branley," his associate warned. "You cannot risk being seen in those clothes by Boney."

"How did you know I was here?"

Lord Randall's face broke out in its usual cheerful smile. "Currently, Paris is half spies and half people being spied upon, and sometimes they are one and the same."

"I am escorting a young woman tonight," Malcolm started to explain.

"Who has caught the emperor's eye," Randall confirmed. "She is the one who spoke for you at the Tuileries Palace, is she not?"

"Yes." Malcolm didn't even want to know how his associate was in possession of such information.

"You must be able to go back into the palace, freely and often," Randall reminded him.

"I know that," Malcolm snapped. "Why do you think I was hiding behind a damned vase?"

"Then don't give the game away now. This woman sounds like someone who can well take care of herself. Boney has an eye for the ladies, but he isn't Henry VIII. She'll be in no danger from him."

In his gut, Malcolm knew Randall was correct. Yet he had never shirked his responsibilities with a female before.

"My duty—" he began.

"Is to king and country, above all." Randall reminded him.

Gritting his teeth, Malcolm looked outside again through the glass panes. He couldn't even see Mademoiselle Renault amidst the revelers.

"It doesn't sit well with me," he muttered.

"Nevertheless, you have a job to do," Randall used his stern tone again.

Swearing under his breath, Malcolm gave in. "Fine. But would you have me simply abandon her? The mademoiselle will understand, but her chaperone and her grandparents will think me mad."

Randall stared at him, then he grinned. "If you care what her grandparents think, my friend, then I guess you care for her. Are you planning on plucking this French flower and installing her in your English garden?"

Poetic bastard! He'd only managed to kiss her. He was hardly ready to get down on bended knee over the chit, just because he found her attractive, intriguing, exciting, amusing and positively gorgeous.

"You look addled," Randall said.

"Shut up," Malcolm told him. "Are you suggesting I leave her here? That's the action of a scoundrel."

"*Hm.* I see what you mean." Randall considered. "I shall go instead and fetch her away from her admirer."

"You?"

Randall drew himself up taller. "Yes, me! Why not me? I have never been near the palace or the emperor, at least, not so he would recall." He winked. "He'll have no reason to suspect me."

"But your accent is hardly better than mine. I doubt he'll look kindly on a crusty Brit stealing away a pretty Parisian mademoiselle."

"I won't speak aloud if I can't get her away from him." Without further words, Randall slipped outside.

Probably the only thing worse than waiting behind a vase of flowers was waiting by a garden door. It seemed interminable, but was probably a mere five minutes before one of the doors opened and Mademoiselle Renault entered, followed by her chaperone and then Randall.

"Monsieur Branley!" Madame Fournier spoke first. "Where on earth did you get to? You missed the most delightful conversation with His Imperial Majesty. Not to mention *biscuits de Reims* and delicious champagne in which to dip them!"

"And sticky *moelleux aux abricots*," Serena said, licking her upper lip, looking satisfied—and utterly desirable.

His attention remained on the woman he'd kissed, realizing how much he'd detested not being able to protect her.

"Are you ready to leave?" he asked.

The mademoiselle nodded. "Absolutely. And your friend . . . ," she turned to include Randall, but he'd already vanished.

LATER IN THE WEEK, Serena prepared to return to the Palais des Tuileries, adjusting her bonnet. So much had happened. Having been kissed topped her list. Thoroughly kissed. Thrillingly kissed. *A heart-stopping, breath-stealing, and making-her-want-more kiss!*

And she'd been to her first ball in over a year. While the entire evening had been entertaining, only the minutes spent with Monsieur Branley had been truly satisfactory. Dancing with others had felt like time wasted, and even chatting with the emperor in the garden after her escort so abruptly disappeared had been merely distracting.

Malcolm, as she thought of him, was quick at disappearing—she would give him that, especially considering his height. It was as if he had vanished in the blink of an eye.

Strangely, Bonaparte hadn't been nearly as exciting as her Englishman.

When a stranger had touched her elbow, managing to move her out of the emperor's circle, she'd been intrigued and then grateful.

Malcolm had signaled a *fiacre* and taken them home. Madame Fournier did all the talking on the quick journey, and they hadn't had another moment alone.

Nor had he made an arrangement to see her again, much to her disappointment. She hoped he'd enjoyed the kisses as much as she had and might want to partake of another one or two.

Stepping out of the carriage, she entered through the gate in front of the Palais des Tuileries, gave her family name to the guard who made sure her wine was on his list before he examined the contents of her basket, and found four bottles. Wondering for a moment how Malcolm would give his name to the guard, she decided he would probably bring a card from the bakery, identifying him.

On the other hand, Serena thought, as she made her way to the cellars to speak with the wine manager, Malcolm might not return, not if he truly had been doing a favor for a friend. Perhaps a real baker from Boulangerie Marineau would next deliver the bread and pastry.

That day, unlike the previous visit, she hadn't brought Michel. If she brought a barrel, then another impending return would be unnecessary, and her chance to discover the emperor's plans would be lessened. For that was her charge from her grand-père—to bring back any tidbits of information. And she was only one of many information gatherers, as far as she knew.

However, instead of being invisible, perhaps wandering through the servants' area and up one of the many back staircases to hear how the emperor planned on defending himself, an Imperial Guardsman found her.

"His Imperial Majesty wishes to see you, mademoiselle."

Those few words started her heart racing. Uncertain, her thoughts flew to the worst. In the blink of an eye, she'd gone from enjoying her game of espionage to hoping she wasn't in any sort of trouble that might end in her imprisonment. Quietly, she followed the uniformed man. To do anything else, including run, would be foolish.

Please, don't let this be because of Monsieur Branley, she thought.

A surprising assembly met her eyes when she was led into a reception room larger and grander than the one in which she'd gathered with the other Parisian vendors. The emperor's throne sat on a raised red dais of five red-carpeted steps, although Bonaparte was not seated upon it.

Instead, he was in conversation with Serena's friend Guillaume, as well as the man who'd sent Monsieur Branley into hiding at the Halle aux Vins.

So this *was* about him!

She curtsied to the emperor and awaited her fate.

"*Bonjour, mademoiselle,*" Bonaparte said, sounding as friendly as before. "I am enjoying your family's wine very much. I believe you know Monsieur Racine."

Guillaume stepped toward her, his expression normal, calm, without malice, and her heartbeat started to calm.

"His Imperial Majesty is concerned about Parisians working with our enemies," Guillaume said, getting right to the point.

Still unsure what they wanted with her, Serena merely nodded.

"This is Monsieur Christoff," Guillaume introduced her formally to the man she thought of as a *tête de noeud.*

He cocked his head and stared at her, and she could only pray Monsieur Christoff hadn't seen the back of her leaving the Halle aux Vins with Malcolm.

When he came forward and gave her a short bow as a greeting, she returned it.

"I recognize you from the wine market, mademoiselle."

She startled before realizing he meant on a regular basis, not while fleeing with an English spy. For surely, she could no longer doubt that was what Malcolm Branley was.

"And I, you, monsieur. You work for Cerise Winery." Her nerves prickling, she turned to address the emperor. "May I ask what Your Imperial Majesty wishes of me?"

"I trust my vintners completely," he said, his dark Corsican eyes boring into hers.

She nearly looked away, but that would indicate disloyalty or weakness, so she held his gaze.

Finally, he blinked and then he smiled. "Those delivering wine move freely throughout the city and talk to many people, especially in the cafés."

"Yes," she agreed.

"I ask only that you, along with Monsieur Christoff, listen to the conversations around you. That's all. In the heart of our great city, I know, there are those who wish me ill and are planning my downfall."

Serena hadn't realized until that moment how the emperor had grown closer, continuing to hold her gaze, mesmerizing her with his convincing tone, until he suddenly reached out and took her gloved hand.

She nearly gasped, but managed to restrain herself. *Gracious!* This was no amusing lark at a Season's event in Mayfair. Their meeting had ramifications beyond these four walls, perhaps for an entire nation and even for a continent. She swallowed, unable to speak past her dry mouth. Surely the emperor had others he could call upon—people more serious and useful who weren't flighty and immature, as her father once called her.

Although at that moment, she certainly felt grown up, even aged beyond her years.

"You are more likely to be welcomed into conversations than either of these brutes, yes?" Bonaparte gestured over his shoulder with his chin.

Guillaume and Monsieur Christoff laughed.

"Mademoiselle Renault is popular," Guillaume added, looking at her warmly. "That's why I recommended her."

Serena couldn't help wishing her friend had kept his admiration to himself, although her grandparents would probably look favorably on the new arrangement.

The emperor gave her another smile before releasing her hand and turning to the others.

"I am most appreciative. Let's have some wine, shall we?"

Serena wanted to get out of the palace and talk to Pépère and Mémère, but one hardly declined an invitation from Bonaparte, who with an apologetic shrug added, "This is not Renault wine, I'm sorry to say."

Monsieur Christoff's face turned florid. "I assure you, Your Majesty, the wine from the Cerise family's vineyard will not disappoint."

Serena knew it to be good wine, although not as good as her family's. As she had already left her bottles with the wine manager in the lower level, Cerise wine would have to do.

Moreover, as a palace servant was summoned and offered her a glass of the ruby liquid, she decided she would have to praise it. Given the circumstances and the sudden alliance in which she'd been unwillingly drafted—and the very real possibility of being under Monsieur Christoff's scrutiny—she would do well to remain on a friendly basis with him.

Although no one had brought it up in her presence, surely he'd told Bonaparte about Monsieur Branley approaching him on behalf of the British, or of the royalists, or both, first at the café and then in the wine market. Yet it was clear the emperor's intent was that none of them would be told too much, either to keep them all safe or keep them all powerless.

As for Guillaume, beaming at her as if she were his protégé, Serena would have to be careful around him, as well. From what Felicity said, he had a romantic interest in her. And a rebuked man could be a dangerous one at any time.

Thus, she smiled back. The conversation turned to Bonaparte's bold plans. He wished to return the French flag from royalist white to the familiar tricolor, which had begun to happen even as he'd marched toward Paris, and he intended to abolish the hated slave trade through the Senate, if they were willing. Serena could find no fault with either aspiration. Indeed, she felt no antipathy toward the dynamic ruler.

If only he hadn't plunged her grandparents' country into so many years of war.

When an officer came in a few minutes later, wishing to speak privately with the emperor, Serena was relieved to curtsy and leave his presence. Unfortunately, she was escorted out by Guillaume and Monsieur Christoff.

"We are going to the Café Montansier. Will you come?" Guillaume asked her. "Felicity will be there soon, and Jean-Paul and Suzanne."

"No, I have been kept longer than expected." She didn't mean to sound censorious.

"It is an honor to be personally asked by the emperor," Guillaume chastised her, his tone annoyingly superior. "That is, unless you don't believe in the cause of a true republic."

"France hasn't been called a republic for six years," she reminded him. "It's an empire, if you recall. A very different thing. But I'm not quibbling with you. It is only that I must get back to my grandparents. They worry when I don't turn up as expected."

"Perhaps you can meet us later." This from Monsieur Christoff. "I had forgotten, but you were at the Aveugles when that idiot Englishman tried to recruit me to the side of the Bourbons." He ended by spitting on the street. "*Pah!*

They can go to hell and their useless king with them. Can you believe they thought I was going to assist them?"

"Hush," Guillaume cautioned. "Better to be discreet, my friend."

At that moment, Serena decided she would go to the café that night after all. Housed in a former theatre, the Café Montansier had become the gathering place for those who supported the emperor. They sang songs in his honor, and were already handing out bouquets of violets, as much a badge of the Bonapartists as the tricolor cockade.

Malcolm's allies, and specifically his faction working in Paris, were depending upon the wrong people if they thought such men as the *tête de noeud* to be potential allies. Perhaps she could discover if any more were behaving as false friends.

And why would she help Malcolm over her friends? She hoped it wasn't solely on account of a perfect kiss.

"I will meet you there later," she promised, letting Guillaume kiss each of her cheeks and blocking Monsieur Christoff from doing the same before she departed.

As she walked away, she heard Guillaume's arrogant laughter at how she'd thwarted the other man from getting close. It sent shivers up her spine. Either man could become a terrible threat if they knew her family's true loyalties.

CHAPTER EIGHT

Malcolm sat in the corner of the Café Montansier in the northwest corner of the Palais-Royal, his cap drawn down, collar turned up, slowly nursing a bottle of wine. He could easily see the entrance and much of the area where the establishment's shows were produced both when it was solely a theatre and more recently, as a café with sideshows of dubious quality. And he was keeping an eye on a table full of young people, including Christoff, the Cerise vineyard wine manager.

So far, the citizens of Paris, at least those in this restaurant, were decidedly on the side of their triumphant emperor. Some had breached the stage, loudly singing *La Marseillaise* while other sang along from the tables. Nearly to a man, they were wearing red caps in solidarity, even Malcolm, and the women had on red bonnets.

"The Revolution is coming back to life!" declared a man a few feet away, and the singing started again. The only dissenting voices were those who feared another long war. And any who wondered such were soon shouted down and told to go elsewhere.

Malcolm was sure it wouldn't be drawn out this time, not over years and decades. Once the Seventh Coalition engaged, they wouldn't let up until Boney was defeated.

What he wasn't sure about was how to proceed, and that, in itself, felt unbearably unusual. Moreover, all his uncertainty centered upon one desirable Parisian woman, and not upon his duty to Britain. He wanted to see Mademoiselle Renault again, despite how his attention ought to be singularly focused on the military and political developments. While the emperor was marshalling troops and presenting extravagant parades to show them off, giving any enemies remaining in Paris no doubt as to his strength, Malcolm was wondering what color Serena Renault's nipples were—dusky pink or peachy. He decided because of her hair color, they were the latter.

The sooner this last assignment ended, the sooner he could go home and start the process of stepping into his role as heir to a viscount. *The process* was the least painful way of considering marriage, and he could hardly recall the faces of the two women he'd deemed acceptable when last considering a wife.

Moreover, if Serena, who had increasingly piqued his interest each time they'd met, gave him a sign she was willing, then he might act upon his inclination to bed her. *After all, how could it possibly interfere with his assignment?*

In the meantime, the Seventh Coalition's plans were moving slowly, as happened when more than one nation tried to work together and all of them wanted to be in charge. Until the time came to act, he would return to the Tuileries Palace by day to sniff out any plans for upcoming acts of war. Boney would decide the next field of battle. Where that would be, no one yet knew.

And in the evenings, Malcolm would circulate through the cafés, especially the hotbeds of insurrection and revolution like the one tonight, listening to the mood of the people and, more usefully, the loose tongues of drunken officers, cavalry, and foot soldiers. Formerly of the French

Royal Army, many were now firmly attached to the Imperial forces.

Randall, lying low after his appearance at Luxembourg Palace, believed Malcolm hadn't been compromised. Only the emperor and some household staff at the palace could identify him as the mute baker.

Except for Serena.

After their searing kiss, although he wasn't a profligate gambler, he would wager at White's she wanted a tryst as badly as he did. A passionate and willing woman was an irresistible temptation. Despite her grandparents insisting on a chaperone, Serena seemed less inhibited than the young ladies of the London *ton*. And her independence bespoke of a more experienced woman.

Not that her being less restricted and more worldly gave him leave to take advantage of her. It simply made the possibility of a liaison while he was in Paris a distinct possibility. She was not the type to demand a marriage contract before a kiss, and he wasn't the type to consider getting serious with a vintner's granddaughter who would never be accepted as the future Viscountess St. John.

Hell! Until a month ago, he hadn't been the type to think of getting serious at all. Yet he was at the age when many of his class were securely wedded and beginning to produce heirs, and he couldn't put it off any longer.

It was frightfully easy to picture babes with Serena's stunning coppery hair and charming green eyes.

Speak of the devil and there she was! She entered the café by herself, but to his astonishment, she went directly over to the table where the brutish beast who'd turned on him at the Halle aux Vins now sat chatting jovially with two other men and two women.

Any foolish notion of saying hello if he saw her couldn't possibly come to fruition while she was with that oaf, Christoff. And now, her vague statements regarding the future of an empire or a kingdom came back to worry him. Quite possibly, she was a Bonapartist through and through, as many of the other Parisian merchants were. She might have helped him simply because she liked him. That brought his thoughts right back to stretching out beside her, both of them naked as a needle, and finding mutual satisfaction.

But she might have helped him in order to keep him close, hoping to learn more, before eventually turning him in.

He passed the next hour and a half gaining no more interesting information than how the two men at the next table intended to turn in their butchers' knives and take up arms for Napoleon should he call upon them to do so.

Malcolm doubted the emperor would stride into either of their butcher shops or this particular café seeking out men with more wine-induced bravado than combat skills. Regardless, the fact they were willing was more evidence this fight must not come to the city itself. Amateur soldiers would make for rich cannon fodder, and the streets would be bathed in blood.

Serena's laughter caught his ear. She leaned close to one of the other women seated at the table, but both Christoff and another man were giving her their full attention. Malcolm doubted she had any idea how bewitching she was. In another few minutes, all of those at her table stood and left. Just before she slipped out of the café's entrance, she lifted her cloak's hood over her head.

Waiting a minute, Malcolm followed them through the same door out into the Galerie du Montpensier. Many people were strolling the Palais-Royal arcades, going in and out of the cellars, most of which had been turned into gambling dens, music rooms, and theatres, and some were even large enough to be ballrooms. Other people were seated in the middle greens on benches smoking or simply chatting. And of course, at that time of the evening, there were harlots in all manner of dress and undress, hanging on men's arms, lounging in doorways, and sauntering along the colonnades.

In the distance, heading north toward the Galerie de Beaujolais, was the cloaked figure of Mademoiselle Renault walking along the piazza with her arm held securely by the other man from the table, not Christoff. The other two women strolled close behind.

Malcolm supposed that should make him feel better, knowing she hadn't taken up with the prick-head.

Turning in the other direction, he crossed the central garden of the Palais-Royal, nodding to the whores who called out to him, before he ducked into a shop on the Galerie de Valois, which spilled him out its backdoor toward his own small apartment. After crossing the next street, he heard a woman cry out.

To his astonishment, up ahead, he saw yet *another* Mademoiselle Renault, this one with her hood fallen back. Her unmistakably glorious hair glistened in the light of the oil lamps hanging on ropes strung between many of the second story buildings by order of Monsieur de la Reynie, Paris's first police chief. Malcolm had thought them a good idea, and now even more so.

A hulking man by his silhouette, undoubtedly Christoff, was attempting to drag her into an alley.

Malcolm was running before he realized what he intended to do.

"Leave her be," he said in English, and then as the man released her, he added in French, *"tête de noeud,"* in case Christoff had any doubt who he was.

With a roar, the brute rushed at Malcolm, but his assailant's size did him no favors, and Malcolm stepped aside to avoid the first bull-like onslaught. His glance caught Serena's, and instead of her appearing distraught, he thought she wore an amused expression.

That distracted him long enough for Christoff to come behind him. Serena winced just before Malcolm received a blow to his lower back, probably his kidneys.

What a damnable fellow! The man was lucky Malcolm had decided not to shoot him but to handle this as a gentleman and beat him to a pulp. His many hours spent at Gentleman Jackson's Boxing Academy were put to good use as he socked the man in his stomach and then, when Christoff leaned over with the air knocked out of him, Malcolm clocked him in the chin, snapping back his ugly, florid face.

"Enough?" Malcolm asked Christoff, glancing over to see Serena leaning against the building, arms crossed, not the least bit bothered.

Christoff came back swinging, managing to catch Malcolm's cheek but luckily not his nose, which he fancied was a good feature of his face. He didn't like to think of it becoming crooked, even if he wasn't going to remain a confirmed rake.

The notion of losing his good looks made Malcolm strike the brute harder, again in the stomach and then in the face. He heard the satisfying crunch of the man's nose, followed by a spurt of blood while Christoff yowled in pain.

"If you come at me again," Malcolm warned, "I shall draw my pistol because I'm tired of this caper."

Then, as any good gentleman, he handed the man, still doubled over, a kerchief from his own pocket to staunch the blood.

"You'll be sorry," Christoff warned, but he ambled away, taking Malcolm's kerchief with him.

"Scoundrel! I can't stand a man who picks on women."

Serena pushed away from the wall and approached him.

"I suppose I must thank you," she said, reaching up and brushing her gloved hand across his cheek where it throbbed.

"You say that as if it's a chore, as if I didn't just save you."

She laughed, the same light sound she'd used in the café, and it infuriated him. Even more when he realized she'd walked off with the prick-head in the first place.

"I fail to see what's so funny."

To his amazement, she took his arm as if they were back at the Luxembourg Palace strolling through the ballroom.

"I didn't *need* to be saved."

"Really?" He thought about that for a moment. Maybe she wanted to go with Christoff down the alley. And thinking how she'd left Café Montansier with a man firmly on the side of the emperor, Malcolm would be a fool to trust her.

"Where have you come from and where were you going?" she asked.

He had to be more careful around her, and not let her beauty and his attraction to her make him loose-tongued.

"I was at the Palais-Royal." *No need to tell her he was watching her all night.* "And I'm headed home."

"Home?" she mused. "Is it close?"

"Yes," he answered tightly, still annoyed at how lightly she'd taken the situation that could have ended in her lying in the alley.

They'd been walking while talking and now, he gestured to the building across the street.

"Right there?" she asked. "But you must show it to me." Then she leaned close and his body twinged with desire, thinking she was about to kiss him on the street. "You don't know this, Monsieur Branley," she said quietly, "but your cheek is bleeding a little. I will come with you and tend it if you'll let me."

Not about to kiss him at all, she only felt sorry for him!

His pride and his ire were raised along with his manhood. The delicious floral scent of her made him long to run his fingers through her copper tresses.

"That won't be necessary, Mademoiselle Renault." His tone was clipped. "Good night."

Releasing himself from her hold, he stalked across the street toward the small door leading to his apartment. Unusual for Paris, there was no concierge's hut, no central courtyard, and hardly any tenants. Merely a street door and three flights of stairs up to a comfortable bed in a clean room. It was all he'd requested from Randall, and all he'd received.

But he stopped at the door. Even though Serena dismissed the attack and his noble rescue, and despite her grandparents' apartment being quite close, Malcolm couldn't leave her alone in the street.

Turning, they nearly collided. He hadn't heard her footfalls crossing the street behind him. The noise in his own head, both persistent rumblings of desire and his blood pumping loudly in his ears, had allowed her to sneak upon him. He was dumbfounded.

"Let me clean off the blood, at least," she said, lifting her arm as if she meant to touch his cheek with a handkerchief suddenly held in her gloved hand

Impossible woman! In the street, even at night, she shouldn't be doing any such thing. Moreover, if he was bleeding, it might soil her pale green glove.

She was such an unpredictable female Malcolm couldn't imagine what she was thinking or would do next. But he'd hoped for a sign she was enthusiastic to be alone with him, to do more than kiss, and he couldn't have asked for a better one.

As long as she didn't laugh at his heroic abilities any more, neither on the street, nor in bed.

Unlocking his door, he realized how shabby the place might appear through her eyes, compared to the small but luxurious apartment belonging to the Renaults. Reminding himself this wasn't his real life, Malcolm brought to mind his comfortably luxurious house in London's Piccadilly neighborhood and the family home in the country that he would one day inherit. If he saw the smallest ounce of pity in her green eyes, he would tell her about them, too.

And wouldn't it be nice to show her both.

Standing by his door after she entered, he hesitated about closing it behind them.

"It's adorable," Mademoiselle Renault proclaimed. "I wouldn't have thought you'd have a garret like this. You seem the type of man who would have a two-story apartment."

That made him grin. "I *am* that type of man," he agreed. "And I would have it if I'd wanted. This suits my purposes. It's quiet and discreet."

As soon as he'd said the last word, her glance flew to his. *Had she just realized the impropriety of her actions?* She'd allowed him to bring her into a private place, a room with nothing but a bed, armoire, and washstand. In fact, she'd insisted. He couldn't believe her to be so naïve, thus she must want him to dip his biscuit, or as the French so elegantly put it, *tremper son biscuit.*

She cleared her throat, then looked around. Seeing the bowl of that morning's cool water, a little sudsy still, she asked, "Do you have a clean rag?"

With those words, she stripped off her gloves, shooting heat straight to his loins.

Wrenching his gaze from her perfect, rosy lips, he reminded himself she might not have come up there for a tumble. But his bed was as rumpled and unmade as he'd left it, and it would be ridiculously easy to tug her down upon it.

If she was willing.

Dropping his own hat and gloves onto the small writing desk, he crossed the small space and drew out a clean handkerchief from a drawer in his armoire. With their gazes locked, he drew close to Serena again and handed her the square of linen.

As their bare fingers touched, he heard her sharp intake of breath, a sound that made his shaft straighten like a ship's mast. He'd best let her minister to him—to his cheek, at least—and then send her on her way quickly.

Or get to the business of some heated rantum scantum.

Again, only if she was willing.

CHAPTER NINE

Serena wasn't sure what had got into her, following a man up to his room. But he wasn't just any man. He was Malcolm Branley, who'd captured her interest in a way she never could have imagined. Her father would be livid, and her mother would weep to see her. Her situation was even worse when she stripped off her gloves so they wouldn't get wet or stained.

Why, she was practically undressed!

Until the moment she'd been helpless to resist trailing Malcolm into his apartment, Serena had assumed she'd matured into a responsible woman, one who'd left behind her impulsive capriciousness. Apparently, she'd been sadly mistaken.

Dipping the clean kerchief into tepid water, her hand trembling slightly, she could feel Malcolm close beside her. Pointedly, he'd left the door open, but he was shuffling from one foot to the next, looking uncomfortable.

"Stand still," she ordered, and reached up to wipe the blood from his cheek. "I think Monsieur Christoff had a ring on. Didn't you feel it?" She was dripping water all over the front of him, and her hands were truly shaking now, although she didn't think Malcolm could see that.

"Not really, no. But it stings now, to tell you the truth."

"I'm sure it does." She dipped the handkerchief back in the bowl and then wrung it out again before dabbing his cheek once more. "It looked worse when the blood was flowing than it is. It's merely a little cut."

Suddenly, his hand grabbed hold of hers, startling her. He lowered her arm gently before taking the handkerchief from her and tossing it into the porcelain bowl where it floated on the pinkish water.

"Thank you. I am fine," he said, his deep brown eyes locked on hers.

In answer to her quizzical look, he added, "I don't want you to get blood on your hands."

Glancing at her hands, she wiggled her fingers in front of him. "No blood, sir. And I owe you an apology. You were very brave, and you got injured helping me. I should have said nothing other than thank you."

"You're right, but now you're placating me." He shouldered past her and grabbed a small mirror from a leather bag so he could look at his face.

If he'd asked, she would have told him he was as handsome as ever and also somewhat maddening. For one thing, she hadn't needed his help because she had her pistol ready to draw out and wave under Monsieur Christoff's nose. And for another, she'd thanked Malcolm sincerely, and now he'd rebuffed her.

Having taken the rash step of coming up to his room, satisfying her curiosity that he wasn't living with some other woman or even a wife, she ought to return home. But she didn't run for the open door.

"I am *not* placating you," she promised. "I'm showing my gratitude, but I had best be getting home." Yet she desperately wanted him to kiss her again, another reason she was moving so slowly toward the exit.

"I cannot believe your grandparents allow you out this late alone."

"Normally, I walk with my friends, but Guillaume and his sister live in the other direction, and Monsieur Christoff offered to walk me home. If the others had suspected he was going to try to steal a kiss—"

Malcolm looked surprised. "Is that what you call him trying to drag you into an alley?'

"He wasn't dragging me into an alley. It was more like an alcove, and I'm sure he simply had the wrong idea."

"You are naïve, mademoiselle." He shook his head, making his lustrous brown hair lift and fall.

With all her heart, she wanted to touch it.

"I know exactly what Christoff was thinking," Malcolm continued, "and unless I'm sadly mistaken, you wouldn't have liked it."

She wrapped her hands around herself as a shiver ran down her spine. She hadn't liked Christoff's manner of staring at her all night. Regardless, she'd stayed the entire evening at the café, letting him boast of his plans and his proximity to the emperor, even as Guillaume tried to hush him.

By listening, Serena played her small part in whatever would happen to France. She hadn't expected Guillaume and Felicity to abandon her to the other man. When she told them tomorrow what had happened, they would undoubtedly regret having done so.

She supposed it could have gone badly if Christoff had managed to take her pistol away.

"I'm glad you weren't terribly injured," she said. And suddenly, she did feel remorse for causing him to be pummeled and cut. Perhaps she was immature and reckless, after all. What could an experienced, confident man like Malcolm Branley want with her anyway? "Good evening, monsieur." With that, she turned to the door.

Malcolm was after her quick as a gunshot. He didn't touch her, but he stood close.

"Do you count Christoff among your allies?" he asked quietly.

She couldn't help looking at his lips, recalling how they felt pressed against her own, before she raised her gaze to his, and his words filtered into her distracted brain.

"Allies? Do you mean friends?"

"Yes," he agreed. "I suppose it got lost in the translation."

But his French was good enough for her to know he'd used *alliés* rather than *amis* on purpose. Plainly Malcolm was wondering if she was aligned with those who wanted to keep Bonaparte in power.

"Monsieur, I have many friends in Paris, including you."

His eyebrows raised. Perhaps he didn't count himself among her friends. She sighed.

And somehow, without even realizing how it happened, Serena swayed against him and his arms were suddenly around her, pulling her close. Tilting her head, she waited for the kiss she knew would come.

She didn't have to wait long. His firm mouth claimed hers, and she felt a sizzle down to her booted toes. Unable to help herself, she reached up and wrapped her hands around the back of his neck. He took a step back into the room, bringing her with him. And somehow, perhaps with his foot, the door shut behind them, closing out the world beyond his small garret.

His tongue licked the seam of her lips, and she parted them. Immediately, Malcolm plundered her mouth, stroking with his tongue, then sucking hers when it met his. She shut her eyes as the sizzling in her body turned to scorching flames, pooling with molten heat at her core.

She moaned, thoroughly enjoying all the sensations he was invoking. With another step and a turn, like a wicked waltz, she felt his bed behind her legs just before they tumbled onto it.

Shocked, her eyes flew open, and she looked up into his serious face. His irises appeared nearly black. *How strange!*

And then she closed her eyes once more when he bent low and took her mouth under his again. At the same time, he ground his hips against the soft juncture between her thighs.

She was pinned, unable to move if she wanted to. But she didn't want to go anywhere, except to separate her legs under him, needing to feel him nestled where she throbbed. Frustratingly, her dress and his weight atop her precluded any such adjustments.

His kisses moved from her mouth to her chin, before trailing a shivery path down her throat, causing her to arch her neck, giving him better access. Without fumbling, he undid the button of her cloak, and it fell open, exposing not only her neck but her décolletage.

He groaned, and she felt the sound deep inside her, turning her muscles and bones to liquid. His mouth continued its devilish exploration across her collarbone to the sensitive hollow at the base of her throat where she could feel her heartbeat pulsing wildly. When his lips trailed a whisper soft path lower to the upper swell of her left breast, she threaded her fingers in his hair, relishing the texture of it, like a thick pelt.

All she could do was hold him to her. When he tugged at the top of her gown, shockingly exposing her, it was heaven. And when his mouth clamped over her nipple, she gasped, instantly rising toward him.

Wishing she could run her hands over his bare skin, she started tugging at his coat, until he rose from her, shrugged out of it, and sent it to the floor.

"You are so beautiful," he whispered before taking her other nipple into his hot, wet mouth.

And she believed his words, feeling extraordinarily beautiful under his wondrous ministrations. She'd managed to part her legs when he'd raised up. As he settled again, his hips fit perfectly against the apex of her thighs, and she could feel the hard length of him through his breeches and her layers of gown and petticoat.

She'd seen images, naturally, both in paintings and in books, but this . . . this! Experiencing the stiffness of a man's arousal was both thrilling and a little scary. She also couldn't stop her body welcoming him, meeting his as best she could.

Yet still she couldn't touch him. Almost frantic, Serena slipped her hands in the small space under his waistcoat and tugged his shirt out from the back of his breeches. At last, his warm skin was under her fingers and palms.

He startled at her touch, before returning to the breathtaking business of teasing her nipples, first one, then the other, leaving both her breasts feeling heavy, full, and sensitive.

And then one of his hands began to draw up her skirts, as many layers as he could, until she felt the cool air across one of her legs. She froze, waiting for what pleasure would come next.

When his fingers, trailed across the sensitive skin of her thigh, she gasped and held her breath. He shifted sideways, allowing his hand better access. And when his fingers brushed against the curls between her legs, she let out a breath and took in another ragged one.

Upon his second touch, he went deeper between her damp folds.

"*Oh!*" she moaned.

In response, he stroked her most intimate area.

Dear God! Releasing her hold on him, she fisted the sheets on either side of her now-tense body. With eyes closed, her entire focus was concentrated on the space between her legs and the small, impossibly arousing movements of his fingers.

Alternately breathing hard and holding her breath, she arched back while a curious sensation built low in her body. She was straining toward something, panting, moaning, desperately hoping he wouldn't stop until she reached wherever she was going.

And then his mouth returned to her breast. As his teeth grazed her nipple, which had pearled, all her muscles tightened and clenched. In another moment, she achieved the pinnacle for which she'd been striving.

A burst of pure pleasure crashed through her in waves, releasing the tension in her limbs and flooding her with relaxing, blissful warmth.

Malcolm seemed to know when the sensations ended, for his fingers left her and he lifted his head, looking into her eyes.

No longer mindless, not gripped in the throes of indulgent gratification, Serena suddenly felt mortified. She was sprawled beneath a man, her skirts up, baring herself to him—if not to his eyes, then at least to his touch. And the man in question was gazing at her with a self-satisfied, smug expression of having done well.

He had! And extraordinarily well as far as she was concerned. But that didn't mean it was right. On the contrary, it was most assuredly wrong.

Wicked, immoral, decadent, wonderful, astonishing, and definitely worth repeating!

No! She stopped her thoughts.

"You look as if you're waging a silent war within," he said, sounding amused.

"Please let me up," she said, her voice croaking and husky.

Slowly, he rolled to the side, kindly dragging her skirts down over her legs as he did.

She supposed that made him a gentleman. He hadn't even noticed her Queen Anne's pistol strapped as usual against her ankle. As she well knew, he'd been focusing on other parts of her.

Sitting up, she watched his gaze lock upon her—

"*Oh!*" she exclaimed, wrenching her bodice up as high as it would go to cover her breasts.

"A tad late," he jested, sounding full of good humor.

A nervous laugh escaped her, although she felt anything but amused. *Was she ruined? Was this what that word meant?*

Running a hand over her hair, she realized her plaited bun had come down. She must be in far more disarray than when she'd fled the dark path in Vauxhall.

"You look beautiful," he said.

Rolling her eyes at his statement, she climbed off the bed. As if it mattered to her whether she looked beautiful to him. It only mattered if she looked presentable when she went home.

On the other hand, she paused then asked, "You think I'm beautiful?"

"I do." He stood and began to tuck in his shirt. "Only a blind man would say otherwise." Reaching over to the armoire, he retrieved the small mirror.

"However, you've been left in a bit of a mess. If I hold this for you, perhaps you can repair the worst of it."

A bit of a mess? That hardly seemed to describe the preceding actions. Nevertheless, Serena found most of the pins still in her hair and set to work. Seeing him watching her so intently over the mirror, recalling the intimacies he'd just performed, her hands shook as she went about coiling her long braid into a bun.

"I hope next time I can see all your hair down," he said as she finished.

Next time? She could only imagine what he thought of her, a strumpet who gave a stranger access to her body. Moreover, he fully imagined there would be a next time, as if she were available to come to his garret on a whim.

"I'm not a harlot," she said, wondering if he knew the French word she'd used. *Prostituée.*

Apparently, he did. His eyes widened. "Of course not. I didn't offer you money, did I? Besides, if you were a whore, I would have expected a little more."

Serena took a step back. It had felt beyond good, and she couldn't imagine anything better. However, she knew he hadn't experienced the same pleasure. While she had panted and gasped, he'd remained relatively calm. With her cheeks warming, it dawned on her what they'd done wasn't what a man normally paid for and enjoyed. At twenty years of age, she knew enough to understand he wanted to do things with his male part, which had felt hard as granite against her.

But that particular act could hardly be classified as merely *a little more*.

She shook her head, thinking it best to stop talking about any of this.

"I didn't mean to offend you," he vowed, "by anything I've said." Then he retrieved his jacket and shrugged into it. "But you've done something with a man before, haven't you? You weren't an innocent."

He seemed to know about the few kisses she'd given and received during her first Season. He spoke as if he were certain of her bad behavior, and she turned, reaching for the door handle.

"I won't let you go, Mademoiselle Renault."

"I beg your pardon?" *Had he formed a firm attachment to her?* Despite how little time they'd known each other, she wasn't opposed to the idea. Quite the opposite since she liked everything about him.

Nonetheless, his previous confession of being a rake seemed at odds with being ready to declare himself after a few minutes upon his bed.

"Out that door alone, I mean," Malcolm clarified. "I insist on escorting you back to your grandparents' home. And I'll brook no argument."

"I see." Feeling a little shaken by all that had occurred, she hadn't thought to argue anyway.

Turning, she had her fingers on the door handle when he said, "Wait."

She imagined he would proffer a tender kiss while they were still alone. Perhaps he still might say something comforting about a future together.

"Your gloves," he said, holding them out to her. "I imagine going home without them might raise questions."

With a sense of disappointment, she snatched them and began to tug them on.

"I confess when you removed them, it was one of the most inviting, alluring things I've ever seen."

Narrowing her eyes, she stared at him. *Was he making fun of her?* Surely, a man who'd done what they had done, and more, whatever that more was, couldn't have found her removal of gloves to be anything interesting.

Yet what did she know of the world? If she hadn't taken them off, *inviting* him, as he claimed, maybe he wouldn't have kissed her or tumbled her upon his bed.

If only she had someone she could talk to about such unknown issues.

"Ready?" he asked, matter-of-factly.

With a curt nod, she preceded him from the garret. A few minutes had changed her, yet she wasn't at all sure she knew precisely how.

When he went to take her arm as they turned the corner toward the Place des Victoires, she yanked it away and put another foot between them.

"Is something amiss?" he asked.

"Not at all," she said, wishing her tone wasn't brittle, but she felt rather fragile and couldn't wait to be alone in her room. It seemed the perfect time for a good cry.

CHAPTER TEN

Malcolm wished he knew what had gone wrong. Serena had grown distant and stiff as they walked. And silent. There wasn't much worse than a silent woman, except a crying one. Or a screeching one, for that matter.

In fact, his mind boggled at all the ways a woman could be annoying, but then there were also so many times they were fascinating, wonderful, exciting as he'd just experienced.

Still, she was plainly annoyed. It wasn't as if he'd pulled down his breeches and nudged her thighs apart. And he was certain she would have let him, too. She kissed like a female who had experience, and she'd willingly come to his room, stripped off her gloves, and let him kiss her. She'd fallen onto his bed as if she'd been tumbled before.

Regardless, he had treated her with respect, going so far as to pleasure her without taking his own satisfaction. And if anything proved she wasn't an innocent, it was how quickly she relaxed at his touch and even more swiftly climaxed.

Beautiful to watch, he might add.

Even while he was worshipping her—which was assuredly what he'd done—he'd decided he wouldn't penetrate her. For one thing, he had no sheath at hand, never expecting to bring a woman to his unsightly garret. If or when he got around to visiting a Parisian courtesan, he would have the necessary protection in his pocket.

And for another thing, something deep inside had demanded he take it a little slowly with her. Maybe in deference to her concerned grandparents, who ought to know better than to let a young female roam the streets alone. They'd invited him into their home, given him wine, and let him escort their granddaughter.

Maybe his slow pace was simply a reaction to how kindly Serena had treated him. He wanted to see her again. If he'd tupped her on their first tumble, that might have been the end of their association, for who knew what this particular female was thinking.

At that moment, though, Malcolm had a fairly good idea she was thinking she wanted to be rid of him as quickly as possible. Her steps sped up when they neared her home, and sure enough, with a few yards of the door, she turned to him.

"Thank you for escorting me home. *Bonsoir, monsieur.*"

Just like that, she walked away.

"Mademoiselle, wait."

She didn't hesitate. In a moment, she'd gone inside.

He stared at the closed door. *What would he have said anyway?* After all, given the company she kept, and her appearance at the Tuileries Palace offering wine to Boney, it was possible she was, in fact, Malcolm's enemy. Such a soft, pretty foe, who smelled like some floral concoction he couldn't begin to guess at but which made his body ache for her.

Trying to dismiss her mesmerizing allure, he walked the short distance home. With ten perfume shops on every street, or so it seemed, she couldn't help smelling so delightful. And it was probably too much Parisian wine making him think her lovelier than any other woman he'd ever kissed.

In any case, he could have given her an apology for offending her in some way, although he knew better than to confess to being confused as to the offense. A man was supposed to know exactly how he'd offended, or it infuriated the temperamental female even more. He had learned that the hard way.

Besides, Mademoiselle Renault certainly hadn't seemed offended when he'd latched onto her sweet, pert nipple and teased it with his teeth.

Grinning to himself, he decided she was simply skittish. After she got her erratic emotions under control and recalled how much pleasure she'd felt when his fingers were stroking her, she would want to see him again.

SERENA HOPED *NEVER TO* see Monsieur Branley again. He hadn't forced her to do anything, nor had he been brutish or unkind. However, by the end of their encounter, he'd made it clear he thought her someone who would return for another tryst when she hadn't meant to have even one. And it seemed he would expect, as he'd said, *a little more.*

But he smelled so good and his kisses were splendid, and his touch had been thrilling. It was easy to get carried away, to forget everything except the wonderful sensations he'd conjured in her body.

Then he'd ruined it by being far too casual about something that had been, to her, quite monumental. Plainly, he thought her loose.

She could at least admit to herself she'd given him plenty of cause, thinking of the garden at the ball. All that must stop now. When she'd walked in the door the night before, her grand-mère gave her the long-awaited good news.

"You're going home," Adèle said.

Her grandparents had received a letter from her father. She was to be sent to England as soon as the current situation "stabilized," as Lord Elmstead put it. Currently, passenger travel on the ferries between France and Britain had been halted.

The news she'd been waiting months for had finally arrived. But her feelings were unexpectedly mixed—all because of Malcolm Branley.

On the other hand, since she'd vowed over her breakfast of fresh bread slathered in butter and spread with strawberry jam to avoid him, she supposed it didn't matter if she hopped a ship for Dover that very minute.

So why did it make her heart ache to think of never again speaking to him? And particularly, the notion of never again seeing his adorable grin caused pangs of melancholy.

Pushing open the door to the Halle aux Vins later that day, she wondered if Monsieur Christoff would dare show his face, not to mention his broken nose. Already, many stalls were open and vintners were dealing with early buyers. Serena wasn't fearful of meeting him, but she also wasn't foolish. She'd told her Pépère an abbreviated tale of the events.

"I kept my ears open at the café," she'd explained the night before, "and then let Monsieur Christoff walk me home." Briefly, she'd described how surprised she'd been by his ungentlemanly behavior, leaving out any mention of Malcolm altogether. Instead, she'd indicated a stranger had come to her aid. She couldn't remember ever lying to her grandparents before.

Her grand-père had come in her stead to open their stall, just in case there was any trouble. And he would stay with her all day.

"I will miss this so very much," she told him after greeting him with a kiss on both cheeks. "I will never be allowed to do anything so interesting back in England. At home, it's all needlepoint and music lessons."

"Probably for the best," Henri Renault said, although he looked fondly at her. "But your Mémère and I will miss you greatly."

They settled into their usual routine, packing crates for Michel and Jacques, sending out the deliveries. There was no sign of Monsieur Christoff, and when they stopped for a midday meal, Serena had nearly forgotten about him. Yet her thoughts about Malcolm had become overwhelming, distracting her from enjoying her time with her grand-père.

"Something is bothering you?" he asked, sipping wine at the Café Procope, just north of the Palais du Luxembourg. The elegant café, open since the seventeenth century, was one of his favorite places to take her ever since they let women dine there when accompanied by a man.

Serena bit her tongue. She couldn't tell her grand-père anything about her conflicted emotions.

"How long do you think it will be before I can travel?" she asked instead.

"Eager to see your parents," he concluded with a nod of understanding. Leaning across the small table, making her do the same, he added quietly, "I think *he* will be gone by August, if not sooner."

She knew very well whom Pépère meant. How he knew so much about Bonaparte, she couldn't fathom. Certainly, it wasn't from the small snippets she'd overheard and passed along, which so far had not been useful as far as she could tell. And now the emperor wanted her to give him information, too.

"Will you tell me something to bring *him* when I go again tomorrow to the palace?"

"Most assuredly," her grand-père said. "Your being invited was a stroke of the greatest fortune. But you will have to be particularly careful when you tell him how you learned your tidbit of news. We don't want to inadvertently point the finger and endanger anyone. Everything must be said like this, 'I overheard two citizens at the Café Lamblin. They were playing checkers. No, I don't recall what they looked like.' Or 'I eavesdropped on citizens strolling on the Quai du Louvre, but it was too dark to see their faces or even their hair color.'" He took a bite of his favorite dish at the restaurant, *langue de boeuf glacée aux epinards*.

When next he reached for his wine glass, he added, "In such a way, you will tell him what we want him to hear."

"Who are *we*?" she asked, not for the first time, wishing she understood if Henri Renault was a faithful royalist or more like the shifting Talleyrand.

He smiled, looking like nothing more than her kindly grand-père.

"MADEMOISELLE," THE EMPEROR GREETED her, "I had hoped to see you but feared you would have nothing to share with me so soon."

"I brought a shipment of wine," she said, making it clear she was a vintner first.

"Yes, yes, but what else?" Bonaparte seemed sure she would have news. "Everything must happen in haste to secure what we are trying to do. After all, it has been a long nine months, watching from afar as the king fails France. No one was happy, not the aristocrats nor the regular citizens, and certainly not the merchants such as yourself. I've had well wishes from all sides and, of course, the revolutionaries, too. Even the clergy has given me its blessing."

Serena was sure some members of all those groups were glad to see the emperor, but many were not. She also knew leaders of European countries and the British were making plans as swiftly as possible with the hope that Bonaparte would get comfortable in Paris and not realize how the forces were amassing against him.

Using the phrasing her grand-père had suggested, she mentioned how news via those who'd recently returned from neighboring countries was floating about the cafés.

"I've heard no one supports the heavy-handedness of the Russians, Prussians, and Austrians. As for the British, French people do not wish to let their old enemy decide who rules Gaul."

"Well done, mademoiselle. It is as I suspected." Then the emperor sighed. "After twenty-three years of war, my people don't want any more of it, nor do I. Henceforth the happiness and the strengthening of France shall be the sole object of all my thoughts. Will you tell that to everyone with whom you speak?"

She nodded, feeling more than a little in awe of him.

"And if anyone is hiding like a mouse, you may tell those who previously turned on me that I have no interest in vengeance. I don't even want to know who betrayed me or what was done in my absence. I shall forever remain ignorant."

With that surprising statement of benign forgiveness, Serena was ready to pledge her support to him as well. The king had not been quite so lenient.

"I am going to meet with my Minister of Public Works and view the progress of my elephant fountain. Do you know of it?"

"Yes, Your Imperial Majesty. It is quite a splendid idea. I hope to see it working soon."

"I'm also going to Saint-Denis to visit with the orphaned daughters of the Légion d'Honneur. Those wicked Bourbons cut their funding. Did you hear about that?"

"I didn't realize." Serena was sure there was a lot she didn't know or understand. All she could do was follow her grand-père's requests.

"I will walk out with you," Bonaparte said.

"Thank you, Your Majesty. I wouldn't put you to any trouble."

"I am going that way, and who wouldn't want to be escorting such a pretty woman?"

She found herself in the unusual position of strolling through the great gallery of the Palais des Tuileries with the emperor, while he pointed out artefacts she might not have noticed, and then they descended the staircase. He even turned toward the servants' area through which she had entered, surprising her farther.

Was he really going to go out through the back door?

"The food was not so good when I was away," Bonaparte said with a rueful smile, as though he'd been on holiday at an unsatisfactory inn instead of in exile on an island. "I like to go through the kitchens and see what I can scrounge. They often have some spare madeleines."

She nearly laughed. He sounded like a mischievous boy instead of the most powerful man in France.

Still, she turned a smile upon him. "I'm sure even if they weren't spare cakes, they would give you one or two."

Relaxed with the emperor, Serena was practically flirting with him.

"You are correct. They treat me well here," he confirmed, as if she might have doubted it. "In truth, on my way back to Paris, I wasn't assured of my reception until I reached Grenoble." Then he smiled at her. "Before Grenoble, I was a soldier of fortune. At Grenoble, I was an emperor again."

She shivered. *Would any of Mayfair's finest gentry believe she, an English baron's daughter, could be keeping company with the Emperor of France?*

"Come with me," Bonaparte invited. "Even if you don't want your cake, I will get double and eat your share."

Now that was spoken like the man who'd expanded France into an empire, she thought.

A guard held the door open as soon as they approached, and at the emperor's behest, she preceded him into the spacious kitchen, nearly colliding with Malcolm in his baker's cap. Stopping abruptly, Serena was pushed forward onto Malcolm's toes by Emperor Bonaparte, who bumped into her.

All her good humor drained away at the shock of seeing him. Even as Malcolm's hand stretched out to steady her, his own expression changed swiftly from surprise to wariness when he saw her imperial companion.

Malcolm bowed low to the emperor.

"Look," Bonaparte said, as cheerfully as before. "Mademoiselle Renault, it is your mute friend."

Thinking of what Malcolm might be there to do and of how the emperor seemed to want only good for his people, Serena felt prickles of discomfort.

"He is *not* my friend, Your Majesty."

Malcolm's mouth flattened at her words.

"But you helped him anyway," Bonaparte said, not appearing to notice any undercurrent of tension. "Very good. A vintner and a baker. If we had a butcher in our quorum, we would have all we need for the happiness of the Parisians. Yes?"

She nodded in agreement.

"Did you bring me any more of your pastries?" Bonaparte asked.

Malcolm nodded and pointed behind him.

"*Bon!* But we are here for madeleines. The palace baker makes a very fine one. Does your bakery make them?"

Malcolm's eyes widened. Serena hoped he would nod because she didn't know a bakery in Paris that didn't make the distinctive shell-shaped little cakes. However, an Englishman might not know that.

He glanced at her, and she offered him a bright smile, which she hoped indicated the correct answer. After a brief pause, he nodded slowly.

"Then bring some next time, my good baker, and we shall see if they compare."

Malcolm nodded again.

Bonaparte called out to one of the kitchen staff, "Four madeleines." Then he said to Serena, "Two for each of us."

Malcolm gave her another surprised look. But the emperor hadn't dismissed him, nor could he say out loud he had to leave.

"I won't bother giving you one," the emperor quipped, addressing Malcolm. "No more than I would insult the mademoiselle by presenting her with a gift of someone else's wine. You must be very busy with all the celebrations in the city," he added. "Don't let my vintner and I keep you."

And with that, Malcolm was at last allowed to go. She could see he wanted her to accompany him, or maybe it was merely her own desire to do so, but she had to stay until dismissed.

Malcolm bowed again to Bonaparte, nodded in her direction, and then departed through the same door by which she had just entered.

In another minute, Serena found herself tasting a golden cake while on the move again, this time toward the front entrance of the palace.

"I don't usually go in and out this way," she confessed.

"I try not to use any other door," the emperor said, and she knew it was a remark filled with political meaning. The ruler shouldn't have to sneak in or out for that matter, reminding her of King Louis XVIII, slipping away from the palace and out of the city under the cover of darkness.

Stepping into the sunshine, they were immediately flanked by Imperial Guards. For the briefest instant, she looked at the people gathered outside, each hoping to catch a glimpse of Bonaparte or even speak with him. Some glanced at her, perhaps wondering if she were anyone important.

She was a nobody, eating cake with an emperor!

And it seemed, he was finished with her. "Come again, mademoiselle. Any time you have news for me."

She curtsied. "Yes, Your Imperial Majesty."

He started past her, heading to his massive fountain project that was currently housed at the Bastille while the elephant was being built.

Suddenly, he stopped and turned, giving her a shrewd glance that made her heart speed up. *Did he suspect her of something?*

"How did you like the madeleine?" he asked.

"It was the best I ever had," she said, feeling a little sorry for the powerful man who had so many forces against him.

"I think so, too," he agreed, "but maybe you'll be here when the baker brings his from Boulangerie Marineau, and we shall compare."

With a tip of his familiar bicorn hat, Bonaparte walked away, through the throng of admirers.

Serena went slowly after him toward the Arc de Triomphe, passing by the guard hut and through the gate before turning left to leave the palace grounds. She'd hardly walked a block when Malcolm fell into step beside her.

She didn't startle. Indeed, she'd been expecting him to turn up again.

"I'm beginning to worry about you," he said.

CHAPTER ELEVEN

Malcolm was starting to get a bad feeling about this female, while at the same time having certain other feelings about her that were only too good.

Mademoiselle Renault glanced at him with her intelligent eyes.

"You needn't worry about me," she said.

"I do if you have chosen the side of Bonaparte. Then indeed, I should be concerned. For make no mistake, he will be removed from power and soon. And when he is, the royalists will be more vengeful than the first time they returned."

"Another difference then," she quipped and kept on walking.

He fell into step beside her. "What do you mean?"

"The emperor told me he doesn't care to punish anyone who betrayed him when he was exiled."

Malcolm considered what Bonaparte had done so far, and he might be telling the truth. Or he might be biding his time.

"Regardless, when he goes, and he will, you won't be safe if you've been seen eating cake with the emperor and smiling at him as if he were your lover."

She stopped in her tracks and looked at him.

"That's ridiculous and insulting. The emperor has gone to visit with orphans at Saint-Denis."

Malcolm couldn't help snorting with derision, understanding the word *orphelins* in any language.

"Bonaparte visits Saint-Denis because it is associated with French kings. It looks good to the people, and believe me, it will be written about in all the papers that are still allowed to publish. It further legitimizes him."

He heard her sigh and wanted to shake her into seeing the truth. The soft sound also made him want to crush her against the nearest building and kiss her senseless.

"Have you heard of the Seventh Coalition?" he demanded.

To his surprise, she nodded, proving again she wasn't simply a vintner's granddaughter. But he'd already known that. There was more to her than her appearance suggested.

"The same countries that were still coming to terms over the newly drawn map and borders of Europe since Boney's exile have created an alliance to oust him again. Austria, Russia, Prussia, and of course Britain have pledged 150,000 men each."

She looked unruffled. "The Parisians do not want war."

"I told you before, the main battle grounds won't happen here."

"There was fighting just outside the city last time," she snapped.

"Bonaparte won't let himself be trapped in Paris," Malcolm insisted. "He'll take the fight to a more advantageous place."

"I hope you're correct," Serena said, sounding like Randall when they discussed the current state of events.

"I've never had a conversation such as this with a woman before," Malcolm confessed.

Serena shrugged. "I've never had a conversation with a member of the Seventh Coalition before."

His ears perked up. She knew exactly who he was.

She cracked a smile at his expression, and even such a small show of happiness squeezed his heart. For the life of him, he couldn't fathom what about this woman caused his heart to race more quickly, not to mention the rest of his body to be at full attention. Not merely her looks, stunning as he found her to be, there was something more.

"We mustn't be seen together again," she said, and his own joy at walking beside her fled.

He hoped her reticence was nothing more than embarrassment over what had happened in his garret, something he would help her overcome. For his part, he had nothing but delightful memories when he thought of how she'd reacted to him, picturing her lips slightly parted and her smooth neck bowed back gracefully as she reached her climax, and her essence moistening his fingers.

With her next words, however, she didn't sound mortified. She sounded threatening.

"Some of my friends saw you at the Café des Aveugles with Monsieur Christoff, the night you insulted him. If they see you dressed in this absurd manner as a baker, they will know you are up to something secretive and sly. Since Suzanne and Felicity heard your English accent, they will assume you are a royalist. I don't want them to put me in the same category as you."

"Because you are strongly on the side of the emperor?" It was important to Malcolm to hear her declare it, one way or the other.

SERENA RESUMED WALKING. THEY had stood long enough in plain sight discussing matters better left unsaid.

"You believe I am a Bonapartist despite how I lied to the emperor on your behalf?"

Malcolm strode beside her. "You also distanced yourself, telling him we aren't friends," he reminded her.

"We aren't," she said quickly, glancing ahead to see trouble. "And unless you are blind, you must see two of my actual friends are coming in this direction. I suggest you disappear."

Without a word, Monsieur Branley ducked into the first doorway, and she knew he'd vanished. Greeting Guillaume and Felicity, it was the first time she'd seen them since the altercation with Monsieur Christoff and decided she should tell them her tale before they heard it another way.

Before she could, however, Guillaume began an effusive apology. While Serena tried to understand what it was for, Felicity jumped in.

"My brother feels terrible for letting you walk off alone with that beast."

Surprised, she looked from one to the other.

"How did you learn what happened?" Serena asked.

"Christoff came by the next day with his nose broken, and said ridiculous things about you. He claimed you led him to a dark place and let an English spy beat him."

Serena's mouth dropped open. She was half appalled at the twisting of the story, and half terrified her friends would somehow discover who Malcolm was and turn him in.

"I knew you would never go anywhere alone with a man. More than any of us," Felicity said, "your reputation has always been spotless."

Again, Serena was stunned to silence. It was hard to fathom that in France, when she had so much freedom, she'd comported herself in such a manner her friends considered her above reproach. Yet after her behavior in Malcolm's garret, Felicity's high regard was no longer deserved. If they ever found out . . .

"I don't mean that Suzanne and I are loose," Felicity added, looking around to make sure no one was listening.

Her brother rolled his eyes. "We know you harbor no love for the royalists," Guillaume asserted. "When Christoff spouted his nonsense, it was obviously a case of a rejected man. I did to him what he was trying to do to you?"

Serena frowned. "You kissed him?"

"What?" Guillaume exclaimed, then he gave a short bark of laughter. "No, I told Imperial soldiers he was a traitor who had met with a member of the Seventh Coalition to plot against our emperor. Felicity told me she'd seen him at the café with an Englishman." Brother and sister nodded at one another. "Christoff has been imprisoned," he said.

Serena felt the blood drain from her face. But her friends were looking at her so pleased with their defense, she had to say something.

"I thank you for . . . for believing in me and protecting my honor." She felt a little ill, however, thinking of Monsieur Christoff behind bars on her account despite his inappropriate behavior.

Moreover, a chill went up her spine at how easily Guillaume had turned on someone who'd been his ally. The two men had stood together before Bonaparte as if inseparable comrades.

"Who *did* break his nose?" Felicity asked. "He certainly looked no better for it."

Her friend had a smile that seemed unwarranted given the seriousness of people being put in jail simply on the word of another citizen. It reminded Serena of tales of the Revolution when people were beheaded on no more evidence than a neighbor pointing a finger.

"A stranger happened along when Christoff was trying to drag me into an alley," she told them. "I didn't get his name."

"I will shake his hand if ever I meet him," Guillaume promised, "and I will always walk you home myself from now on."

"What about me?" Felicity teased, although she wore a smile, obviously approving of her brother's romantic interest.

"We'll find you a nice man to walk you home," her brother said and put his arm around his sister.

Serena no longer wanted to participate in this teasing banter. Things had changed, and her previous carefree life of working in the Halle aux Vins during the day and enjoying evenings with her friends was over. At work, she would be wary of Monsieur Christoff's associates who might somehow blame her, and in the cafés, she would listen intently both for those who sought to betray the emperor and for those who would turn Malcolm in to the Imperial Guards.

MALCOLM DESCENDED THE BACK stairs at the Café de Chartres. The news from Randall was alarming. Jules Versanne had disappeared entirely, and no one believed it was of his own volition. Somehow, he'd been discovered as a royalist, and they were cracking down especially hard on anyone who might be the wily Fox himself. *Le Renard* had eyes and ears everywhere, or so it seemed.

More than that, the supposedly closed catacombs under the Left Bank of Paris had seen recent activity. It was true that bodies were still taken there occasionally, but coalition spies had seen men who were very much alive traversing the main gate at the top of the very steep and long steps. Malcolm had been tasked with descending into the tunnels and having a good look around.

Seeing Serena at a table with her friends, he paused. An idea was coming to him, but he couldn't talk to her with anyone around in case they started asking why she knew a British man.

Running back upstairs, startling Randall, he snatched a piece of paper off the table and took the pen from his associate's hand.

"What are you doing?"

"Your letter to Prinny can wait," Malcolm said.

"It's to Wellington, actually."

Malcolm hesitated, then quickly scrawled a note inviting Serena to meet him the following day an hour before sundown at the Jardin des Plantes, very close to the wine market.

"Organizing a little tryst, are you?" Randall asked, reading over his shoulder.

"Hardly," Malcolm said. "She's a helpful, resourceful woman."

"That doesn't mean she's not worthy of a good tupping."

Malcolm nearly turned on him. Yet refusing to rise to the bait, he shrugged. It wasn't the time to defend Serena's honor, especially when he did so badly hope to tup her before he returned to England.

"The best time to get into the old mining tunnels is at dusk," Malcolm said. "One guard is there all day, and he locks up directly after dark. Odds are he'll be bored in the hour before he bolts the gate and leaves."

"And what better alleviator of boredom than a beautiful redhead," Randall agreed.

Why did it sound rather distasteful when his associate put it so plainly?

Handing the note to the man who guarded the second floor, he instructed its delivery to the ravishing copper-haired beauty in the dining room, then watched from the recesses of the stairwell to make sure it was delivered.

As soon as she read the note, she glanced around the dining room before tucking it into her reticule. Immediately, she resumed chatting with the man across from her. Malcolm had no idea if Serena would agree to help, nor even if she would keep his request secret from her friends.

LATE THE FOLLOWING AFTERNOON, while pacing the circular brass temple at the summit of the Jardin des Plantes'

impressive hedgerow labyrinth, Malcolm began to fear the worst. For all he knew, an Imperial Guard might show up in Serena's place. Naturally, that was why he'd chosen the hill at the botanical gardens, giving him an expansive view of Paris and of anyone approaching.

And then he saw her coming up one of the winding paths. To him, she was unmistakable despite her ordinary spencer and bonnet that looked like any other female in Paris. Having been intimate and having touched her body, Malcolm could pick her out even if she was draped in a coarse feed sack simply by the way she walked and by the shape of her.

"Thank you for coming. I hope it hasn't caused you any inconvenience," he said, deciding to begin with formality. Inside, he was simply glad she hadn't betrayed him.

"Not inconvenient at all," she said. "After being indoors all day at the Halle aux Vins, it is a treat to be here. Such a gorgeous view." She gestured across the Seine that sparkled like a necklace as the sun sank lower in the sky. "The tiresome part was last night, when my friends all wondered if I'd received a *billet-doux*."

A love note! "I'm sure that happens often," Malcolm said. He could think of a dozen ways to praise her, and many would be romantic enough for a poem.

Yet she rolled her eyes, dismissing his assertion. "I told them it was a wine order. Speaking of which, I brought two bottles, as you requested."

"Thank you. That was well done," he said. "I'll get to the point. Have you been under the city?"

"Under, monsieur? Do you mean the catacombs?"

"Yes, but specifically, the ossuary, not the miles of abandoned mine tunnels." At least, Malcolm certainly hoped he wouldn't have to explore miles of catacombs to figure out what was going on underneath Paris.

Visibly, she shuddered. "No. Some people like that sort of amusement, but I have no wish to see a million bones. Besides, they closed it to the public last year."

"Last year, naturally," he agreed. "It's difficult to police a city if people are wandering around under it, and the new king didn't want any lingering Bonapartists hiding down there. But I thought all Parisians went down for a lark at one time or another." And she seemed like the adventurous sort who would've done exactly that.

However, she shrugged and said nothing more.

"In any case, simply because it is closed, mademoiselle, that doesn't mean it's not being used. With all visitors being prevented from entering, what better place to hide people who are your political enemies?"

She frowned, obviously considering. "Why not imprison people in the regular jail?"

Serena looked adorable, and he wanted to reach out and smooth the furrows on her brow. He resisted. She might take offense and snap at his hand like one of the stray dogs he'd seen around the city's street.

After all, she'd still been angry with him when last they'd parted.

"Napoleon said he isn't going after his political enemies, isn't that correct?" he asked.

"So he told me," she said.

"No one in power, especially with as precarious a hold as the emperor currently has, allows his enemies to mill about undeterred," Malcolm pointed out. "He may not do anything about them publicly, but that leaves him two options. Take them outside of Paris and kill them, or hide them below the city, and maybe kill them down there, I suppose."

She scrunched up her mouth in disgust. "I dislike the way you speak of killing as if it is nothing."

"No, mademoiselle, I don't think it is nothing. I value human life and wish we hadn't experienced two decades of war already. It has gained all of us, British and French, very little. I'm simply being realistic. I've lost contact with a friend whom I fear has been taken down into the catacombs, hopefully to be detained and nothing more. But that is bad enough, don't you think?"

She nodded.

Should he ask her? There was something capable and calm about this woman, at least on the exterior. If the situations she found herself in frightened her, such as the incident with Christoff, she didn't show it.

"You helped me so well at the Tuileries Palace. I wonder if you would help me again."

"Do I have to go underground? It is supposedly sixty-five feet down, and the limestone mining tunnels spread out for miles."

It seemed he had stumbled upon a small crack in her tough exterior.

"The section that used to be open to the public, with a marked trail, is only a mile, I believe," he said.

"Only?" she repeated. "It would feel to me like being buried alive."

Malcolm hoped it wouldn't come to that. He didn't relish poking around down there either, but he had to. She, however, did not.

"No, you don't have to go below," he promised. "Remember when I said I wouldn't have played the part of a baker at the palace if a friend hadn't disappeared?"

"Yes, I remember. And this friend may be in the catacombs?" she asked.

He appreciated her astute grasp. "I believe so. I wouldn't ask you to do anything dangerous. Nothing more than chat with the guard who stands by the entrance gate. You could ask him questions and distract him while I slip through the gate and search."

"I suppose I could," she said, sounding less than enthusiastic.

"I have no right to ask you, but I could certainly use a diversion such as you can provide."

To his surprise, she barely hesitated.

"Very well. I'll do it."

SERENA WAS GLAD THEY were going directly to the catacombs that very moment. If she'd gone home, she would have been unable to keep the plan from her grandparents, and they might have forbidden her. However, as long as she didn't ask, they couldn't tell her no.

It was a rather underhanded way of keeping her independence, but she knew this task was important. And she was, in fact, rather honored to have been asked. It seemed a more important role to play than any she'd had so far. As long as she didn't have to go underground, she couldn't see the harm in flirting with a soldier for a good cause.

And now she understood why Monsieur Branley had asked her to bring two bottles of wine that didn't carry her family's label.

They approached the main public entrance that had been closed ever since she'd arrived in Paris the year before. Malcolm disappeared somewhere behind her into the shadows awaiting an opportunity to enter the gated stairwell. She would lure the guard—only *one* if the intelligence had been correct—a little way away so her English spy could slip inside the iron gate in the stone archway and descend to the ossuary below.

She shuddered again at the thought. When she was younger, and they'd traveled to France during times when the war was not raging and her mother was desperate to see her parents, even then Serena wouldn't go down into the catacombs when invited, not even with her Pépère. Malcolm was right, though. It was a caper which most every Parisian engaged in, looking at the massive collection of bones and the limestone carvings, and the so-called Quarryman's Bath.

A few feet from the guard, she nodded to him and smiled as if passing by. Assured of his attention, she tripped on a stone of her own imagination.

"*Oh*," she cried out, stumbling, nearly dropping her basket and making sure to push one of the bottles out so it crashed to the ground. "Sweet mother!" she exclaimed.

The guard rushed over immediately.

"Mademoiselle, are you hurt?"

"The emperor's wine," she said, gesturing to the broken bottle and the blood red liquid seeping into the dirt. "I am so clumsy."

"The emperor's wine," he repeated.

"Our family calls it that now," she said, "because His Imperial Majesty is so fond of it. I go to the Tuileries every other day with a shipment." However, what she had with her was her grandparents' friends Charles and Sophie's wine since they were safely out of the city.

"You are a long way from the Tuileries," the guard pointed out, but his eyes took her in from head to foot, as well as noticing the other bottle in her basket.

"Yes. Today, I was at the Halle aux Vins," she gestured back toward the Quai Saint-Bernard, as the sun began to set. "Then I met a friend in the gardens of the Palais du Luxembourg."

"A lover?" the man asked with impudence.

She ignored the question but smiled coquettishly, unsure whether having a lover made her less or more desirable while she tried to keep his interest.

"I thought the catacombs were closed," she said, taking a few steps away from the mess at her feet. As she'd hoped, the guard followed her. "Why do they make you stand here all day?"

"You know how people like to go down there," he said and shrugged.

"Do they?" she asked innocently, still not able to imagine why there was such a fascination. "Whyever for?"

"To see how the bones have been stacked up. Not just the skulls, but also the femurs—the legs, you know. It's done in an artistic way."

He stopped walking, and she knew he would venture no farther from his post. In fact, he began to turn back toward the entrance.

"Wine," she offered to keep his full attention, "since there is no one here."

The guard grinned at her. Over his shoulder, she saw Malcolm already creeping toward the iron gate. Serena could only hope it didn't squeak.

"Why not?" the guard asked. "It would be churlish of me to turn down a lovely woman."

She smiled again and drew from her pocket a simple brass corkscrew that she nearly always had with her since sometimes buyers came to the Halle aux Vins and wanted to taste the wine.

"I have no glasses," she said, holding out the bottle.

"That's no matter," the guard said, "but ladies first."

She took a small sip, wiped the top with her sleeve and handed it to him. He took a healthy swallow, and by then, she knew Malcolm had made it through the gate and must be already descending the steep, circular stairwell.

The guard handed it back to her, but she only pretended to drink more.

"Do you like it?" she asked.

"Very much," he said.

"Then you have the taste of an emperor."

They laughed together. Serena kept him talking and drinking, until it felt as though an hour had passed but could hardly have been ten minutes.

"It's getting dark," the guard said. "I can close up soon, and then I am free for the night."

Oh dear!

"We must finish the bottle first, *mon copain*," she said. "It will not keep."

He laughed as if she'd said something outrageously funny, but he grabbed the bottle and drained the last third. Then he hurled it with all his might into a nearby bush.

"Now you don't have to carry it home, mademoiselle, or to wherever *we* go next."

He walked back toward the gate, not quite in a straight line. Her heart pounding, Serena barely thought before she said her next words.

"I've changed my mind. I would like to see the catacombs. I've never been down there. My friends tease me over this because I've always been afraid. But with you taking me, being my guide, I would feel safe, even if we are completely alone down there, in the dark."

This drew the expected response—a broad, sly grin and a vigorous nod.

"I would be happy to escort you down and give you a personal tour. But we don't have to be in the dark. There are shafts to bring in the last of the light, although with the sun nearly set, they won't be much help. We shall take a lamp, and there are lamps down there we can light, too."

She was relieved. The notion of being in the pitch black in a mass grave with a drunken stranger were just about the least desirable things she could imagine. Except . . .

"Are there spiders?" she asked.

"Honestly, I don't like crawlies myself," the guard disclosed, "but I vow I have seen none down there. Take my hand."

Setting down her basket, she found herself ushered through the iron gate and going to the last place in Paris she wanted to go.

CHAPTER TWELVE

The journey five stories underground was not as bad as she'd feared, since the guard, whom she now knew was named Pierre, had a steady lamp in his hand and went ahead of her. Moreover, the stairwell was not too cramped, and she could stand up perfectly straight, although the steps wound dizzyingly around and around, seemingly forever.

As they descended, the air grew colder. Serena tried not to think of how much land was over her head, nor of the cave-ins from the previous century, and after one hundred steps, she stopped counting.

The catacombs themselves were chilly, but the walls weren't slimy, and there wasn't a spiderweb in sight. Moreover, it smelled like the dirt in her grand-mère's garden at their vineyard in Saint-George-sur-Loire and not at all unpleasant.

There was no evidence of Malcolm when they reached the limestone floor in a moderate-sized chamber with a table bearing neatly stacked papers, and two curiosity cabinets with glass fronts. When Pierre held up his lantern, she could see one had a sign above it with the word *Mineralogy* and the other proclaimed *Pathology*. Sure enough, the first had many rocks inside and the second displayed pieces of bones.

"They have some printed information about the ossuary," Pierre told her, gesturing to the table, but he strolled past it and entered a long, arched tunnel, which stretched forward into pitch blackness.

"Don't worry," he said, as she gripped his arm. "The first thing you see will be something beautiful, not bones."

She hoped the first thing she saw wasn't Malcolm getting caught trespassing. And in order to warn him of their arrival, she began a steady stream of loud conversation, which Pierre tolerated, probably thinking her an incessant chatterbox. At least if Malcolm had found his friend and was trying to free him, he would know to be quiet and stay out of sight.

Pierre led her into a chamber where someone had carved directly into the limestone, creating intricate buildings and fortresses.

"They *are* beautiful," she agreed, having read of them in a book her grand-père had given her about old Paris and its outskirts.

"Monsieur Decuré was a quarryman," Pierre said. "They say he carved these on his lunch breaks. That one," he added, nodding to the largest sculpture that looked like a medieval castle, "was a place he was imprisoned during the war."

He said that as if there'd been only one war, but Serena already knew the carving represented Port Mahon, a Spanish fortress where the miner had been imprisoned after the Seven Years War, so she asked nothing further.

Besides, the only other thing Pierre might tell her was how the unfortunate quarryman had died in a cave-in, which she'd also read about and didn't want to be reminded.

Suddenly, the guard held his lantern up high so she could read the inscription over the passageway they were about to enter. She gasped.

"Arrête, c'est ici l'empire de la mort!" Stop! This is the empire of death!

Under the bodice of her dress, Serena's skin felt cool and clammy, and she longed to turn around. Instead, she kept going.

In a few steps, she was surrounded by walls of bones, both skulls and legs, as he'd promised. A stone plaque told her the remains were from the Cemetery of the Innocents, placed there when the Parisians complained of the terrible smell of the obscenely full cemetery in the heart of the city, right near the bustling markets. Even worse, bodies had begun to come up in nearby cellars during rainstorms. Finally, by 1780, the city had closed the cemetery and almost immediately began exhuming the remains and dropping the dead down the wells into the catacombs. Eventually, the bones were arranged with some artistry and respect.

Countless people, countless tales to tell. Serena hurried past, but the guard held her arm.

"I wish we had more wine," he said, his back to the stacked, arranged bones as if they were nothing more than patterned wallpaper. "Your family produces the drink of love, don't you think?"

She gawked at him. If he thought the ossuary was going to arouse romantic feelings in her, he was sadly mistaken. Her skin prickled and she desperately wanted to be back above ground, breathing fresh air and seeing any stars she might view through the Parisian chimney smoke.

"Let's keep moving," she said. "I'm cold."

"I'll warm you up, mademoiselle."

"I would like that," she lied, "but not near the bones."

He chuckled. "Very well. Let's keep going."

As they rounded a passage, the guard suddenly halted.

"That's odd. There is lamplight coming from up ahead, perhaps in the next chamber. Stay here," he ordered.

It had to be Malcolm, so even though Pierre was only a few yards away, she called loudly, "Where are you going, monsieur? What's in that chamber?"

The guard didn't answer. As the last vestiges of her voice echoed around her, she trailed after him, determined not to be left behind without a lamp.

MALCOLM KNEW OTHERS WERE in the tunnel besides him and Versanne, whom he'd located and just managed to get out of his chains. A lockpick, nearly as useful as his pistol, was always in his pocket.

"These idiots think I am the Fox," the Frenchman had explained. "I wish I were *le Renard.* I would run circles around these fools."

"We need to run like foxes now," Malcolm said. Then he realized one of the voices he heard coming closer was Serena's. "Are there others being held down here?" he asked, hating to leave any poor soul behind in the catacombs.

"I don't know. I was brought here and left. A guard brings me food and water once a day and lets me relieve myself. If there are others, they haven't been around for a party yet," Versanne finished wryly.

Malcolm helped him to his feet, surprised by how much weight the man had lost and how unsteady he appeared. He wouldn't be running circles around anyone. They would be lucky if he could make it out of the catacombs considering how many stairs they had to climb. It would probably take until dawn.

"Just stand there," Malcolm said to Versanne. "But when the guard comes make some noise. Keep talking to him. I'll be close by."

As soon as he slipped around the bend into the shadows, he heard the guard exclaim in surprise.

"What are *you* doing down here?"

"As if you didn't know," Versanne retorted. "I have lost track of how long I've been in this hell."

The guard probably told the truth and hadn't known, or he wouldn't have brought Serena into the catacombs. It didn't matter. The man worked for Boney, and Malcolm couldn't let himself be seen.

Stealthily, he tiptoed around the corner. The guard's back was to him, his gun drawn and pointed at Versanne. And Serena stood a few feet behind. An angel in the darkness, her hair reflected the lantern light like a shining sun brought down to Hades.

"I don't know how long I've been held down here," Versanne said, talking loudly. "Is this how the emperor treats the citizens of Paris?"

The guard was undaunted. "If Imperial soldiers put you here, then they must have a—"

Malcolm launched himself onto the man's back, and the guard dropped the gun with a yelp of surprise. Even Serena cried out at his sudden appearance. Wrapping his arm around the man's neck, he used a practiced hold until the guard went limp, and Malcolm instantly released him to the floor.

Serena was in his arms nearly before the man hit the limestone. He could feel her trembling, which startled him since she'd been so brave in all other situations. He wished he could hold her until she calmed, but they needed to get moving.

"The guard won't be asleep for long," Malcolm said, setting her from him and moving toward the chains he'd left on the cavern floor.

"What are you doing?" She looked horrified.

Being careful not to give Versanne's name, he said, "My associate is not strong at the moment—"

"Bah!" Versanne said. "I'm fine, *Anglais.*"

Malcolm ignored him. "It's going to take us a while to get back to the top. I have to chain this man so he doesn't come after us."

"But we can't leave him down here in the dark," she said, sounding revolted.

"They left me," Versanne said.

"He said he didn't know you were here," she pointed out, turning on the Frenchman.

Malcolm had to put a stop to her interference and the quibbling. After he'd chained the man's hands and feet, he snatched up the second lantern.

"Let's go."

"No," she said stubbornly, "we cannot leave him."

"If he came after us, I would have to shoot him," Malcolm explained. "This is better. The same soldier who has been bringing my associate food and water every day will find the guard tomorrow and set him free. Now come. We'll go out the way we came in. It's closer than the exit at the other end of the catacombs."

As Malcolm expected, Versanne needed assistance getting back to the entrance and even more help going up the stairs. Letting Serena go first and light the way since she seemed desperate to escape, he got his old comrade onto the steps and moving sluggishly upward. Each time Versanne faltered, Malcolm pushed him from behind. It was gruelingly slow.

Before they'd made much progress, the sound of many feet up above, quickly descending, made them all freeze.

"We are sunk," Versanne announced in his usual optimistic view.

"Hurry," Malcolm said, determined to get off the stairs since Serena was in the direct line of fire. Practically dragging Versanne, he pivoted, and soon they were back in the entrance chamber.

"Behind the display cases?" Serena suggested.

Malcolm glanced at them. They were enormous, and it was unlikely he could shift them although he appreciated her faith in his strength.

"We have to go back into the tunnel," he announced.

"I hate this," Serena said, hurrying along behind them. "I hated it the first time, and I hate it even more the second time."

"How do you think I feel, mademoiselle?" Versanne quipped. "I fear I shall never breathe the rank air of Paris again."

"We shall all breathe it again if we keep our heads," Malcolm said. "Although it's about as fresh as London air," he added, thinking of the sooty, smoky air of home, longing for it now more than ever.

Soon, they were back in the ossuary and coming up to the guard who'd awakened.

"I thought you'd left me," he said, sounding half terrified, half relieved.

"We have," Malcolm said, keeping his face averted and racing past, still assisting Versanne as they entered the next chamber. Behind them, he heard Serena mumble an apology, and the guard yell beseechingly after them.

The man had surely alerted their pursuers, who would be coming even more quickly. Malcolm had no idea how the Imperial Guard had known he was in the catacombs rescuing Versanne, but there must be a hundred places to hide, and he would get them safely into one of them.

Passing a well and a large cross, they left the ossuary and were presented with more tunnels as well as the second staircase leading up to freedom. By this time, however, Malcolm could hear the footfalls echoing behind them. If they started up the steps, over a hundred and thirty of them if he recalled correctly, they would be captured.

"We must venture into one of these tunnels. The soldiers, hopefully, will assume we've gone up. By the time they realize differently—"

"We'll still be sitting here like easy prey," Versanne said, wavering as if he might sit on the limestone right where he was.

"No," Malcolm said. "We could go back the way we came and up the front steps."

Versanne sighed. "I haven't had this much exercise since I was a youth."

Meanwhile, Serena who'd remained silent, held her lantern up to chase the darkness away and peered down the two tunnels forking before them.

"They'll be upon us soon," she said. "Much as I detest saying it, I think we need to pick one of these passages and hope there is a hiding place."

"Brave woman," Malcolm said, trying to keep Versanne upright. "Right or left, it makes no matter."

Serena chose the right tunnel, and after a few feet, they realized, there were in fact openings in the walls.

"In there," Malcolm directed.

Serena hesitated, but it was impossible for him to go first since Versanne was all but collapsing except for Malcolm holding him up. Footsteps growing louder spurred her to glance again at him before she held up her lantern and disappeared between the limestone walls into the darkness.

Her piercing scream caused the hair on Malcolm's head to stand up. Without hesitation, he dropped Versanne and dashed into the cavernous opening behind her.

CHAPTER THIRTEEN

"Good God!" Malcolm exclaimed at seeing a dozen men, some seated, some lying down, all in chains.

They were greeted by those who were able, but some merely groaned.

"Are you all royalists?" Malcolm asked, stooping down to start the task of freeing them.

A few answered warily in the affirmative, but it didn't really matter. Malcolm couldn't leave them there to die. He had unchained three men when the footsteps of their pursuers arrived in the tunnel. Instead of rescuing everyone, it was more likely Malcolm and Versanne would end up joining these hapless souls. He could only hope the Imperial Guard would have the decency to take Serena back to the surface.

Just outside the cave, Versanne was in conversation with them, and a moment later, two men entered the dark cavern. Malcolm had already drawn his pistol.

"The Fox sent us," the first one said.

Behind Malcolm, a cheer came up from the men with enough strength to do so. And suddenly, the notion of shooting his way out or being imprisoned in the catacombs gave way to relief.

Working with the others, he helped unchain the rest. Serena had already gone to wait with Versanne, and by the time Malcolm left the cavern, helping one man to walk, she was seated beside his gruff associate, making him laugh.

"Now that I see the state of these poor souls," Versanne said, "I am thankful they kept me in the other chamber with the old bones." He chuckled. "Can you believe they thought *I* was the Fox?"

Some went silent, some chuckled with him. Malcolm wasn't sure any of them knew the answer to that mystery. He certainly didn't.

"Do you think there are more prisoners?" Serena asked, drawing all eyes to her.

Malcolm felt a surge of pride and protectiveness, as if she were his.

One of the men answered her. "The Fox said about a dozen have gone missing."

"Then this is all," Malcolm said. "Let's get to the surface."

"I think you and your lady friend have done enough," Versanne said. "We will be a slow lot. You should take her up and away in case we are discovered."

He looked at Serena who had hope in her verdant eyes that she was about to be set free from this subterranean nightmare.

Malcolm offered her his hand, which she took. Drawing her to her feet, he nodded to Versanne. "I'll speak with you tomorrow at the usual place if you're well enough."

And then he led her away with the sounds of cheering and even a few bawdy words called after them. Malcolm rolled his eyes. *The French!*

SERENA STOOD IN THE chilly night air and breathed in great gasps, still clutching Malcolm's strong arm. She never wanted to let go.

"I know there was plenty of air down there," she said, noticing him staring at her. "But from the moment I descended those endless circular stairs, I felt as if I couldn't breathe. The less so, the deeper I went."

"Then you were doubly courageous. You never seemed panicked."

"Knowing you were down there, I couldn't walk away and let that guard lock you in."

He drew her into his arms. "Have you breathed enough fresh air?" he asked softly.

"Why?"

"Because I want to kiss you, and I would hate to make you faint. I've already lugged Versanne around for the past half hour. I don't want to carry you all the way back to the Rue Coquillière."

She smiled. "I'm lighter than Monsieur Versanne. Is that his name?"

"Dammit!" Malcolm exclaimed. "Alone with you for one minute, and I've already broken the sacred trust of my organization."

She laughed at his woebegone expression. "I won't tell anyone. Are you still going to kiss me?" She hoped so, because her entire body, on edge from the evening's caper, was tingling and ready for his touch.

In answer, he claimed her mouth under his, and she relaxed against him, even as her insides seemed to melt. She slid her hands behind his neck, causing her breasts to lift and crush against him.

"Mm," she said, already forgetting the horrors of being underground. She wished they could be alone somewhere more comfortable. And then she recalled how angry she'd been at him and how she'd been ready never to see him again.

But she was hopelessly besotted. When he was close, her anger evaporated. He made her want only to be in his arms and to experience things she knew she should save for her marriage bed.

"Do you think we might find a taxi if we walk a little?" he asked.

"If we walk back along the Boulevard d'Enfer—"

"The Boulevard of Hell, yes," he translated before slipping back into French. "You Parisiennes have such a way with words. I saw a street named for a woman with no head and one for a cat who fishes," he added.

She shrugged. "What about the Londoners with their Haunch of Venison Yard and Cock-Pit Steps and Cock Lane!"

He was staring at her. "How on earth did you know about those?"

Oh dear! How indeed! "I have read books, monsieur. And people from London visit," she added quickly, "and they've described their city."

He looked unconvinced, even puzzled, so she quickly returned to the topic at hand.

"There will be *fiacres* for hire just past the Boulevard d'Enfer on the Boulevard du Montparnasse."

They turned their footsteps in the correct direction.

"Your grandparents will be worried," he guessed, putting to words what she'd been thinking. "We had best hurry before your grandfather calls out the gendarmes."

All at once, she wished she could tell him she would be leaving soon, but that would cause too many questions. *And for what purpose?* A part of her wanted him to ask her to remain in Paris. Or if he discovered she was going to England, how lovely if Malcolm promised to see her again upon his own return.

A foolish fantasy. She certainly didn't want him suddenly declaring his love for her simply because he learned she was a baron's daughter.

"You've become silent," he said, squeezing her arm. "You must be cold and tired."

"A little of both yes." The only time she'd felt warm and exhilarated was when he'd kissed her.

As she'd predicted, they found a *fiacre* easily. In a few minutes, they'd crossed the Seine and she was on her way home. With Malcolm's arm draped across the back of her shoulders, she decided to enjoy the time she had left in his company and snuggled against him. After all, perhaps they would indeed meet on one of those streets in London they'd been discussing.

Thinking she felt his nose upon the top of her head— *was he sniffing her hair?*--Serena turned her face to his. As she'd hoped, he kissed her again. With the touch of his mouth to hers, now-familiar delicious warmth flowed through her, and she squirmed at the sensations pulsing in her body.

It would be easy to divert the hired carriage to his garret. And then she would be exactly as he suspected, a blowsy strumpet.

"You were beyond helpful as usual," he said. "I don't know what I would do without you."

His words tore at her heart, and again, she wanted to confess her impending departure.

"Why did you help me?" he asked suddenly.

What could she tell him? "I suppose because my grandparents have instilled in me a sense of duty to France."

"But I am an Englishman."

"Helping the French," she said. "At least I believe you are doing your best."

Turning to her, he threaded his fingers into her hair and held her face still. In the dark, she could hardly see his expression, but enough light caught his eyes. She would be happy to stare into them for the rest of her life. He'd confessed to being a rake, and she knew that meant a man who dallied with women for sport and pleasure before moving on. Perhaps she was foolish to think herself special.

"What do you want?" he asked, his tone husky.

If she said *I want you*, what would he think? She supposed he meant what did she want for France's future, but the answer she gave was closer to her heart.

"I very much want a dog of my own."

Despite moving closer a second earlier, perhaps to drop another kiss upon her lips, Malcolm leaned back, looking astounded as if she'd said she wished for an exotic giraffe or her own ship. Surely a dog was a reasonable wish.

"A dog?" he echoed, and his mouth lifted in an attractive grin. "Any particular type? Something for hunting perhaps? Or protection? Or chasing wild boar?"

She laughed. "Not a dog with any purpose. Just for being good company, I suppose. For walking with and stroking. And even for hugging."

"Hugging," he repeated, his tone incredulous.

She sighed. "Dogs are warm and soft, and they make me laugh. I feed the mongrels in my grandparents' courtyard, yet I don't know why we have so many milling about."

He chuckled. "Because you feed them, silly girl."

Oh! She hadn't thought of it like that. He was right, of course. When she'd first moved into her grandparents' flat, she'd only noticed one sandy-colored dog, and she'd given it scraps. Soon there had been two, then three, then the small pack that had taken up residence. No one seemed to mind. In fact, she'd seen other tenants feeding the good-natured mutts who were often simply lying in the sun on the warm stones of the central courtyard.

"In any case," she persisted, "I want my own dog, one I can name and leash and bring indoors with me."

"Dogs are so permanent when one actually owns the beast," Malcolm pointed out. "They tie a man down. It means one must stay put."

Odd how he would say that. Serena supposed it cut to the heart of being a rake, the very image of which was a man who didn't want to stay with one woman.

"And a wife doesn't do that? Tie a man down, I mean?" she asked, trying to make light of it.

Cocking his head, looking so disarmingly handsome he practically stole her breath, he said, "I wouldn't know, having not yet had a wife. Nor am I particularly eager to find out."

Yet Malcolm seemed to think a little dog would be reason enough to settle down. He was a riddle indeed, one Serena wished she had more time to understand.

Taking in this scrap of information, however, she reminded herself firmly he was not suitable for marriage. She ought to cease at once the fond feelings that had been steadily growing inside her, strengthening each time she was in his company.

While pondering this, the carriage came to a halt.

"Thank you," he said, sounding entirely genuine, "for your help."

"You're welcome." She wanted to thank him for kissing her so perfectly and bit her tongue to stay silent and proper.

After he helped her down like a gentleman, she let him take her into the central courtyard of the apartments, past the concierge's little hut. Even the stray dogs were already sleeping.

At the foot of the staircase leading to her grandparents' home on the second floor, she stopped him.

"I'll go alone from here, monsieur. *Bonsoir.*"

He hesitated. "I would like to see you again, but I can't think of an excuse."

Serena simply could not keep herself from smiling at his honesty, as the thrill of conquest raced through her. *He enjoyed her company, too!*

Then he added, "But I can think of nowhere we can be alone except my garret."

Her exaltation plummeted. He had one thing upon his virile, rakish mind. She would not behave in such a manner again, leaving him with the wrong impression just before she disappeared from Paris.

"Only because I don't think after tonight, you should be seen with me," Malcolm said by way of explanation, softening her impression that he was merely trying to get her into his bed. "Too many men saw me with Versanne tonight, and you with both of us."

"But those men were prisoners. They are not our enemies," she protested.

He shook his head. "We don't know who they are, only that the emperor thought them a danger."

Malcolm was a cautious member of the British spy network, and she was too careless, as evident by her prior actions.

"You are right," she said.

"So how will I see you again, mademoiselle?"

"I don't know, monsieur. But if you work for the Prince Regent as I suspect, then you will find a way."

His face broke into a grin, a little lopsided which made her heart flip.

"I said you were a clever woman. I shall find a way." And his lips met hers once more with a heart-pounding kiss before she turned and ascended the stairs.

If she didn't receive a severe dressing-down from her grandparents, she would be shocked. But the entire adventure had been worth it.

CHAPTER FOURTEEN

True to his word, Serena received an invitation from Malcolm. Under her grand-mère's watchful eye, she opened it. Not exactly a *billet-doux*, nevertheless, it made her heart race.

"An assembly at the Louvre," Adèle said, reading over her shoulder. "To celebrate Monsieur David's painting of the emperor. I suppose that will be acceptable. And it's a masquerade, too. *Très amusant!*"

In fact, Malcolm couldn't have chosen better since her grand-mère loved the museum and thought an artist's talent was a gift from God. Although it was a day-time reception, showcasing pieces the emperor had obtained from conquered countries and brought to Paris, everyone would be in festive finery.

Malcolm had chosen the masquerade for obvious reasons, and Serena practically laughed out loud at her good fortune—another chance to be with the fascinating Englishman who made her insides quiver. And with Madame Fournier, no doubt.

Her grand-père, however, wasn't so easily persuaded.

"You are a clever girl, but you take too many chances," Pépère said, having not stopped scowling since she'd confessed to the events in the catacombs.

"But the Louvre, Henri," her grand-mère intervened. "It is safe."

"The masquerades at Carnival weren't exactly tame," Pépère said.

Serena had heard stories of how wild Carnival was especially the last of the six "fat" days, *les jours gras*. She couldn't imagine her grandparents engaging in the revelry of the night before Ash Wednesday, when the anonymity of masks gave license for all types of wickedness. Banned for a short while after the Revolution, Serena had Bonaparte to thank for allowing masquerades once again at the turn of the century.

"But this isn't Carnival," Mémère scoffed. "Just a daytime party with masks. She is young, Henri. Let her have fun before she returns to stuffy Britain."

"Hm," he said.

Serena took that as a good sign. Not exactly a blessing, but an indication she would be allowed to go.

Wearing a gown of mostly white silk with little purple flowers around the bodice and at the bottom of the skirt, she draped a lavender-colored, soft Kashmir shawl over her shoulders. Although not as expensive as the imported kind, since it was from French goats rather than Indian goats, still the shawl was one of her favorite pieces.

When topped with a white lace cap trailing purple and green ribbons and a lavender silk mask, she felt perfectly in the pink of fashion.

When Monsieur Branley came to fetch her, he entered their parlor wearing the full black cloak of the traditional Venetian domino costume. And again, her grand-père gave him a serious stare.

"Be very careful with my granddaughter," Henri said.

"Yes, monsieur," Malcolm answered seriously.

When he swept the simple cape over his shoulder so he could easily take her arm, Serena noted his regular clothing underneath, a pale gray jacket with cream-colored breeches and black boots.

"And a mask, monsieur? her grand-mère asked.

"It's on the seat of the carriage," he promised.

Madame Fournier rose from the divan. Unlike Serena and Malcolm, she wore a full costume. Serena watched Malcolm's expression of surprise, quickly tamed to one of utter neutrality.

But Madame Fournier wanted praise. "Aren't you going to say anything about my appearance, Monsieur Branley?"

"Of course. You look utterly fetching as a . . . a fishgirl?" he trailed off.

"What?!" she exclaimed. "I am a peasant girl, not a fishgirl."

Serena could almost hear him thinking Madame Fournier was far too old to be a *girl* of any type, but luckily, all he said was, "*Je m'excuse.* The stripes confused me."

"A traditional fishgirl costume has a red and white skirt," their chaperone declared.

"Except the Calvados fishgirl," Serena's Mémère added. "Then it could be blue and white."

"Yes, naturally," said Madame Fournier before rounding upon Malcolm. "But obviously, I am a peasant girl." She turned slowly, showing off her costume consisting of a short red-and-black striped petticoat with a gold cashmere overskirt. This was artfully pinned up to show its red lining. Over this she wore a black velvet bodice, a white apron, and a dainty muslin cap.

Serena watched him take in madame's gold-and-red stockings and gaudy black shoes with gold buckles. Then his gaze came back to her face with its bright spots of rouge painted upon each cheek. He was holding back a laugh with some difficulty.

"I can see plainly now you are a peasant girl," he said. "Your plaited blonde hair should have given me a clue."

"It should have," Madame Fournier agreed with a sharp nod, before leading them out the door.

As they entered the carriage, Malcolm had to snatch his mask from the seat just before Serena's chaperone sat upon it. They exchanged a glance.

Madame Fournier started chatting immediately about the collections and what she'd seen in the past, and how she hoped there would be champagne.

"The emperor may be there," she mused. "I wonder if the purpose of the evening is for him to rename the Louvre as the Napoleon Museum the way he did before his exile."

Serena's gaze shot to her English spy, but he looked unbothered. She supposed the odds of running into Bonaparte were slim in such a large place. And with his costume, even if he did, it was unlikely Malcolm would be recognized as the mute baker.

As if making sure, he took the opportunity to tie his black silk mask securely, immediately taking on the classic domino air of intrigue, adventure, conspiracy, and mystery—perfectly suited to Malcolm Branley.

When they arrived, the festive air was obvious. Carriages lined up along the Rue de Rivoli, and soon, their party of three were entering the stately museum, once a medieval fortress, and strolling the elegant Grand Gallery.

"Did you know Bonaparte married the Archduchess Marie-Louise in this very hall?" Madame Fournier asked, addressing Malcolm.

"A mere five years ago," he said. "Were you an honored guest?"

Serena's chaperone blushed, darkening her cheeks under her rosy makeup, and fanned herself while offering a coquettish smile.

"Oh, no, monsieur. But I did see them come out of the building afterward. The empress's gown was beautiful, and they both wore ruby red robes. They were most majestic."

"Majestically imperial," he said, teasingly.

"Or imperially majestic," Serena quipped.

The older lady nodded. "Either, I suppose," she said, not noticing how they teased. "Now, let's see what paintings are past those columns."

When Madame Fournier was a few steps ahead, still talking as if her charge were next to her, Serena stopped in front of a painting and Malcolm halted, too.

"Are you working tonight?" she asked him quietly.

He shot her a curious look. "Working?"

"Yes, gathering information for the Prince Regent or the Seventh Coalition? Isn't that what you do?"

He sighed. "We shouldn't talk about that."

"You don't trust me," she concluded. It stung, especially after all she'd done to help him already.

"It's not that. Some things are simply better left unsaid. We're here today because we enjoy each other's company, and I hope we will see some impressive works of art such as no Englishman had been able to see for two decades before last year."

"Because of the wars," she said.

"Because of the wars," he agreed.

"There you are," Madame Fournier exclaimed. "I was halfway along the gallery when I realized you weren't beside me."

"We were struck by the beauty of this painting," Serena lied, glancing at what they were standing in front of, a particularly gruesome depiction of someone having just been beheaded by a particularly large sword.

"Were you?" asked her chaperone slowly, staring at the painting and then back at Serena.

"Mademoiselle meant the attention to detail is quite astonishing," Malcolm said. "It must be a Flemish artist."

Serena looked again at the perfectly depicted drops of blood on the lacey collar of the hapless victim. Quite frankly, it was grisly.

"Well, I prefer some of the still lifes with flowers and fruit," Madame Fournier said. "They look realistic, too, without the . . . *um* . . . the violent aspect."

"Show us," Serena said, eager to leave the painting behind.

As her chaperone had hoped, there was champagne being served from silver trays, and soon they came across one of Napoleon's prize pieces, the *Apollo Belvedere*, a statue which he'd taken from the Vatican after conquering Rome.

Serena was trying not to stare at Apollo's manhood but couldn't keep her eyes from the realistic sculpture, wondering if Malcolm's manly parts looked similar. She dared a glance at him only to discover he'd noticed her interest.

Feeling her cheeks heat, knowing they now resembled Madame Fournier's rouged skin, she looked quickly away.

"Rumor has it our emperor spends his free time enjoying the theatre," Madame Fournier whispered loudly, "as he is quite taken with Mademoiselle Mars."

"But he is married," Serena protested. And the empress was reputed to be an attractive woman. *Why on earth did he need to take up with an actress?*

Madame Fournier shrugged. "Our emperor's wife has refused to return from Austria to be by his side, or so people say."

"Our emperor is a rake," Serena concluded, making her chaperone gasp.

"Every man with a mistress isn't a rake," Malcolm protested, causing Serena's ire to spike.

"Are you defending his philandering?" she asked, hoping even a declared rake would have some set of morals.

"This is most certainly not appropriate conversation," Madame Fournier complained, even though she'd started it.

But Serena wasn't finished ascertaining Malcolm's thoughts.

"Is that Mémère's and your good friend Madame Archambeau?" she asked, looking past Madame Fournier.

"Where?" Her chaperone's head was suddenly on a swivel.

"There, madame, by that large landscape painting."

"Why, so it is. I'll go say hello. You two stay where I can see you."

"Of course, madame," Malcolm said affably.

As soon as her chaperone was out of hearing, Serena demanded, "Why do you say men with mistresses are not rakes?"

"I think Madame Fournier is correct," Malcolm muttered. "This topic is inappropriate."

"Tell me anyway," Serena commanded.

He shrugged. "A man can be upstanding *and* have a mistress. That is all. He isn't necessarily doing anything one might call rakish."

"Only adultery," she pointed out.

"An adulterer is not necessarily a rake," he explained, "although a rake can be an adulterer."

"Are you mincing words?" she asked while sticking out a finger and nearly touching Apollo's thigh before she realized where she was and snatched her hand away.

Malcolm didn't seem to notice.

"Not at all," he promised. "A rake is hardly ever a married man like the emperor. That's all I mean. Because rakes don't wish to marry. They are usually unsettled men who enjoy a bevy and bounty of women either at the same time or sequentially, although the term *rakehell* used to be applied to more of a dissolute and debauched individual."

He tugged on his cloak and brushed off an imaginary piece of lint from the front.

"Referring to a man who participates in far too much gambling and drinking," he added, "and thus not at all like myself."

Serena tipped her champagne glass toward him. "Drinking?"

He laughed. "Not anything so refined as champagne," he said, and sipped from his own. "More like bottle upon bottle of gin."

She couldn't help wrinkling her nose at the idea of drinking such vile stuff. But her thoughts were spinning at

Malcolm's explanation of various levels of debauchery and rakishness.

Madame Fournier returned. "Shall we move along?" And she strode ahead of them from one room to the next, giving them an unceasing view of her swaying red-and-black stripes.

"I feel like a child," Malcolm quipped under his breath. "All we need is for her to attach our leading strings."

Serena laughed.

"*What* is so amusing?" Madame Fournier called over her shoulder before stopping next to Veronese's *The Wedding at Cana.* "Nothing inappropriate, I hope."

"No, madame," Serena promised, and she wished right then that rules of decent society didn't prevent her being alone with Malcolm. Assuredly, they would get up to exciting trouble, which was why those strict precepts existed in the first place.

Whoever had invented the notion of chaperones must have had a wayward daughter, she thought.

"You look as though you're in a tweague, mademoiselle," Malcolm remarked.

"No, not annoyed, monsieur. Merely feeling a little restricted," she glanced at Madame Fournier, who was signing her name in a guest book, and then back at her escort.

"Are you going to sign?" she asked him.

"I think not. Rather imprudent of me given the circumstances, wouldn't you say?"

Just then, Madame Fournier exclaimed loudly in surprise, making Serena jump.

CHAPTER FIFTEEN

Following her chaperone's gaze, Serena saw her grandparents unexpectedly making their way toward them, not in any sort of costume except the obligatory half masks to show they'd made an effort. After she kissed their cheeks, as did Madame Fournier, and after Malcolm shook Henri's hand, her grand-père explained how he couldn't resist bringing his lovely wife to such a grand event.

And why shouldn't they come out and enjoy the museum? However, they weren't usually impulsive, and Adèle's eyes appeared wary.

"Is everything fine, Mémère?" Serena asked.

"Of course it is, dear one." And the older woman threaded her arm through hers. "Let's go see the new painting."

They walked through the gallery under the brilliant sunlight streaming in from the cleverly placed windows in the ceiling. Finding *The Coronation of Napoleon*, recently lent to the Louvre by its painter, Jacques-Louis David, upon the emperor's return, would not be difficult. It was reputed to be at least thirty-two feet long and nearly twenty feet high.

Madame Fournier stayed with them, and Pépère walked behind with Malcolm, who'd raised his mask to the top of his forehead while they spoke.

When Serena came upon the painting, she gasped. With her grand-mère on one side of her and her chaperone on the other, they stood far back in order to take in the scene of Napoleon's coronation at Notre Dame. Depicted in their finery, a large group of courtiers and the Pope, himself, were practically life-size. It appeared so realistic, Serena almost believed she could step directly into the great cathedral.

Distracting her, however, were the men of her party who had yet to admire David's magnificent work, but instead were talking a few feet away. At something her grandfather said, Malcolm's gaze shot directly toward her.

She doubted they were discussing rakes. Raising an eyebrow, she hoped Malcolm would tell her later. At that moment, however, all he did was frown and look away. A minute later, he and her grand-père joined them to exclaim over the Louvre's newest piece.

With its brilliant reds and golds and the shimmering play of light, Monsieur David had captured the moment when Napoleon, having crowned himself, made his first wife an empress, holding a crown over Josephine's bowed head. The solemnity of the occasion had been painted on every face, and the symbol of an emperor's vast power was clear.

When they turned as a group to enter the next hall, Serena feared she would never get another moment alone with Malcolm that day. Yet when her grand-mère chatted with Madame Fournier, and her grand-père was examining a painting by Monsieur Gros depicting a victorious Napoleon visiting a Prussian battlefield with cadavers strewn in the foreground, Serena took up a place by Malcolm's elbow.

"What were you and my grand-père discussing?"

"Your grandfather was worried about any misbehavior," he told her.

"But we had a chaperone?" she protested, embarrassed her Pépère was thinking such things, no matter if they could be true.

"Not between us," Malcolm explained with a wry grin, but his glance fell to her mouth, and Serena's insides tingled with awareness. Then he shook his head to break the spell.

"Monsieur Renault was thinking more of trouble between soldiers and anyone suspected of being a royalist."

Serena felt her heart sink. "Surely, nothing will happen here at the Louvre. Would anyone risk the national treasures being damaged?"

Malcolm shrugged. "Your grandfather said he has heard soldiers are combing the city because of a certain incident at the catacombs."

They stared at one another in silence. Then she whispered, "Are you saying my grand-père came to warn us of—"

Shouting came from the front of the building interrupting her. Quick as a whip, Malcolm herded Serena in the opposite direction, away from the noise. Henri was just as swift to grab Adèle Renault by the arm and also Madame Fournier, and the five of them went deeper into the museum's galleries.

"An unwelcome turn of events," Malcolm said, dragging his mask back into place.

Serena agreed. A pleasant afternoon had suddenly become another possibly perilous outing.

The initial sounds, which she'd identified as men calling out orders, had quietened, but a wave of whispers carried through the museum halls, until Serena thought she heard *"la rousse."*

A red-haired woman!

Deciding she must be imagining it, she started to ask the others if they thought they should simply try to leave. After all, Malcolm could be in danger. However, her grand-père's severe expression and Malcolm's clenched jaw made her hold her tongue.

And suddenly, blue-and-white uniformed grenadiers were upon them, soldiers who personally served the emperor.

"That one," said an Imperial Guard in the front, a shiny sabre hanging from his belt.

Another approached, the red plume in his tall, black bearskin hat swaying as he walked.

"Possibly," he said with a distinctly Polish accent. He was one of the *chevau-légers*, volunteers who had followed the Emperor into his exile on Elba and helped him to return.

"Take her along with the other two," said the first.

Serena's grand mère and Madame Fournier both exclaimed aloud in dismay.

"What is the meaning of this?" Henri Renault demanded. "You cannot take my granddaughter."

"We can, monsieur. The emperor commands it."

Serena glanced toward Malcolm, expecting to find only an empty place where he'd been standing. Unlike at the Palais du Luxembourg, however, probably because of his costume, he stood steadily by her side.

"Why are you taking her and where?" he asked calmly.

"To the Palais des Tuileries," the first grenadier said. "The why of it, I cannot say."

"She is innocent," Adèle said, grabbing Serena's arm.

"If she is innocent, madame, then she has no reason to fear," the Polish-accented guard replied.

By Serena's side, Malcolm was bristling with restrained energy, but there was nothing he could do under the circumstances. Then, to her surprise, Pépère pried her grand-mère's hand off her arm, much to Adèle's consternation.

"She has done nothing wrong. You may take her," her grand-père said, "but I will go with her."

"I'm afraid you have no say in the matter, nor can you go with us."

"It is improper for you to—" Madame Fournier spoke up, trying to do her duty.

She was interrupted immediately. "We are taking other females. If you and your party wish to follow behind, you may wait at the gates of the palace with their families."

Serena didn't want her grandparents to argue with the Imperial Guards any longer. After all, Bonaparte had always been kind to her. She was his favorite vintner. He'd said so himself.

"I will go with them." She sent Malcolm a quick glance, wishing she could see more of his face, but the firm set of his lips spoke of the situation's gravity. Regardless, she plastered on a bright, undaunted smile and turned to the soldiers. "I am ready, messieurs."

The uniformed men looked impressed, and Serena felt courageous until she took a few steps away from Malcolm and her grandparents with the grenadiers flanking her.

"Do not worry," her grand-mère called after her.

But Malcolm and her grand-père's silence filled her ears. If they were worried, she probably had cause to be as well.

MALCOLM RAN VERY FAST until he was back in his garret and snatching up his baker's disguise. Shedding his costume and his normal garments, he donned the loose, rough clothing of the baker before heading to the boulangerie. Frustrating him, Monsieur Marineau had already closed for the day.

"Blast!" He could hardly show up empty-handed since the palace guards always examined his basket.

Thinking of where he could turn at that hour of the late afternoon when most of the bakeries, open since dawn, had sold their wares and shut their doors, he headed for the Palais-Royal, praying the owner of the Café de Chartres could help him.

Cursing the delay, he went up the back stairs two at a time and tried to push past the armed guard who stopped him. Raising his cloth cap, he let the man see his face. With a lift of his eyebrow, the man let him pass.

The room was empty. No Randall, no Versanne. Feeling frantic, knowing Serena had been taken because she'd helped him in the catacombs, Malcolm was ready to storm the palace with only his own arsenal of two pistols.

"Don't be a fool," he told himself and headed downstairs to find the restaurant's owner.

Shortly, armed with a basket of bread and cakes, he left the café. It was a quick jaunt, only a few turns to get to the palace. Sooner than he'd thought possible, he was slipping through the back gate, waved in by the guard after inspecting his wares.

Now what? He was in the cellar, but Serena was surely two floors up in a reception room or even in the emperor's private chamber, facing what charges, Malcolm didn't know.

WITH TWO OTHER RED-HEADED women, both looking immensely terrified, Serena was taken across the immense esplanade behind the Louvre and through the Arc de Triomphe. They entered the Palais des Tuileries under its great square-walled dome and into one of the reception rooms in which she'd previously met with the emperor.

A butterfly seemed to take up residence in her stomach, but the presence of her Queen Anne pistol against her ankle comforted her. And knowing Malcolm was somewhere nearby helped as well. She didn't know how she knew, she simply did.

"Only three ladies with red hair," came Bonaparte's voice as he entered from the next chamber wearing his customary white uniform with dark blue accents and knee-high black boots, spurs at the ready.

He didn't look his usual amiable self, however, and Serena didn't think he was about to offer her madeleines.

They made eye contact, and for the first time, she saw something in his gaze that was both ruthless and unforgiving.

Swallowing the fear rising in her, she curtsied along with the other women.

"It's no matter," said a familiar voice from the corner where a man had stood unnoticed. "Your guards have found the right one."

Monsieur Christoff stepped forward, and she sucked in a shocked breath. Then he pointed directly at her.

"She's the one working with the traitors."

Serena felt the blood leave her head.

"You may go," the emperor said to the other two, who curtsied, murmured words of thanks, and scurried away quickly to their families waiting at the gates.

Her grandparents would see at once she'd been detained. *Only her.*

"Where are my manners?" Bonaparte asked, gesturing to the sofa.

Since her knees were knocking, she gratefully wobbled to where he indicated, and she sat. The emperor also took a seat, but he didn't invite Monsieur Christoff to do the same.

"This man said you helped him escape from the catacombs. Is that true?"

How had she and Malcolm not noticed him? And after being saved from such a horrid fate, Christoff had repaid her with a treacherous act. *How despicable!* Yet it was never supposed to be his fate in the first place since he was a Bonapartist through and through.

"I was in the catacombs recently," she said cautiously. "I was touring them."

Monsieur Christoff snorted loudly. "You did a lot more than tour them."

She leveled a stare at him, one she'd seen her father use. Oddly, it seemed to work, for he pursed his lips and said no more.

"Will you tell us, Mademoiselle Renault, what happened?" The emperor's words were not unkind, yet his tone was icy.

"Yes, Your Imperial Majesty. Let me think. I was walking past the entrance when I stumbled and dropped a bottle of wine . . . ." She explained the whole evening and how she'd ended up innocently wandering the catacombs and even holding a light while someone she didn't know unchained prisoners. After all, she couldn't possibly know why men were being kept down there, nor could she stop others from freeing them.

Serena told the tale without incriminating herself at all.

"As you see, I was like a leaf upon the Seine, drifting along while around me were the torrents of intrigue, none of which I, a vintner's granddaughter, had any part of."

"You left the catacombs with an English spy," Christoff insisted.

She stood up, outraged, causing Napoleon to stand as well, his gentlemanly manners surprising her since he was their emperor and could do as he liked.

"How was I to know he was a spy?" Serena demanded. "Wasn't he the same man with whom *you* had a meeting, just the two of you, at the Café Aveugles a few weeks ago? My friends will attest that we saw you break bread with him. I wonder if *you* are the one who is working with a spy. Why were you tied up in that cavern if you are loyal to his Imperial Majesty?"

And just like that, the emperor turned upon Monsieur Christoff. While Bonaparte's back was turned, she wanted to stick her tongue out at her accuser, but she remained with a saint-like expression on her face, entirely placid.

"Your Imperial Majesty, as I explained before," Monsieur Christoff began, "I was sent there by unfortunate mistake. I do not hold your guards responsible. It was this woman and her friend who told them lies about me."

At least Serena could show true outrage this time. "I never said a word to any guards about you." She made the sign of the cross upon her heart, over her Kashmir shawl. "I vow before God."

"Then your friend did," Monsieur Christoff insisted. "But we are not talking about me. We are here because you have shown up too many times in the Englishman's company."

Serena took a breath, sighed, blinked, hoped she looked entirely calm if not bored.

"Your Majesty," she addressed Bonaparte, looking at him squarely with her green gaze she'd been told was frank and trustworthy, "I believe you would be interested to know why my good friend, Guillaume Racine, unquestionably loyal to the empire, worried about the trustworthiness of this man. I'm sorry to report, Monsieur Christoff attacked me on the Rue Croix des Petits Champs, near the Bank of France!"

"What is this?" the emperor asked. "Are you a barbarian?" He turned on the florid-faced man.

"No, I . . . ," Monsieur Christoff began.

"Any man who attacks a female, especially a fellow citizen of France, cannot be trusted. I don't want such a monster in my army. What do you say for yourself?"

Monsieur Christoff took a step back. "I thought she would return my affection."

Serena made a noise of disbelief. If he'd been smart, he would have denied it outright and made it his word against hers. But he wasn't finished trying to drag her down.

"I admit I should not have tried to steal a kiss—"

"*Oh!*" she exclaimed, intimating he'd done more than that.

"I admit it," he continued, "but why did the English spy come to your defense?"

This time, Serena shook her head. "I was alone with you when you became a wild man," she embellished. "It's true that a stranger answered my screams for help, but only you say he was an Englishman and a spy. You are seeing spies everywhere, or pretending to."

"But the *tête de noeud*," Monsieur Christoff insisted.

"What are you saying?" the emperor demanded. "Are you mad? Who are you calling a prick-head?"

"No one, Your Imperial Majesty. I swear it. *I* am the *tête de noeud.*"

Bonaparte clapped his hands, and two guards entered through the open double doors.

"I've heard enough. Take this man away."

"Your Majesty, I beseech you," Monsieur Christoff began.

"The way this young lady undoubtedly beseeched you as you tried to violate her. I will not tolerate such things in my capital. To jail, this time," he added to his guards. "He's not only a scoundrel, he's half insane."

The brute did not go quietly, hurling accusations against Serena and Guillaume, as well as the British. He tried to fight his way free before the guards overpowered him and dragged him away, still yelling.

Feigning offense, she put a gloved hand to her forehead as if his words had greatly upset her. When the last echoes of his invectives had died away, she and Emperor Bonaparte stared silently at one another for a moment.

Then he turned and strode the length of the room before coming to stand before her.

"You must tell no one of anything you heard or saw in the catacombs, mademoiselle. I wouldn't insult you by saying there are things going on you do not understand."

"Thank you, Your Imperial Majesty."

"However, you must let events play out as they should. Too many men think they can shape history with a whisper here or a shout there. It is not for them to do. All power resides within the throne. I alone represent the people and will guide our destiny."

"I understand," she said, although Serena knew the emperor couldn't control the members of the Seventh Coalition or those seeking to oust him from his throne of power. He couldn't even control Malcolm.

Bonaparte looked at her a few seconds longer, and then he nodded.

She was being dismissed. Curtsying low, she couldn't believe she was about to walk out of the palace, a free woman.

"Don't think I am sending you away, mademoiselle," the emperor added. "Not forever. As before, if you hear of anything useful, I welcome your return. Not for my sake but for France, I know you will come again. With your wine, of course. The Renault family is important to me now."

She wished he hadn't mentioned her family. *Was it a threat?*

As she turned, Bonaparte offered one more word of caution.

"After all, it would be foolish for anyone with your unusual hair color to attempt the dangerous pastime of subterfuge. Only see how easily you were picked out from a crowd."

She smiled. "You are correct, Your Imperial Majesty." Her grandparents had asked her to wear a bonnet that was more concealing every day when she first arrived, but she'd been too vain. Today, it could have cost her dearly.

"Good day, Your Majesty," she said, but he'd already walked away toward his private inner chamber. And with that dismissal, two of the three thousand servants reputed to be part of his household came instantly to usher her out.

They left her when she reached the first floor, and as swiftly as they did, Malcolm appeared. The juxtaposition from the tense moments she'd recently endured to his silly disguise as a baker made her want to laugh.

He shook his head, walking past her and out the door toward her family. She followed behind. Malcolm went past her grandparents, his head down, not stopping, nor did they seem to recognize him.

And then she was being hugged.

"Mémère, Pépère," Serena greeted them. "I'm fine."

"Of course you are," her grand-père said. "You are a Renault first and foremost."

Her grand-mère nodded, took her arm, and directed her toward the waiting *fiacre*.

"You will tell us every word he spoke," Adèle said, "as soon as we are home."

CHAPTER SIXTEEN

S erena wasn't surprised when Malcolm showed up at the Halle aux Vins the next day in his disguise. Her insides fluttered as usual, although she wished it were otherwise. Of all the men to have captured her interest, Malcolm Branley was certainly not a good choice. *A spy and a rake!*

Telling Michel she was going for a walk in the sunshine, she joined Malcolm, appearing as two working-class people strolling along the quay.

"Bonjour, Monsieur Boulanger," she greeted him as if he were a baker. To her surprise, he didn't appear amused.

"This isn't a game," he scolded.

That sliced with a shard of truth. She had treated it as such for a long while, the way she treated all of life. The way she'd behaved during her only Season in London. And every day, Serena readily played the part of a French female as if it were indeed an amusement. Moreover, while her grandparents' well-being was vitally important to her, whoever ruled France was less so. Until lately.

Now it seemed she had to make a choice and stick to her convictions because people on one side or the other could be hurt.

Regardless, she didn't care for a fellow Englishman taking her to task.

"I am fully aware this isn't a game," she insisted. "And I am not a chess piece, a mere pawn for you to use." Although that was precisely what her grand-père had done, and Serena had willingly allowed him to. As for Malcolm, she'd fallen into helping him almost unintentionally.

"A pawn, no," Malcolm said, looking at the dappled light on the water and not at her. "How about a queen? Or at least a viscountess, were it possible."

She caught her breath. *What was he saying?* He was teasing her, she supposed, and she would call his bluff.

"What's stopping you? I am perfectly happy to be a viscountess." *As long as she was his.*

He turned to her, his expression unreadable, but they both stopped walking. *Was he a viscount?*

Once upon a simpler time when she was about to enjoy her first Season, she'd been presented to Queen Charlotte at St. James's Palace, and it had sorely rattled her nerves. Serena had performed a deep curtsy with as much grace as she could muster while wearing the outdated but mandatory court fashion of a high-waisted gown paired with a full-hooped skirt. With the obligatory train that nearly tripped her as she'd backed away upon being dismissed and despite the tall ostrich feathers that had collapsed over her face, Serena had been relieved when her ordeal was over. Luckily, by then, the queen had no longer been looking at her.

All in all, going to court was a nerve-wracking experience from the long wait until the difficult backward exit. But lately, she'd strolled with an emperor. And now, in her plain green-and-white striped cotton dress, she felt brave and fearless, and she imagined being a viscountess could hardly be so very difficult, even on a daily basis.

Malcolm offered her a rueful smile and then pronounced an entirely inaccurate statement.

"You know nothing of my world," he said beginning to walk again. He directed their footsteps to the old Pont de la

Tournelle, a bridge which took them across to the Île Saint-Louis. They were surrounded by four, five, and six-story buildings in the elegant old neighborhood first developed for aristocrats and politicians in the seventeenth century. The most fashionable Parisians were strolling in the midday sunshine on their small island in the middle of the Seine.

"A viscount's wife, or indeed, any female member of the *ton*, has many social duties and little freedom, nothing like you have here in Paris. Your life would be a series of restrictions and demands. And you would have to be above reproach and beyond any suspicion of French support, or they would eat you alive."

"An English paragon of virtue?" she asked. She hadn't been one before, and she doubted she would be considered one now.

"Something like that," he agreed.

"Are you truly a viscount?" she asked.

"No," Malcom said. Then to her surprise, he added, "Not yet."

Oh! Suddenly, her view of him shifted for the worse. A handsome lord and heir to a viscountcy could do quite a bit of damage as a rake.

"You, as a male member of the gentry, can do exactly as you please without consequence. You may take a lady down a dark path at Vauxhall and be considered in no less good-standing if discovered, while she would be all-but ruined."

He frowned. "How do you know about such things?"

She shrugged. Since they'd reached halfway along the Rue des Deux Ponts and she had no wish to walk across the second bridge to the Right Bank, she turned around. While she might be thinking of life as a viscountess, on this particular day, Serena needed to get back to her work at the wine market.

"Anyway," Malcolm said, "you're wrong. Gentlemen, especially noblemen, are expected to behave well, and if they don't, they get a reputation."

"As a rake," she surmised.

"Exactly. And then they aren't as welcome as they once were, although not ruined, to be sure. If single, they aren't considered quite as good a match for the young ladies, and if married, all the sympathy goes to the wife, as it should."

"I wouldn't want sympathy," she told him. "I would want revenge."

His eyebrows rose questioningly.

"If a man pledged his troth to me," she explained, "then I would expect his fidelity. That's not such a difficult or unreasonable concept, is it?"

"No, not at all," he agreed, "which is why I haven't pledged my troth or anything else to anyone yet. I wasn't ready to keep such a promise."

"That makes you *not* a very desirable match, as you said."

His cheeks flushed a darker shade. Either he was embarrassed or annoyed at her for pointing it out.

"In any case, I was speaking about French sympathies," he explained, "not fidelity to one's spouse. Neither a viscount nor a viscountess can be suspected of harboring favorable feelings toward the country with which we've been at war for so long. And that's all I meant about you not being a suitable viscountess."

"I see." She glanced down river so he wouldn't see her disappointment, wishing she could flounce her skirts and look majestic. Instead, she had to settle for the small swish of her plain cotton dress. But she wasn't French, and her only loyalty was to her grandparents. That didn't preclude her from acceptance among the *bon ton,* as long as they'd forgotten her earlier indiscretions.

In truth, she would willingly accept a promise from the tall man beside her if he was prepared to settle down. Her heart was more than ready to disclose its preference for Malcolm Branley—*or Lord Branley, which he must surely be called in England*—over any other man she'd ever met.

Luckily, her head was too smart to say anything of the sort to a confirmed libertine. For even if she was suitable to be his viscountess, he had clearly reiterated he wasn't going to make any promises or take a vow of fidelity.

"Why did you come to see me today?" she asked, something she should have wondered when he first showed himself at the Halle aux Vins.

"To make sure you are well." He said it as if his concern for her was the most natural thing in the world, almost as if she mattered to him.

"You saw me leave the palace unharmed yesterday," Serena reminded him. "I saw you there."

"And I was prepared to get you away from the guards if they'd tried to imprison you."

"I know," she told him.

He sent her a genuine grin. "Did you?"

"Yes, I trusted you would rescue me if need be. Luckily, the emperor let me go. Monsieur Christoff was my accuser, by the way."

Malcolm shook his head in astonishment. "How? Why?"

"We saved him, you and I, along with the others from the catacombs."

"Careless of me," Malcolm muttered. "I'm terribly sorry."

"I had to mention his brief assault in order to cast doubt upon his character. And he has been locked up again." She sighed. "Bonaparte expects me to bring him anything I hear or see that might be useful."

"Will you?" Malcolm's words were clipped.

Feeling irritated by his question, she didn't answer.

"Never mind," he said. "As long as you don't turn in the mute baker, I am grateful."

So that was his main interest in seeing her! She was more than a little disappointed. Although she supposed in his business, he had to be wary.

"I will not. It would only reflect badly upon me," she added, unable to help the bitter tone. He hadn't been thinking of her as a potential wife, only assuring himself he could continue to do his duty.

Stepping off the bridge, they returned to the Quai de la Tournelle, mere yards from the wine market.

"You shouldn't come any farther with me. It might look suspicious," she said. "Good day, Monsieur Branley."

He didn't argue. "Good day, Mademoiselle Renault."

And she walked away, wondering if she'd seen the last of him.

"Boney's planning the where and the when, even as we speak," Randall said.

"I heard." Malcolm had, in fact, already been talking with a pretty scullery maid in the palace who'd heard from a chamber maid who'd heard from her lover, a footman in the emperor's private apartment, that a cartographer had been summoned.

Certain key officers had also arrived, including the emperor's Chief of Staff, Marshal Jean-de-Dieu Soult, General de Grouchy, and Marshal Ney, who by all accounts was at loggerheads with Soult.

"I suppose I should get a look at those plans if there's anything in writing," Malcolm mused.

"It's always in writing," his associate promised. "I've never known a military commander who didn't want to see his bloody perfect battle plans in black and white. And our Boney is a soldier general as much as he's an emperor."

"True. Louis would have expressed some vague orders," Malcolm said, "and then left it up to his officers to sort out the how of his brilliant strategy."

"If he'd even bothered," Randall muttered.

"Remind me why we want to sit fat Louis once again upon the French throne."

Randall smiled at Malcolm's irreverent question.

"Precisely because he won't bother with anything to do with war, at least not with Britain. And I would like a few years of peace now we've tasted almost a whole year of it."

"It was nice while it lasted," Malcolm agreed.

"Then let's restore King Louis and peace," Randall said. "When can you get a look at those plans?"

Malcolm didn't mind any task that returned him to the palace because it was the only place he might run into Serena Renault by chance. He had no believable reason for strolling through the Halle aux Vins. And if he sent her an invitation to anything in the city, there was a great risk to her should they be seen together by the wrong people.

Besides, her grandparents might not let him in their door again, not after the last dangerous outing to the Louvre.

But at the Tuileries, he could run into her, perhaps find a secluded area where he could kiss her again. From there, it wasn't too far to his garret if she wanted to explore their mutual desire further. And he was entirely certain the feeling was mutual. No woman could kiss a man so passionately if she wasn't feeling sparks.

Still, he wished his conscience wasn't pricked by the idea of beginning a satisfying affair with her—tupping her daily if she'd let him—only to leave her behind when he returned home.

What was the alternative? He couldn't seriously consider taking a Parisian vintner's granddaughter back to jolly old England and hoping she would fit in. There would be wolves aplenty due to her nationality. On the other hand, the warm twist to his heart when he thought of her made him more than willing to have a go at protecting her from those wolves. Surely, he could keep her safe and make her happy.

And the idea of having her in his arms, under his roof, in his bed for the rest of their lives made *him* happy! He was surprised by how much.

SERENA DELIVERED HER LATEST false message to the emperor. In the cafés where everyone knew foreign agents lingered, talk was that the Seventh Coalition would amass their forces *only* to the east of Paris, she told him, and the enemies of France were counting on Parisians going over to their side.

Of course, nothing could be further from the truth. In fact, the alliance of powers was hoping to march on Paris from all sides and, as her grandparents discussed, the Coalition intended to crush the smaller French army sooner rather than later. It could happen tomorrow!

Napoleon listened and thanked her. Curtsying low, she took her leave and made her way through the long hallway to the top of the main staircase when she heard male voices through an open door.

Glancing behind her, seeing no one, she moved closer. Perhaps she could discover whether the emperor planned on waiting for the enemy to come to his door or would choose an advantageous battlefield. And where that might be!

Loitering a moment outside the open door, she realized the men were indeed officers, but they were discussing food rations. At first, she thought it unimportant, until she realized they were touting numbers of troops, not only the Royal Army that Emperor Bonaparte had inherited, which was about two hundred thousand, but also men who were responding to his call to arms, another one hundred thousand at least.

More than that, they discussed the country's police and naval units also being turned into foot soldiers. And the emperor was even considering reinstating the mandatory conscription the king had abolished as so many hated it. The men debated and calculated how much food they would need if all these men were going to march across France.

To where? she wondered, listening carefully. *Where would Bonaparte take his army if he didn't wait in Paris to be attacked?*

"Eh, mademoiselle, what are you doing there?" came a voice from the other end of the corridor. *Not the emperor*, she realized with a sigh of relief. Undoubtedly, it was one of the palace guards.

The voices in the room beside her halted. Without turning around to allow whoever was addressing her to see her face, she swiftly descended the stairs. In the corridor below, she looked for a place to hide.

With her heart beating fast, she opened the first door she came to and disappeared inside. Surely, anyone following her would continue down another floor toward the entrance.

Pressing her back against the door, she realized she was in a meeting room, with maps strewn across a long table and small white porcelain cups contain the last dregs of coffee residue.

Maps! Creeping forward, she saw *Armée du Nord* scrawled across one and *Armée du Rhine* across another. She swallowed, determined to comprehend what she was looking at before she had to flee.

Moving a large map to one side, she revealed more, stamped with *Armée du Jura, Armée des Alpes,* and *Armée du Var.*

Eyes wide, she wondered how she could recall and convey anything she was seeing. *Could she roll them up and put them under her skirts somehow?*

At a swishing sound behind her, the hair on the back of her neck rose, and she stood up straight, scrunching her eyes closed with dread. If she were the fainting kind, she would have done so on the spot. Footsteps behind her sealed her fate. She would be taken outside and executed. No one would believe she'd wandered into the room filled with secret plans by mistake.

Too frozen even to turn around, she held her breath and waited to hear her fate.

CHAPTER SEVENTEEN

"Serena!"

Whirling at the sound of Malcolm's voice, she faced him in his baker's costume. Next to him was a slit of darkness from a narrow opening in the wall, indicating how he'd entered without using the main door. The relief flooding through her made her momentarily light-headed. Then she dragged in a breath and staggered forward.

"We must get out of here. I heard two officers upstairs, and I just left the emperor, and they will all be coming down here to go over these plans." The words spilled out of her like water from a fountain.

Malcolm nodded calmly and walked around the entire table, lifting the large sheets of stiff paper, taking it all in far better than she could.

"Only twenty-thousand troops to protect Paris," he mused.

"Hurry," she urged. "Are you going to take them, perhaps crumple them and stuff them under your shirt or in your breeches?"

He ignored her, continuing to study map after map, and she realized Malcolm was committing information to memory. Her own mind had already scrambled much of what she'd seen, and she doubted she would have anything useful to tell her grand-père so terrified was she at nearly being caught. She alternately held her breath and expelled it slowly, trying to remain calm and silent.

"I have finished," he said at last. "Let's go."

She turned to the door.

"Not that way," he said before propelling her toward the open panel, covered with wallpaper and affixed with its own small piece of chair rail. When closed, she hadn't noticed it at all, and it appeared to be part of the wall.

Without hesitation, desperate only to be hidden, she headed into the dark passage, barely as wide as a man's shoulders, only to nearly trip over his empty basket. She stepped into it and out of it the other side. Then she turned.

"Hurry," she urged, wanting him to close the panel and secure them inside.

Stooping, she lifted the thick woven straw, hoping to get it out of the way, but its size wedged it between the narrowly spaced walls. She wasn't thinking straight. She should have turned it sideways. Now, it blocked the entrance with Malcolm on the other side.

Exclaiming in frustration, she tugged while he pushed until at last, it gave way, popping past the narrowest part of the opening, and knocking her backward. He followed it. Quickly, he swung the door closed by pulling on a small rope attached to the inside until it clicked. They were plunged into darkness.

"You should have left it," she began, but he put a hand over her mouth, finding her by the sound of her voice.

To her horror, she heard men entering the room they had been standing in mere moments earlier. She shook her head to dislodge his hand, but then she went completely still.

In silence, they waited until the sound of chairs being drawn out provided a little cover, and as softly as possible, they crept down the small dark, servants' passage.

Without room for Malcolm to pass her and lead the way, Serena remained in front, trailing her gloved hand along the wall to guide her. She could see nothing at first, yet she thought it was lighter up ahead so she kept walking slowly. However, the edge of his infernal basket which he now carried continually bumped her in the back, making her startle each time.

When they had gone for many feet, she was beginning to think there was less air and she could barely breathe. It was almost worse than the catacombs. *What if a spider web touched her face?*

Stopping abruptly, she braced herself as he bumped into her again.

"This is intolerable," she said.

"There are openings ahead, signified by ropes hanging off the door panels. Let's switch places," he offered, and she heard a thump at their feet. "I'm stepping into the basket. She felt his hands grasp hold of her arms and draw her towards him. "Step in, too. Don't worry if you land on my feet."

She let him draw her in, and sure enough, she was perched on top of his boots, facing him.

"You understand," Malcolm began, "I couldn't leave the basket behind. It would have declared my having been in the room as surely as if I'd left a message scrawled across one of the maps."

She did understand, but her awareness of his touch, heightened by the darkness, was distracting. Their bodies were pressed against each other, and yet she could only feel one heartbeat. Hers or his, she couldn't tell.

His familiar spicey scent of carnation and bergamot, so English, so utterly Malcolm, elicited a reaction deep inside her. Vividly, she recalled what this man could do with his lips and his fingers. She swallowed.

"Of course," she agreed, trying to focus on the important matter at hand, escaping the palace. "And you can't leave it anywhere in this passageway for the same reason."

"Exactly," he agreed, his tone softer, a little husky. His mouth was closer, as if he were bending toward her.

Her skin was tingling under the grip he still had upon her, and low between her hips was already tingling as well. In fact, she had an absurd notion of how delightful it would be if he were to press her back against the passageway wall, as long as there were no spiders. She wanted to feel the length of his firm body.

This was a terrible time to be aroused, with the risk of detection looming. But they were in such close quarters, Serena couldn't deny the spark of attraction had become a roaring fire.

As if he knew everything she was feeling, his mouth descended upon hers, landing half on her cheek at first until he corrected its course, then firmly taking her lips. She slipped her hands behind his neck and held him tightly as the kiss deepened. Amazingly, he did what she'd hoped, pressing her against the wall behind her, grinding his hips precisely where she was most sensitive. At the same time, her breasts were crushed against his chest.

A kiss more intense and satisfying, she could not imagine. At the same time, it made her yearn for more. Ever since their encounter in his garret, in the recesses of her mind, she'd wanted to see him naked and to let him satisfy her with all the skill he had. Perhaps they could do something right there, standing up.

Someone whistled loudly on the other side of the wall panel behind her, cooling her ardor instantly. People, some of them dangerous, were mere feet away.

Breaking off the kiss, Malcolm leaned his forehead against hers as they listened to the booted feet of soldiers, perhaps searching for them.

When it grew silent again, he whispered against her ear, "Step out of the basket in the direction I was."

He held her hand as she stepped back, and then he joined her, picking up the basket that was now in front of him before starting onward.

The passage grew brighter, and when it turned at the building's corner, suddenly there was light ahead. A small window was cut in the wall to her right, and light came in from the interior courtyard. At the same time, she realized there was a rope hanging to her left to indicate one of the secret door panels.

"We can go through here," he said, "but it would be safer if we continue to the servants' stairs and go down to the next level where I started."

Although she desperately wanted to get out of the tight space, she knew it would be safer to go downstairs.

"Let's continue," she said.

"We may run into a servant coming in our direction," he reminded her. "You should do the talking. Tell them we were seeing the sights, admiring the palace after making our deliveries, even though we knew it was wrong. And if it's a man, batt your gorgeous green eyes at him."

"And if it's a female, you should do the same," she said.

He chuckled. "Batt my eyes?"

"They are a lovely warm brown," she told him. Although she couldn't see his face, she knew he was grinning.

Up ahead, after passing two more ropes, suddenly, the floor dropped away to a dark, narrow staircase winding down without even a railing. Luckily, with the diffused light behind them, they were prepared. If it had been nighttime, Serena believed they would have tumbled head over heels.

To their left was another rope indicating a door.

"Through the palace or down the stairs?" she asked, already knowing the answer.

He looked into the pitch black of the servants' stairs, and she peered past him, doing the same.

"We'll take our chances with the darkness," he said. "Keep a hand on each side to guide you. I'll go first. If you fall, you can crash into me. I won't let you tumble down the stairs."

"And if you fall?" she asked, as they started to descend.

"Then I'll probably break my sorry neck," he quipped.

Travelling the path that all-but invisible servants had used for centuries, they ended up at a dead end, probably having missed half a dozen doors that the true palace staff knew by heart to get them into each room.

When they could go no farther and a solid wall was in front of them, Malcolm pushed to the left and a door opened, letting in the dim light of the cellar. It seemed as bright as the noonday sun.

Blinking, they crept out. Cavernous areas under stone arches housed rounds of cheese, bottles of wine, and root vegetables. Naturally, servants crisscrossed their path, carrying baskets of this and trays of that, but with Malcolm dressed as a baker and Serena in her plain daytime dress and a cotton bonnet on her head, no one gave them a second glance.

They still had to escape the palace and the grounds, but they had gone down one level too far.

"Sorry," Malcolm said. "I believe I overshot the mark, as they say."

"I don't relish going back in there," Serena confessed, nodding at the passageway door.

"Let's take the regular stairs to the kitchen," he suggested. Ascending the crude wooden staircase, they came up beside the main kitchen area, next to a storage room filled with sacks and crates.

"A little better," Malcolm quipped since they could see an exit beckoning them outdoors. Together, they moved swiftly toward it.

"Mademoiselle Renault," she heard behind her just when she thought they would escape undetected.

And this time, Serena recognized the voice most certainly belonged to the emperor. Turning slowly, she noticed he had a madeleine in each hand and a questioning expression upon his face.

"We've been looking for you," he said. *"La Rousse."*

"I . . . that is . . . I," she stuttered as terror threaded her veins, stitching her feet to the floor.

"Hurry," Malcolm implored her as he took a few steps toward the door and freedom.

Napoleon's eyes narrowed. "Well, baker, you are not mute today, I hear."

Serena gasped, realizing Malcolm had destroyed his disguise for her sake. She gasped again as two Imperial Guards rushed down the main stairs.

Napoleon's usually pleasant face became an unreadable mask.

"She is there," he said casually, gesturing to her with one cake before biting into the other one. "And take him, too."

"Serena!" Malcolm's voice awakened her from her frozen fright. Grasping her skirts, she raced for the door leading to the courtyard.

Malcolm had pushed the heavy door open before she reached it, so she slipped easily through. Outside, they climbed a short flight of stone steps from the servants' level and found themselves in the courtyard at the back of the palace.

With armed guards behind them, they didn't slow down.

"Keep running," Malcolm urged, grasping her hand and directing her as he had when they'd waltzed.

"That was easier than I'd thought it would be," she said in jest to chase away the fear.

He squeezed her hand. "Easy as falling off a horse," he agreed. "Except for the guards chasing us and the others marching about the yard, and the gates on three sides. The sooner we—"

A shout followed by another came from the other side of the enclosed courtyard, and more guards swiveled in their direction.

"It's me they're after," she said. "I was seen listening outside a room in which officers were talking."

"This way!" Malcolm took a sharp right toward the gate, but then suddenly, he changed course, slipping down the narrow way between the building and the wrought iron fence on the river's side of the palace. There were steps down to the quay, if they could just reach the other side of the enclosure.

"We're trapped," she said, feeling her heart hammering.

Without hesitating, Malcolm pulled her forward. "There is a way over the fence. I have a friend who has made sure of it."

Ignoring the yelling behind them, they used a perfectly placed crate as a stool to clamber over the iron fence, the only casualty being the hem of Serena's dress, which got caught upon one of the spikes, tearing as she jumped down the other side.

Crossing the Quai du Louvre, they ran toward the Pont Royal to cross the Seine, where they could disappear into the streets of the Left Bank.

"There are guards ahead," Malcolm said, grabbing her hand. Instead of venturing onto the bridge, he dragged her down the steps beside the quay to the Port Saint Nicholas and directly into the path of three men.

CHAPTER EIGHTEEN

After a moment of abject terror, Serena breathed a sigh of relief when she recognized two of those who now stood before her.

"Excuse us, *mes amis*," she said to Guillaume and Jean-Paul. "We are in a hurry." Behind her, she could hear shrill whistling and the calls to apprehend *"les espions!"*

Malcolm started to push past the men, but they barred his path.

"Are you *with* this man?" Guillaume demanded.

"With him?" she asked. "What do you mean?"

"He is English!" he spat out. "Felicity told me. He is the tall man from Café des Aveugles. Clearly, he seeks to overthrow our emperor. So I ask again, are you with him, this *baker*?" Guillaume said the word with scorn, knowing Malcolm was in disguise. "Serena, do you side with the Seventh Coalition?"

She hesitated. However, her loyalties were not torn. She stood with her family always. And her grandparents stood for peace over any temporary ruler. They'd always worked to maintain or restore peace in any way they could, no matter the regime, republic, empire, or kingdom.

"*Je suis pour la France!*" Serena told him firmly and tried to push past.

Guillaume's hands were suddenly restraining her, holding her by the shoulders.

"Then why are you helping him?" he gestured his head toward Malcolm, who quick as a whip, knocked Guillaume backward with a shove to his shoulder, effectively freeing her.

Guillaume bristled, raising his large, fisted hands in front of him. "If you are by his side, helping him to escape, then you are not for France!"

She knew with every second the guards were getting closer. This wasn't the time for discussion, neither patriotic nor philosophic. It was a time to take up arms.

"*He* must be handed over to the emperor's guards," Guillaume concluded.

She didn't bother to tell him it was she they were after. As Jean-Paul and the stranger stepped forward, clearly intent on restraining them, she bent down and slid her pistol from its holster. Smoothly, she stood, leveling her gun at her former friends, only to realize Malcolm was doing the same. She hadn't even seen him draw out his gun.

They glanced at one another, and he frowned.

"Don't you think I can protect us?"

"I am not a useless female," she said.

"I never said you were. But I'm the one who is on a mission."

"I already told you I would help," she reminded him, and then she waved her small pistol around, "so I am helping."

Guillaume's head, and those of the other men, were swiveling back and forth as she and Malcolm bickered.

"We have to go immediately," he reminded her. "They're after both of us now."

She nodded. Keeping their guns trained on the three men, she and Malcolm circled them. As soon as they had skirted Guillaume's blockade, they ran along the Port Saint

Nicholas dock and up the short flight of steps at the other end.

"I'm impressed," Malcolm called to her as they left the quay and ran across the Pont des Arts to get to the other bank.

"As am I," she said. "I thought the Imperial Guards would have captured you by now."

"I think I've just been insulted," he intoned.

From the Quai Malaquais, Serena could still see her friends on the other side of the Seine, speaking with the guards.

"Let's get away from the river," Malcolm suggested.

"Where?" she asked.

"Not too far. I know a safe place. An associate lives nearby."

"A friend?" she asked, hurrying to keep up.

"An associate," he repeated.

"Another spy," she confirmed. "English or French?"

He shrugged, saying nothing more. When they were a few blocks down from the river, Malcolm turned right onto the Rue des Marais, a quick left, right, left, and they finally turned right onto the Rue du Dragon.

"Here," he said, grabbing her by the arm and swinging her into a doorway under the eaves. After rapping three times, he waited, and knocked thrice more before pushing the door open.

Malcolm drew her into a dim sitting room.

At first, Serena didn't realize it was occupied. Then a heavy-set man, with his own weapon drawn rose from a chair in the dark corner.

"This is my associate," Malcolm said. "And if you don't knock properly at his door, he will blow a hole through you."

The stranger gave a grimace, which Serena realized was a smile. "I might do so in any case," he said. "To you, *Anglais,* but not to her."

She realized he was the man from the catacombs, the one they'd rescued first.

"May I introduce Mademoiselle Renault," Malcolm said, as if they were at a dinner party instead of fleeing for their lives.

"The vintner's granddaughter," Monsieur Versanne said. Then a moment later, "Where is your mother?"

Serena took a step back. *What did this burly man know about her family?* She looked from him to Malcolm, who nodded.

"Ma mère n'est pas à Paris." That her mother wasn't in Paris was all she would tell him. If this stranger already knew Hélène Renault had married an Englishman, then he would probably disclose it, and Serena's secret would be known. She held her breath.

"I haven't seen her in years," Monsieur Versanne said, "but I remember her working in the old Halle aux Vins, and your grandparents, too." He squinted at her. "You are the picture of your mother, except for your hair. That color comes from Madame Renault."

Malcolm looked at her curiously. After all, she hadn't told him anything about her parents, and he probably assumed, as her Parisian friends did, that they were dead. It was easier to let everyone believe such a thing rather than explain how she'd been exiled for her own foolish misbehavior.

"You are looking better, monsieur," she added, hoping to win over the gruff Monsieur Versanne.

He simply scowled and switched his attention to Malcolm.

"What trouble have you brought, *Anglais?*"

"The Tuileries' guards have taken a dislike to me," Malcolm quipped. "I'm not Gallic enough for them."

"For me, either, but you're fortunate I'm not trying to capture and torture you for information."

"Actually, Bonaparte recently learned I'm not a mute baker, so I will have to make myself scarce. But first I need to get Mademoiselle Renault safely back to her grandparents' home on the Rue Coquillière. Obviously, she can no longer be seen with me."

She didn't like how he disclosed the address so easily, but assumed he trusted this man entirely. Even more distressing was how it seemed he was washing his hands of her.

"You know I cannot stroll along the Champs-Élysées either," Monsieur Versanne said. "Especially not with your fiery-haired lady friend. She is like a beacon."

Serena's stomach cramped with worry, and she tugged her bonnet over her hair more tightly. It did little good. With all the running she'd done, most of her hair was hanging down around her shoulders.

"With her unusual hair," Monsieur Versanne said, "she may not be safe in Paris if Imperial Guards saw her helping you leave the palace."

"I believe *I* was helping *her*," Malcolm pointed out.

"Pride!" Monsieur Versanne scoffed. "Were you both seen or not?"

"Yes," she admitted, "not only by the guards but by my friends."

"Who are not your friends any longer," Malcolm pointed out.

She stared at him. In one short afternoon, everything was ruined. She'd lost her important connection with the emperor and would no longer be useful to her grandparents. Her friends now considered her their enemy. And most importantly to her, she was going to be forced to stop all contact with Malcolm.

It was unbearable. Somehow, he'd become keenly important to her happiness.

"Mademoiselle, take that ugly hat by the door," Monsieur Versanne instructed. "You can tuck all your pretty locks up inside of it."

Serena looked at the shapeless black cotton, feeling a twinge of disgust at seeing its stained brim, but she took it down from the hook.

"When you are out of your apron and cap, *Anglais*," Monsieur Versanne said to Malcolm, "maybe if you grow a mustache, it will help." Then he cocked his head. "But you're a whey-faced son of a Brit. Can you grow a mustache or a beard for that matter?"

"Your humor is unwelcome," Malcolm said, his tone serious. "Her safety is all that matters. My height is a problem. Your figure and face are less well-known than mine. Put on a hat, stick a pipe in your mouth to cover your ugly visage, and I trust you will escort Mademoiselle Renault safely home."

"I will," the burly man said, glancing at her again. "Even if I am caught only to be hanged, drawn, and quartered."

Malcolm rolled his eyes, but Serena didn't want either man to get into further danger because of her.

Quickly, while they talked, she set the hat down and plaited her hair before tucking the braid under the collar of her spencer. Hardly any of the red showed, and she decided there was no need for the Frenchman's greasy hat.

"If they really think her a threat," Monsieur Versanne said, "they will discover her residence soon enough or wait for her at the Halle aux Vins."

Serena sucked in an unsteady breath. She hadn't considered the ramifications, but it was obvious, she would have to go into hiding immediately. At that moment, however, she desperately wanted to go home and tell her grandparents everything that had transpired.

"I don't need an escort," she declared, causing both men to look at her. "In fact, I'll look less conspicuous traveling alone than with Monsieur Versanne since I was last seen in the company of a man."

The stranger just stared at her, but Malcolm started to shake his head.

Serena decided it was time to reclaim her independence.

"Good day, messieurs." With that little warning, she spun about, yanked open the door, and stepped outside.

Hearing Malcolm call out behind her, she slammed it shut and went running up the street.

AS SHE'D FEARED, HER grandparents prepared her for a quick departure to their vineyard and winery in the Loire Valley. There, she would wait until they'd arranged safe passage across the Channel to England.

"You will have to leave earlier than planned," her grand-père said. "A pity. You were situated so well at the palace with Bonaparte none the wiser."

Serena couldn't blame Malcolm. She'd caused this calamity herself.

"Don't look so sad," her grand-mère said. "You gave helpful information regarding both the maps and the numbers of troops the emperor's officers discussed feeding. And you were leaving soon anyway. We must put your safety above all else," Adèle added, echoing what Malcolm had said. "It's time for you to go home."

Home. Returning to England at last was supposed to be a joyous occasion, but it felt bittersweet. Naturally, she wanted to see her parents and her brothers again, but her grandparents had been wonderful to her. And then there was Malcolm. They'd been growing toward something special until . . .

She stopped herself. That was all in her head. He'd said he wasn't going to pledge his troth, and she wasn't going to become someone's mistress, or worse. She wasn't sure what was worse, but there was probably something. Moreover, now he couldn't see her, neither in his regular garb nor in his disguise as a baker.

"When am I leaving?" she asked.

"Before dawn," her grand-père said.

"Are you coming with me? It might not be safe for you here anymore." Serena's greatest fear was that she'd endangered her grandparents with her carelessness.

Henri sent his wife a sharp look, but it was Adèle who answered. "We must stay here, dear one. We are in the middle of things."

"I know you are," Serena said, "but if the soldiers come for you—"

"They won't," Pépère said. "Even if they do, we are not their enemy. We'll be fine."

How could he be so sure? Even a fox was sometimes captured and killed during a hunt.

"Michel will go with you," Mémère added.

"What about the emperor's fondness for our wine?" Serena slapped her fist into her palm with frustration. Everything was changing so fast. "Napoleon will be suspicious. He may send Imperial Guards to the Halle aux Vins."

"If a request comes from the palace for our wine, Jacques will deliver it," her grand-père said. "If guards come to the market place, they will find themselves unwelcome."

"Even if Jacques goes to the palace, he cannot get close enough to the emperor to learn anything," Serena fumed.

"We will manage," her grand-père insisted. "The Seventh Coalition will manage, too, even without our help."

It was the first time Henri Renault had mentioned forces larger than solely the French people themselves deciding their fate.

Serena sighed. It was out of her hands. Maybe for the best. Perhaps it was her place simply to watch the events unfold and not to have a hand in shaping them. She couldn't even say goodbye to Suzanne and Felicity. She would never see them again.

〜

IT WAS JUST AFTER noon, and Serena was in one of her favorite places, the Renault Vineyard. The same sunlight that ripened the grapes throughout the Loire Valley came streaming in the front windows of the small white-stone manor. With no formal entrance hall, instead, the solid oak front door opened directly onto the sitting room. Watching the play of light across the cheerful buttery-yellow floor tiles, she felt anything but cheery.

Michel had gone outside to see why the horses were fussing. The housekeeper, Madame Lucie, was nearby hanging laundry, and Serena had to sit on her hands to keep from pacing. Unable to settle down during the past few days of her latest banishment, she could neither read nor knit, and she'd spoiled a batch of jam and burnt madame's cakes while trying to help in the kitchen. She had no patience or concentration lately, only a disturbing sense of despair at leaving . . . Malcolm.

The thought of never seeing her Englishman again weighed heavily upon her, squeezing her heart painfully when she let her mind ponder her fate. This was what her mother would have felt had Serena's father not offered for Hélène after compromising her, the pain of unrequited love.

Luckily, her father had been equally smitten.

And Serena knew what she felt was true love. *Why else would she have saved Malcolm more than once and taken his side over that of her friends?* And then there was her behavior in his garret, allowing him to take outrageous liberties. All because she was falling for him and hoping he would feel the same.

Ridiculous as it was, she had wanted him to fall in love with Serena Renault, the Parisian girl, not with Miss Elmstead, a baron's daughter. Finding out she was not so far beneath him socially, he might suddenly have decided she would be a suitable future viscountess, after all. It would have been far too convenient for him, and a matter of head over heart.

Slumped in a chair, she contemplated each of the times she'd encountered Malcolm over the past weeks. Maybe if she'd figured out a way to say goodbye in person, had her grandparents had allowed her, then he would have—

The door flew open and a figure, backlit by the strong sun, filled the opening. For a second, she believed it was Malcolm, conjured from her thoughts. Obviously, it must be Michel. And yet, she knew by the shape, it was not.

Rising slowly to her feet, she felt the first tendrils of fear tickle her. Then she realized who it was.

CHAPTER NINETEEN

"Guillaume? What are you doing here?"

He was brandishing a pistol and breathing hard. Closing the door behind him, he moved closer.

"I had to see for my own eyes you had truly fled Paris like the other royalists. Because you fear our emperor."

"I am *not* a royalist," she said truthfully. As for fearing Bonaparte, she was far more afraid of her former friend who had the fervent look of fanaticism blazing in his eyes. Her grandparents had lived through the terror of the Revolution. They'd told her stories of those who turned against not only the crowned heads but anyone around them whom they suspected of being a royalist. Inflamed by the fire of revolution, people had become zealots, overturning previous civility and friendship.

Looking around, he set his gun upon the oak card table. "You are safely tucked away in your family's vineyard and yet your trunks are packed. Why?"

She glanced behind her where her two trunks were stacked by the archway to the staircase leading to the bedrooms. She and Michel awaited word to head to the coast, a message which they expected hourly.

When she said nothing, he took a step closer. "I had hoped you and I could be together."

"I will return to Paris soon," she said. "That's why my trunks are packed."

"Liar!" he spat out. "I sent Felicity to speak with your grand-mère, and she said you would write to her. It did not sound as though you were returning to the city. And yet, plainly, you are going somewhere with that man who works with you at the Halle aux Vins."

She gasped. "Where is Michel?"

"Is he your lover?" Guillaume crossed his arms.

"No! He is a family friend, not that it is your business. Where is he?" She repeated, starting forward, frightened now that her family's loyal employee had been harmed on her account. He had a loving wife and two young sons who needed him.

Guillaume's arm shot out and restrained her. "He is merely having a little rest."

Her blood ran cold. "Did you harm him?"

Guillaume stared down at her. "You are the only woman I want. I have shared my thoughts with you and my hopes for the future on many an evening in the café. A future I thought would be ours."

"That's not possible," she said gently. "I don't think of you in that manner."

"You led me to believe otherwise," he insisted, stroking a large hand down her arm.

"I didn't. I swear. At least, not intentionally." With each word she spoke, he appeared more annoyed. "Guillaume, I thought we were all friends. You and Felicity, Suzanne, and Jean-Paul. But nothing more. You shouldn't have come all this way for nothing."

He didn't respond. Instead, grabbing her by the shoulders, he held her in place.

"Maybe when we kiss, you will feel the passion I feel."

He swooped down, trying to land his mouth upon hers. Twisting her head to avoid his kiss, not expecting any help, she screamed from sheer outrage and a healthy dose of fear.

The door behind him burst open. Malcolm appeared, and Serena's mouth dropped open. He was like one of the famed mesmerizers at Covent Garden whom she'd seen perform conjuring tricks when she was a girl. Suddenly—impossibly—he was in the sitting room of the Renault vineyard house when she'd imagined him many miles away in Paris.

And he had a two-barreled pistol trained on Guillaume.

"I hope you are unharmed, Mademoiselle Renault?" were his first words.

Still gaping like a fish, so stunned was she, all she could do was nod, although if they were alone, she would have run into his arms already. It seemed everyone she knew from the city was showing up. She half expected Bonaparte himself to stride in.

A moment later, she wished it *was* the emperor arriving with his distinct air of civility. Instead, Jean-Paul strode in, holding a Charleville musket, old but effective.

"I heard Serena scream," he said, but his gaze, one of confusion, was trained on Malcolm. "I never even saw him slip by," he mused.

"Because you are an idiot," Guillaume berated him. "And what of her other protector?"

"Tied up behind the shed."

Serena closed her eyes with relief. That sounded promising. If Michel was tied up, he was alive. But what a ridiculous farce this was! Guillaume wanted her. She had no interest in him. She wanted Malcolm who didn't reciprocate her affection, at least not to the point of marriage. And Jean-Paul was just in the way.

At that instant, she wished all these manly men with their hostile posturing and their guns would disappear so she could determine Michel's condition and get on with her escape to England.

"We are at a stand-off," Malcolm said.

"Hardly a stand-off," Guillaume said. "Drop your weapon, or Jean-Paul will have to use his."

Serena stared at Guillaume, hardly daring to look at Malcolm because his being in danger made her heart beat faster and caused her to feel even more vulnerable.

"Please, Guillaume," she implored, "go home."

"I will," he said, "but I'm taking this British spy with me."

Fear choked her throat.

"Even if your friend shoots me," Malcolm said, his eyes never wavering from Guillaume's face, just as the aim of his pistol never left her former friend's barrel chest, "I will manage to shoot you, too."

Guillaume shrugged. "Jean-Paul won't shoot you," he said calmly. "He'll shoot her."

"What?" Jean-Paul exclaimed, and Serena knew her cheeks had paled from the blood leaving her head.

"Put your gun down," Guillaume ordered Malcolm, "or he *will* shoot her."

But Malcolm shook his head. "He won't shoot her, but I will gladly shoot either one of you through the heart."

As if knowing it for the truth, Jean-Paul rightfully blanched at the threat.

Slowly, reaching behind him, Guillaume picked his weapon off the table and raised it to Serena's chest.

"Gui!" Jean-Paul exclaimed.

Serena didn't believe Guillaume would hurt her. After all, he'd been sorry when Monsieur Christoff had tried to steal a simple kiss. Yet now, all three men had their weapons raised. It was only getting worse.

"I am not such a besotted fool as you think," Guillaume said. "She's shown her loyalties don't lie with the emperor. I couldn't possibly take her for my own."

Good! Serena didn't want him to take her at all. Yet she also didn't want to be shot. Glancing at Malcolm, she tried to quell her rising fear at a situation which was quickly spiraling out of control.

"We haven't killed the other man," Jean-Paul said, his perseverance clearly wavering. "We aren't here to commit violence."

"My friend is right," Guillaume said. "We are not here to murder anyone. We should all put our guns down, starting with you." He looked at Malcolm. "We will leave her in peace with no more violence if you will come with us."

Malcolm hesitated, and Serena shook her head. He couldn't go with them. In Paris, he would be executed.

Yet Malcolm came to a decision and lowered his weapon, sliding it back into his pocket. As soon as he did, Guillaume swiveled his pistol toward him.

"Grab his hands behind his back," he instructed Jean-Paul, who had already laid down his own weapon.

"Are we taking him back?" he asked.

"If he survives," Guillaume said.

"Guillaume, please," she said again. "What are you doing?"

Following orders, Jean-Paul tried to take hold of Malcolm's arms, but it was clear the Englishman was better trained in fighting and kept slipping from his grasp.

Guillaume yelled, "Stop, or I will shoot you as a spy *and her* for a traitor."

For a tense moment, Serena thought Guillaume might be so stupid and brutal as to do what he threatened. However, as soon as Malcolm allowed Jean-Paul to draw his arms behind his back, Guillaume pocketed his pistol.

Just as she sighed with relief, he delivered a solid blow to Malcolm's stomach, making him double over.

"No!" she screamed, rushing forward and grabbing Guillaume's arm.

He laughed. "You don't think this British *lopette* deserves a sound beating for meddling in the affairs of France."

"No, I think you need to leave my family's vineyard at once. You have no business here."

Guillaume paid her no mind and punched Malcolm again.

"Oof," Malcolm expelled a breath, struggling to free himself from Jean-Paul. "I should have shot you," he added, although Serena didn't know which man he was speaking to. *Probably both!*

Guillaume hit him again, making Malcolm double over so only Jean's grip was holding him up.

"I won't let you hurt him any further," she announced to Guillaume's back.

He stiffened and turned on her.

"Oh, yes, I'd forgotten. You have your own little pistol, don't you?"

Merde, Serena swore silently in French, thinking it less damning to her soul. She should have kept quiet.

"Of course not," she lied. "Not in my own sitting room. That's only for the streets of Paris."

"Prove it," Guillaume ordered. "Lift your skirts."

She rolled her eyes, hoping she looked entirely truthful and nonchalant, instead of increasingly terrified.

"Fine." Sending Guillaume a look of pure annoyance, she turned and grabbed the straight-back chair at the table where she and Michel played chess and cards in the evenings. Twirling it around so the seat faced her, she set her right booted foot upon it.

The room fell utterly silent. Keeping her gaze trained on Guillaume, she slowly raised her skirts to show her unadorned ankle with no holster.

"Satisfied?" she asked, starting to lower her skirt.

After a pause during which Guillaume did nothing but stare at her leg, and then at her face, he said, "Not yet. You and I will go to the bedroom, *ma cherie,* and I'll give you another chance to understand what we can have together. Or at the very least, you'll discover what you'll be missing by betraying me."

"Gui," Jean-Paul warned. "What are you doing? We were only going to bring her back to Paris."

"I've changed my mind," Guillaume growled. "Keep this one—"

Before he could finish, Malcolm broke free. "You bastard!" He lunged at Guillaume. "Serena, run."

But she stayed frozen in place. Guillaume had raised his pistol once again, and this time, it was pointed at Malcolm's forehead.

"*Serena*, do you say?" Guillaume looked between her and Malcolm. "I think you have been too familiar with our French women. In fact, I think you deserve to die for your crimes against the empire. Why should I waste my time taking you back to Paris?"

"Guillaume, no," she said, inching her left hand down her leg.

"No?" he asked. "You care for him?" His voice grew louder. "Do you play the filthy *pétasse* for this *Anglais*?"

"Gui," Jean-Paul warned again. Yet when Guillaume cocked the hammer of his flintlock, Jean-Paul stepped back, clearly fearing being shot by mistake.

Seeing no other choice, Serena swiftly drew her pistol from the holder strapped to her left ankle, wondering that her friend had never noticed she was left-handed.

Fearing she would be too late, she fired, hearing Guillaume do the same.

However, Malcolm stayed standing, and it was Guillaume who fell to the ground, his pistol having discharged wildly to the side when she shot him. Jean-Paul took a long look at the blood seeping from the wound in his friend's side and ran out the door.

MALCOLM COULDN'T BELIEVE HOW quickly things had gone from bad to worse, nor how lucky he was the

Frenchman's hand had wavered when he'd been shot. And Serena had enjoyed the advantage of being so close to the man she couldn't have missed.

Bending down, he turned the one she called Guillaume over. The bullet had entered from low in the small of his back and remained inside him, clearly having done mortal damage. Malcolm had seen wounds on the battlefield, and it would certainly have been better if the bullet had come cleanly out.

Instead, blood was trickling out of the side of Guillaume's mouth as well as from the wound. Straightening, Malcolm looked at the woman who had saved his life. She was deathly pale and her gorgeous green eyes were wide.

In his heart, he already knew she was destined for him. Indeed, he'd chased southwest across the countryside to catch her and tell her so. And he didn't give a tinker's damn she was French and a mere vintner's granddaughter. He didn't even care if she was experienced in the ways of the flesh. He would make her his wife and then his viscountess and let the *ton* go to hell.

He took a step toward her and she stumbled against him. Wrapping her tightly in his arms, he rested his chin atop her head and simply held her. In a flash, he imagined telling their children how brave their mother was, how she'd walked beside an emperor and defended a kingdom. Maybe he would leave out the part about how handy she was with a pistol, at least until they were older.

Regardless, he loved her and would happily abandon his immature, rakish ways and be honored if she would marry him.

She already had his heart, and he owed her his life. *Again!*

But she was staring at the dying man, and it was not the time to ask for her hand, which was even then trembling where it touched him, as her whole body began to shake. Malcolm could do nothing for Guillaume, but he could make it easier on Serena.

"Sit," he ordered. When she didn't move away from him, he pushed her gently down onto the chair she'd used to show her ankle. Knowing Serena had drawn her little Queen Anne pistol with her left hand outside the Tuileries Palace, he'd felt a surge of relief when she'd exposed her right leg. His only worry had been how quickly she could draw her weapon, which had been very fast as it turned out.

"Serena," he said her name, but she continued to stare at her former friend.

Concerned by the glazed look in her eyes and how she quaked under his touch, Malcolm quickly took off his coat and draped it around her slender shoulders. She was suffering from the shock of the situation.

"Just stay right here," he said and brushed his lips across her forehead.

She'd barely blinked and didn't respond. Quickly as he could, he grabbed the dying man by his boots, not sure if Guillaume had breathed his last yet, and dragged him out of the manor's front door, leaving a trail of blood on the cool, square tiles.

As Malcolm made his way with his burden across the gravel drive, a woman in an apron appeared around the corner of the house, gasping at the sight and dropping the basket she carried. A small dog that had been trailing behind her stepped in front, alternately baring its teeth and yapping like a banshee while performing a little dance of darting forward and retreating.

"Do you work here?" Malcolm asked.

She nodded, obviously frightened.

"I mean you no harm. Mademoiselle Renault is inside," he said. "She needs tending. Some tea or maybe brandy if you have it."

Without a word, the woman hurried past him, calling her dog to follow, before disappearing inside the manor and closing the door. He dragged Guillaume farther away from the house, onto a grassy patch beside a paddock fence.

Next, Malcolm searched for the other man who'd been mentioned, the Renault employee he'd been expecting to find, not two dangerously unpredictable Bonapartists with no plan and even less brains.

In a few minutes, he found him tied up behind a shed with signs he'd been ambushed and overpowered.

"Is she unharmed?" the man asked as soon as the gag was out of his mouth.

Malcolm explained what had happened while he untied him. After being helped to his feet, the man staggered.

"You're injured," Malcolm said. "Were you shot?"

"No, monsieur. But my head feels heavy as lead." Reaching behind and touching the back of his skull, he brought his hand forward, and Malcolm saw it was smeared with blood.

"Let me look," Malcolm said, examining the man's head. "It's not bleeding anymore, and you're lucky it's not cracked open. But you have an egg."

"An egg?" the man repeated, looking mystified.

Malcolm wasn't sure what euphemism the French used for a bash to the head, so he gave up. It wasn't important.

"Do you know your name?"

"Of course. I am Michel Anselme."

That was a good sign. The Renault employee hadn't been knocked senseless. Draping Michel's arm around his shoulder, Malcolm started back toward the manor house, but after a few steps, the man doubled over and vomited onto the dirt between his feet.

Malcolm handed him a handkerchief as he would to a crying or sneezing female at a ball. Gratefully, Michel rubbed his face with it.

"That hurt like hell," he remarked. "I think I've got a broken rib. Maybe two."

Malcolm could well understand why. Guillaume had packed quite a punch, and his own mid-section felt decidedly tender.

"I hoped you could help me with a burial, but you're in no condition. I'll get you inside and see if there is someone else who can assist me."

"There are workers in the field, tending the vines." Michel pointed to the hills beyond the paddock. "Ask for Pierre. Tell him what happened. I can get indoors by myself."

Malcolm watched him go, moving slowly, stopping to wretch again. Then he set about finding help and burying the body. He supposed the other man, Jean-Paul, would be hell-bent for Paris by now. He had a feeling that one hadn't wanted to be there. He certainly hadn't wanted to play a part in Guillaume's violence. Nevertheless, if Jean-Paul spoke into certain ears, it could bring more trouble in the form of Imperial Guards, racing from the city to find Serena before she escaped their reach forever.

Malcolm was determined to make sure they were too late.

CHAPTER TWENTY

Serena watched Madame Lucie clean the blood from the tiles with vinegar, just as if they were common red wine stains. The housekeeper's little dog, Mignon, lay nearby watching everything.

Shuddering again, unable to stop doing so, she took another sip of the brandy madame had given her and tried to make sense of the past half hour.

How could her small part in all this have turned deadly? She never would have guessed she could pull the trigger. When she'd drawn her gun at the Tuileries, it had been only to frighten off Guillaume and Jean-Paul. Everything had still seemed like an exciting adventure, especially when she and Malcolm had escaped the guards together.

Yet Felicity's brother had dropped to the floor, his eyes fluttering closed as he'd died. But she couldn't let Guillaume murder Malcolm. The Englishman had her heart firmly in his grasp, and thus hers would have stopped beating along with his. Surely, she would be forgiven for saving his life.

When the door opened again, Michel entered, looking gray in the face and barely able to make it to the divan, where he collapsed and closed his eyes.

"I just need to sleep," he muttered to her, his hand clasping his stomach.

She and Madame Lucie exchanged worried glances. He didn't stir when they examined him for wounds, but she discovered his hair was matted with dried blood. Hopefully, when he awakened, he would feel better. She doubted they could move him upstairs, even with Malcolm's help, so she covered him with a quilt and let him be.

How much time had passed, she didn't know, but it seemed to be hours. Madame Lucie had started dinner in the warm and welcoming kitchen in the back of the manor, overlooking the vineyard. Gently rolling hills surrounded them, and she'd always thought it as lovely as any piece of English countryside. Wisteria climbed the sides of the house and lilacs lined the wide dirt and stone drive. Much appreciated apple and pear trees shaded each of the verandas, one at the front and one at the side of the house. And all around them, a sea of grapevines drank in the brilliant sunlight and gave back the very best wine, as it had done for decades.

Wafting through the house was the mouth-watering scent of Madame Lucie's *coq au vin*. As a cook, she rivaled any in Paris. But Serena had no appetite, seated on a soft chair beside the divan, watching Michel, unable to set foot outside for fear of seeing Guillaume's body.

Finally, the door opened, and a sweaty, dirty Malcolm appeared.

Uninjured, healthy, hale, and perfect. Regardless of the consequences, she rose from her chair and launched herself into his arms.

They clamped around her, holding her against him. Close to tears, she bit her lip to stop herself and wrapped her arms around his middle, laying her cheek against his chest. Silently, they remained locked together until finally, she looked up at him.

"How are you?" he asked.

"I am not hurt," she told him.

"I meant how do you feel?"

She didn't want to talk about that. Not yet. She'd killed a man. Turning away, she gestured to Michel, now snoring on the long beige divan.

"I'm concerned for him."

"He probably will have a bad headache and be unsteady on his feet for a few days," Malcolm guessed. "And he might have a broken rib."

All bad news, but not as bad as it could be, she thought. She wanted to ask Malcolm where he'd buried Guillaume, but she couldn't get herself to put it into words. That Felicity's brother was now a body was absurd. That he was under the ground at her grandparents' vineyard seemed impossible.

"Why are you here?" The question had plagued her since he'd burst through the door.

He hesitated. "That should be obvious. I'm not on a tour of France's wineries. I came to find you."

"But why?" she pressed. "Aren't you needed in Paris?"

"I can't go back to the Tuileries as a baker." He gave her a wry smile as they recalled their last time there together. "In fact, my usefulness is in question at the moment. In any case, I had to make sure you were safe."

"Thanks to you, I am." She still had a journey to the coast, but for the time being, Serena felt perfectly secure.

"You've come a long way and then . . . ." She didn't want to mention how he'd spent time digging and burying, so she said nothing more.

"I could use a bath, both to clean up and to cool off," Malcolm agreed. "It's hotter here than in Paris. I feel more like a raisin than a grape."

She could almost smile at his little joke.

"We have a wash room and a large tub. I'll show you. Do you have a change of clothes?"

"I'll get my saddle bag."

It wasn't long before Malcolm was clean and in fresh clothing, seated beside her in a single-breasted green jacket and beige breeches on the back terrace. He ate heartily from a plate of Madame Lucie's dish of tender braised chicken, bacon, mushrooms, and pearl onions in a buttery red wine and garlic sauce.

"*Coq au vin,*" he repeated when she told him what it was. "Absolutely delicious."

Her stomach growled, and she stopped pushing the food around with her fork and took a bite. It was a comforting, satisfying dish, and she would be foolish not to keep up her strength before whatever came next.

Should she write to Felicity? What could she say to her?

"I couldn't let him kill you," Serena blurted, then set her fork down with a clatter, not having meant to say out loud what had been circling in her mind.

Malcolm reached over to cover her hand.

"You *could* have," he said, "and thus, I am eternally grateful you didn't." Squeezing her fingers, he added, "You are not a soldier. It will be easy for you to blame yourself for that man's death, but he chose to come here and to draw his weapon. He brought the fight to your door when he could have easily left you alone. And then he confronted you and threatened me."

Malcolm released her with a shake of his head. "You shall have to let this go, mademoiselle. The blame is not only Guillaume's. It is also mine. I should have shot him myself as soon as I walked in. Instead, because he was your friend, I thought he would be reasonable. If he'd been threatening to shoot you and I'd killed him, would you think any less of me?"

"No," she said.

"Well, then."

He was right, although she wouldn't let herself off so easily. If only Guillaume had stayed in Paris.

The terrace door opened, and they were both on their feet before the man had taken a step. Malcolm raised his pistol, which had rested on the table beside him, but Serena held nothing but her fork. Regardless, she recognized him as an associate of her grand-père.

"There is no concern," she told Malcolm. "I know him. Monsieur Bowes, is it not?"

"*Oui,* mademoiselle. Henri sent me with the message it is time to go." He handed her a leather satchel. "There is a letter from him with instructions, money for passage, and another letter for the captain of a ship in Saint-Malo."

"Saint-Malo?" Malcolm asked. "Not Le Havre?"

Serena introduced the men, and Malcolm laid down his pistol while her grand-père's friend took off his riding coat, draping it over his arm, looking dusty and weary.

"Le Havre is not safe," Monsieur Bowes explained. He cocked his head. "There is a ship in Saint-Malo that no one bothers about when she comes and goes."

Serena understood then that she would depart upon a smuggler's ship. Her grandparents had told her how French wine was still a welcome commodity in Britain, and authorities turned a blind eye to most of the traders in exchange for a fee.

"I saw Michel in the other room," Monsieur Bowes added. "He doesn't look well at all, but your grand-père says you must leave tomorrow. Everything has been arranged."

She looked at Malcolm. "Michel will not be able to travel by morning, will he?"

"I doubt it. But that doesn't matter," Malcolm said, leveling his gaze at her. "I'll take you myself."

Serena blinked to fight back tears, even as her heart sang. *How inappropriate to take pleasure in being forced together at what cost to others, and when the stakes were so high.*

Moreover, she had to be sensible. It was dangerous for Malcolm to be gallivanting around the countryside.

"Perhaps Monsieur Bowes can take me."

The man shook his head. "Alas, I cannot. We expected Michel to be ready. I have to return immediately, and then head to Vienna. My life is all on horseback right now."

"But surely you'll stay the night," she offered.

"I will, at least for most of it." He looked grateful.

"Would you care to join us?" Serena invited him, gesturing toward the table behind her.

Monsieur Bowes glanced from her to Malcolm. "If you don't mind, mademoiselle, I'll go see Madame Lucie and eat with her. My wife is her niece, and I have news to share."

With a nod to each of them, he disappeared into the house's interior. They heard Mignon bark at the intrusion before he quieted.

"You don't wish for me to take you to the coast?" Malcolm asked directly, and she could have sworn he wore a wounded expression. "In fact, as things stand, I can escort you all the way to England."

"It's not that I don't wish it," she said, then added. "In fact, I welcome your company."

"Then it's settled."

MALCOLM FINISHED HIS MEAL with satisfaction. Serena was leaving France, but she was going to England. It was as though fortune were smiling upon him. If she'd been traveling deeper into the Continent, to Russia for instance, the likelihood of convincing her to start a life with him after he finished his service would be far more difficult.

He intended to declare himself and ask for her hand after she got past feeling shaken over killing a man. That might be later that evening or while they were on the road to Saint-Malo or even on the ship. Once he got her safely ensconced in England, and after his return to Paris to help Randall as best he could in a less visible position, then he would pay Prinny a visit and retire for good.

"Your family's wine truly is superior," he said, wishing she wasn't so quiet. At least she'd started eating, but she was not the babbling, lively female she'd once been. He would have to work hard to distract her troubled thoughts.

"We'll leave early. Are you ready?"

She nodded.

"Do you have a wagon, something we can abandon? While I would prefer to travel on horseback to avoid delays on the roads, you would have to leave your trunks behind. I assume you want your trunks."

Again, she nodded, not looking particularly interested.

"We should go to bed early, then."

Her gaze flew to his, and her cheeks uncharacteristically reddened.

Malcolm tried hard not to smile. Perhaps he knew the best way to bring her out of her doldrums and to distract her.

"I'll show you to your room," she said.

They both rose from the table, and for the first time, he went upstairs. The home was not elegant or fastidious. Rather, it was quaintly shabby but with an air of old graciousness, and it was certainly comfortable.

She led him into a modest-sized bedroom and lit the lamps. No chambermaid had been in to light the fire or turn down the linens.

As if reading his thoughts, she said, "You won't need a fire tonight. And there are extra blankets in that trunk." She pointed to the base of the bed. Then while looking as if she had more to say, she scooted toward the open door. *"Bonsoir, monsieur."*

Should he let her go? She was still jittery, on edge, and moody. Recalling how relaxed she'd been after their tryst in his garret, he moved quickly after her and snagged her arm.

"Would you stay a moment?"

She looked to where his hand encircled her upper arm, then into his eyes. "What for?" The little tremble in her tone was endearing, but her green glance was wary.

"We aren't strangers to one another, and we're alone." He thought that explained everything.

"We aren't alone," she protested. "Madame Lucie is nearby as well as Monsieur Bowes, not to mention Michel, who might need help in the night."

"And there are grape harvesters and horses in the stables, too, but none of them matter." He turned her to face him properly, gauging her reaction. If she resisted even the slightest, he would let her go. But he desperately hoped Serena would remain.

Leaning down, he brushed a kiss across her lips, and then another across her fine cheekbone, ending by nuzzling her temple.

"Stay with me," he whispered.

She stiffened. Then, after a brief pause, she turned her face so he could claim her lips.

When their mouths melded, she slipped her hands around his neck, and he swept his hands under her, lifting her off her feet. Gently, he placed her on the bed, bending low so their kiss wasn't broken.

After a moment, she moved over to give him room. But when he climbed onto the mattress, instead of lying beside her, Malcolm covered her body with his, leaning upon his elbows and resting a leg on either side of hers.

His heart was already pounding, and as they touched, he could feel hers, too.

"You make me happy," he said before he thought about it.

Her eyes widened at his confession. To diffuse the vulnerability he felt, he nearly joked about how she'd rescued him so many times. After all, who wouldn't be happy with a clever, beautiful woman coming to his aid, even in front of the emperor. But he didn't want to bring her thoughts back to the day's events.

"I want to make you happy in return," he offered, hoping she understood his meaning.

She nodded, before reaching up and drawing his head down to hers for another kiss. It was a strange notion to be in love with a woman he knew so little about. But something inside him longed for her, with the certainty he needed her with him for the rest of his life. He'd never experienced anything like it.

She moaned against him as he deepened the kiss, stroking her tongue with his. That she might have been with other men, maybe her Parisian friends, didn't deter him a whit. He was confident he could be a better lover, and clearly, she hadn't given her heart to any of them.

And it was her heart he most wanted, even as he intended to enjoy her body.

Rolling to his back, he took her with him, and while she was suddenly splayed across him, he easily unfastened the single button at the back of her dress. Now, he had only to start drawing up her skirts so he could deal with her other layers, for he wanted her entirely bare this time.

She wriggled until he stopped. And then, to his wonderment, she tilted her head, lowered her mouth to his, and kissed him. He even felt her tongue at the seam of his lips, as he had done to her.

Reaching up, he clasped the back of her head, just below her coiled bun, and held her in place while his other hand palmed her breast, aching to feel her soft skin. Opening his mouth to her explorations, their tongues seemed to dance a sensual waltz, rubbing along each other.

But he wanted more. By the feel of her pearled nipple through her gown and shift, she did, too. This was becoming torture.

Breaking off the kiss, he rolled again so they were in danger of falling off the far side of the bed. But he could look down into her face once more. Dropping a kiss on her chest, just above the valley between her breasts, he felt her shiver beneath him.

"Serena, I want you."

To his chagrin and surprise considering she looked flushed and willing, she shook her head.

"No, I don't want you?" he asked, unable to keep from smiling. "Or no, you don't want me?"

"Neither," she said. "Will you kiss me again?"

"I will," he said, "but it's becoming increasingly difficult not to wish for more."

Still, he obeyed, lowering his mouth to hers, fearing he'd lose his sanity when she lifted her hips, writhing against him. He found himself grinding against her, feeling like a randy youth.

Raising his head, the words were pulled from him again. "I want you."

Again, she shook her head.

"Serena!" he exclaimed exasperatedly.

She shrugged. "You don't know me," she said in her perfectly lilting French.

Hadn't he just been thinking how strange it was to feel so deeply about a woman he barely knew? But that didn't change how he felt.

"I care for you, and I want to give you pleasure. What else do I need to know right now?"

She sighed. He would have chuckled at her expression if his groin didn't ache for her.

"I will be happy to learn all about you," he promised, "and we can spend hours talking while we make our way to Saint-Malo."

She brightened. "Yes, I would like to learn about you, too."

There was a lot he could tell her, and a lot he never would. A decade of furtive assignments held many ignoble and savage tales she had no reason ever to know.

"But that doesn't mean we can't enjoy ourselves now," he pointed out.

He felt her press her legs together more firmly beneath him. *Was she ashamed?* It would be ridiculous for her to feel shame with a rake who'd enjoyed too many ill-spent hours spending himself *inside* or *beside* too many ill-chosen women.

"It doesn't matter to me what you've done in the past," he promised. "I am not judging you for being experienced."

Her expression shuttered, and he feared he'd said the wrong thing in an effort to reassure her.

"I didn't mean to offend you. It's only I wanted you to know despite how practiced you might be—"

She started to struggle before he could even begin to say something flowery and charming. He ought to have started with the words, "I shall marry you anyway," but now it was too late.

When she beat her fist on his shoulder, he sighed and rolled off of her. And directly onto the hard floor.

"*Ouch!*" His shoulder throbbed. The first time in all his years, he found himself having fallen out of bed while a lovely woman remained in it, angry as a summer wasp despite how he'd not yet done a damn thing.

In the next moment, he looked under the bed as her feet touched the planks on the other side.

"I will see you early tomorrow, Monsieur Branley. *Bonsoir.*"

Childishly, he made a face at her retreating ankles. Then he lay his head down and looked at the ceiling, willing his body to calm down. A viscount's son lying on the floor amidst the dust balls, yearning for a female who ought to consider herself lucky he wanted her.

"Ha! You idiot!" he scolded himself aloud. He didn't believe it for a second. She was a coppery, shining star, and he would be lucky if the green-eyed goddess let him kiss her ever again.

CHAPTER TWENTY-ONE

Early, with the sun just cresting the east vineyard, they bid Michel and Madame Lucie goodbye. Riding side-by-side on the seat of a sturdy, uncovered wagon used for transporting grapes or barrels, Serena wished Malcolm didn't take up so much room. Their shoulders were touching, as were their thighs, and it would be a long way to the coast.

With her trunks in the back, Malcolm's horse pulled them along at a good pace. Monsieur Bowes had already left, heading northeast to Paris with messages from Michel to his wife and from Serena to her grand-père relating how Guillaume and Jean-Paul had shown up. She couldn't explain what the two had hoped to accomplish, but she told Henri Renault the deadly results.

"We will have to find a place to stay tonight," Malcolm said into the silence they'd shared since setting out.

A very long trip indeed, Serena repeated silently, if she couldn't overcome her peevish annoyance over his bold assumptions about her virtue. He seemed to think she'd been dancing the hornpipe jig with every male she met. While she had herself to blame for his low opinion of her, he was the only one who'd truly compromised her innocence.

Taking a long moment in which she tempered her tone to one of cool neutrality, Serena spoke.

"If we make it to Saint-Rémy-du-Plain, Pépère says there is a winery where we can spend the night."

"Most of the vintners are for Napoleon," Malcolm said, looking at her, but she continued to stare straight ahead.

"The working class and merchants of Paris are for Napoleon, including many vintners. But most of the people, as you know, simply want peace. They don't want to go back to a time of war. It hurts business." She thought a minute, then added, "Still, it would be best if we don't declare any allegiance at all when we get there."

"Agreed," he said. "Now that you're speaking to me again, will you tell me about your parents? I expected them to be at the winery."

Serena bit her tongue and wished she hadn't started speaking at all. As soon as he knew her to be a baron's daughter, everything would change. Given her true position in society, he might be shocked at her behavior with him, which she knew had been truly outrageous. On the other hand, he might suddenly declare her suitable to be a future viscountess.

In either case, they would no longer be plain Serena and Malcolm, nor could she allow him to kiss her or carry her to bed, ready to tup. Without her French accent and working-class disguise, she would feel too vulnerable.

Moreover, he would still be a rake.

Deciding to let him remain entrenched in his wrong-headed notions until she was ready to disabuse him of them, she considered what she could tell him.

"Presently, my parents live happily in the countryside of England."

"Why? Where?" He sounded utterly confounded.

"Are you taking me all the way to them, or only to the Devon coast?" she asked.

"I intend to get you safely to the British shore and into a coach bound for your home before returning to France at once."

"Then you don't need to know where my parents are, or even why."

"Very well. I shall tell you stories of my own life and bore you to tears."

As it turned out, none of Malcolm's stories were boring, as he'd had adventures at university and then many more while in service to the Crown.

"I have grown weary of it," he confessed. "And my parents would like me to settle down."

"I am sure any parents of a renowned rake would prefer he at least give the appearance of domesticity and responsibility by taking a wife, but can you really stop your philandering ways?"

He didn't hesitate. "I would not take a wife for appearances' sake, I assure you. The female I intend to marry will hold my interest and excite my passions and keep me utterly captivated."

"That seems a tall order for any woman." *If he was waiting for such a gifted female, he might be unwed forever.* "You need a *Pandora*," she added.

"A guitar?" he asked, cocking his head, making him look utterly boyish and charming.

But what was he saying? "Excuse me?" she asked. "A guitar?"

"A *pandura*, like a guitar, maybe more of a lute or a mandolin," he said, slipping into English. Then back to French as he added, "While I enjoy music, I would rather have a wife."

She smiled at his confusion, which made him smile back, and suddenly, her heart gave a little kick at how much she loved him.

"No, monsieur, I meant you need a woman like Pandora for your future wife. You know, the Greek goddess. She was all-gifted. An impossibility, I think."

"I think not," he retorted. "I think it entirely possible. In fact, probable."

She turned her head at his tone and was rewarded by his expression of pointed interest. *Was he saying . . . ? Did he mean . . . ?*

Serena couldn't even form the thought in full, so astounded was she that he might be inferring he thought *her* to be such a woman.

Feeling the heat creep up her cheeks, she turned away.

"I fear I offended you last night, Mademoiselle Renault, and I must apologize and tell you it was the last thing I meant to do."

Obviously he hadn't meant to, for it lost him the easy enjoyment he'd been expecting. But it stung nonetheless, the way he'd magnanimously excused her supposed immorality in order to make love to her. As if she was supposed to thank him for his generosity. *Should she have forgiven him for being a rake?*

Sighing, she wished she didn't feel flattered by his interest at the same time as she felt insulted. She should have slapped his face the first time he'd touched her. Instead, she'd encouraged him. She'd wanted him desperately, and she still did.

By the time they'd eaten the food Madame Lucie had packed for them and made it as far as the winery in Saint-Rémy, Serena had decided she'd been too harsh and too hasty. Fearful of a libertine's reputation for dallying with women, she hadn't taken into consideration how Malcolm had treated her rather decently so far.

When he suggested they pretend to be a married couple—"for safety's sake and your reputation, too," he'd explained—she went along with it. Thus, at the Louis Defleur winery, where her grand-père had said she would be able to stay, Serena found herself shown to a spacious room with one bed.

"You are most welcome here," said Monsieur Defleur.

"You certainly are," agreed his round wife. "The granddaughter of Henri and Adèle! You're the very picture of your mother. Except for your hair."

Everyone always said the same thing. For a moment, she feared Madame Defleur knew her father was English, but instead she exclaimed with delight that they'd come so recently from the capital.

"You must tell us all the news of Paris over supper. I imagine there are celebrations going on every night."

Glancing at Malcolm, Serena nodded after he gave the slightest shrug. After all, the kind vintners were hardly going to hold them and try to turn them over to Bonaparte's Imperial Guards.

"We have seen little difference so far," Monsieur Defleur said when they sat down to eat. "Nothing much happens this far away, and it is said the emperor traveled through the Rhone valley without opposition, all the way to Paris."

She and Malcolm took turns telling what they knew, even about the Seventh Coalition, carefully remaining neutral until Madame Defleur exclaimed what a shame that the peace of the land might be disturbed again.

"The other nations should stay out of it," her husband declared.

"On the other hand," Madame Defleur said, "Bonaparte took us to war many times and King Louis did not."

Serena let the two of them debate the matter. It was all out of her hands now anyway. Malcolm, too, seemed content to let the Defleurs come to their own conclusions as to the best ruler.

When she yawned broadly, hiding it as best she could behind her hand, their hostess jumped up.

"You newly yoked young people must wish to go to bed, yes?"

Serena had managed to put aside the thrilling yet nerve-wracking situation that awaited her upstairs, a single bed for the two of them.

"Thank you," Malcolm said. "We hate to be rude, but we have to get up early and be on our way."

Far too quickly, she found herself alone in a bedroom with Lord Branley, a viscount's son, a self-confirmed rake, a man who was grinning from ear to ear.

"Stop it," she said.

"Stop what?" he asked, as innocent as a babe.

MALCOLM DECIDED HE WAS going to be a saint. He was going to lie quietly beside the most enticing woman he'd ever known, with her luscious curves and sweet valleys, and he was going to do absolutely nothing. Not even sleep if his overly excited body had anything to say about it. But he was certainly not going to make advances toward her.

After they each took a turn at the washstand, using toothpowders and washing their faces, he undressed discreetly in one corner. Facing away from her to give her privacy, he shrugged out of his braces and slid his breeches down his legs. His shirt hung low but still he heard her gasp.

Whipping around, he found her staring at him, looking at his bare legs and anything else she could see beneath the hem of his linen shirt.

"I thought you would turn around," he said, feeling unfairly spied upon.

"I thought you would let me get undressed and under the covers before you started baring yourself," she said.

"I'm not baring myself," he protested. "I'll sleep like this."

"How do you normally sleep?"

He made a wry face, giving her the answer.

"Never mind," she said. Then she frowned. "Even in winter?" she asked.

"Maybe you'll find out some day," he quipped. It was only May, and he hoped by the winter they really would be a wedded couple, and she could see for herself he slept bare all year round.

When she still stared at him, he had to ask her.

"Do you need help?" he asked, determined to enjoy being with her even if the frustration killed him.

His delight at their situation was undoubtedly evident in his tone, for she rolled her eyes and turned her back on him. He held his breath as she drew her gown over her head and laid it over the chair for morning. Her petticoat and her stays joined it.

She was a vision in her lightweight cotton shift, through which he could see her round bottom. He clenched his fists since his fingers were twitching at the thought of squeezing those perfect globes.

Without looking directly at him, Serena slid under the covers and rolled to face the window. A moment later, he put out the oil lamp on the bedside table, and climbed into bed, giving his pillow a hearty punch before laying down his head. As a gentleman, he faced away from her.

Ten minutes later, Malcolm was trying to hear whether she had fallen asleep. It felt like ten hours.

Damn! His heart was hammering at such a rate, one would think he'd never been near a woman before without tupping her. His body was at full attention and ready to perform, even though there was to be no performance.

Come to think of it, he had *never* been in bed with a woman if they weren't making the two-backed beast or some variant of the act. It was almost unnatural to be lying quietly beside a desirable female. He couldn't imagine how a married couple ever passed a night without swiving. *What an excruciating thought!*

Rolling onto his back, he stared at the ceiling. There was nothing to see, no canopy over the bed with a pattern he could trace with his eyes, no cherubs floating upon clouds, not even cracks in the plaster.

He sighed without realizing it until she moved.

"Did I awaken you?" he asked hopefully.

"I wasn't sleeping," she answered. "Just thinking about tomorrow and the voyage and all the days after that."

Good Lord! And he'd been contemplating the ceiling!

"That's a lot to think about while trying to fall asleep."

"I suppose it is," she agreed. "And you?"

"I was calculating the time and distance to Saint-Malo," he lied.

"Very well. I shall try to sleep. *Bonsoir, monsieur.*"

"*Bonsoir, mademoiselle.*"

A few minutes later, she stirred again. This time, she rolled onto her back.

"Do you think we might run into trouble in the waters off the coast of Devon? Being on a smuggler's ship, I mean."

"I think your grand-père wouldn't put you in any danger. The captain has probably been in his business a long while, and the authorities on the other side are paid well to let him alone. In fact, London wine shops, not to mention Prinny himself and half of the noblemen in Mayfair, also pay the authorities to let the smugglers' ships land. I've heard the constables and the magistrate in Cornwall and Devon are extremely wealthy because no one wants to stop the flow of French wine from reaching British lips."

"British lips," she repeated and giggled.

The sound made his rod as hard as the mast of a smuggler's ship. Maybe harder, he thought. If only she would go to sleep so he could remain in peaceful solitary torment.

"I think Renault wine is better than what we had tonight," she said, lowering her voice to a whisper.

He said nothing, thinking of how much he wished she was whispering with her mouth against his mouth, or against his . . .

He groaned. Suddenly, she sat up, resting on her elbow and looking down on him.

"You don't agree?" she asked. "You like Defleur wine better than Renault?"

"What are you talking about?" His brain was clouded with lust, and she was making no sense.

"Well, what are you groaning about?" she demanded.

He could be truthful at least. "I groan at having your beautiful body so close to me while I'm bloody well behaving myself."

"Oh," she said softly. Then she flopped back down onto the bed, staring up again. Finally, she turned only her face to him. "I suppose you could stop behaving yourself."

He clenched his fists.

"I could," he agreed. She was testing him, staring at his right ear, but he wouldn't even look at her.

"But then you would get angry again," he reminded her.

"I wouldn't," she insisted.

"You might," he said.

"I'm not who you think I am," she said into the darkness.

CHAPTER TWENTY-TWO

Malcolm turned his face to hers, trying to see her better. "Are you an Imperial spy?"

"An Imperial . . . No!" Then she started to laugh, which was even harder to ignore than her sweet giggle. It was a gloriously sunny sound, making him want to lie down in a field of flowers and look at a blue sky with puffy clouds. As long as she was there, beside him, laughing, and preferably naked.

"What's so amusing?" he asked.

"That the first thing you think of is which side of this awful conflict I'm on."

In the darkness, he shrugged. "What else can you be hiding?"

"For one thing," she said, "I'm not experienced."

"You handle a gun very well," he said.

"No, you addlepated fool. In bed, I mean, or outside of bed, for that matter." She no longer whispered or laughed but spoke seriously. "I am not in any way *experienced*. Except with you."

His brain did a strange shift in perception, realizing the import of her words. His heart felt a little lighter, and he realized he'd harbored an unreasonable jealousy toward any man who'd touched her before him.

"Are you saying I was your first kiss?"

"No," she confessed. "Well, yes."

"Which is it?" he asked.

"I suppose I had a few hurried pecks, but yours was the first real kiss. With any passion," she added. "Or tongue."

He nearly laughed when she said that, but was glad he didn't when she continued confessing.

"And you were the first to touch me *anywhere* else for that matter."

"I see." His independent French woman was as innocent as any protected lady of the *ton*. *How marvelously unexpected!* And yet, it didn't make him love her any more than he already had.

Yet her quiet words had been a gift. He lay beside a woman who had just told him *not* to behave, and she wasn't saying such a thing because she already knew the joys of coital pleasure. She was saying it because she wanted him.

He recalled his garret and how quickly he'd pounced, assuming she'd known what it was to kiss and be caressed and to climax. Then he'd intimated she would want to do it again on a casual basis. No wonder she'd been annoyed at him.

"I'm sorry for my previous assumptions. I thought a female with as much freedom as you seemed to exercise would also be free in other areas."

"Quite incorrect," she assured him.

"Yet we've ended up lying here in bed together, and I was determined not to compromise you further, despite not knowing I'd been the sole compromiser."

In fact, he ought to be given angel wings for his extraordinarily good behavior.

"I confess, Malcolm," she tried out his name, and frankly, it thrilled him to hear it from her lips. "I know it's wrong to desire you outside of marriage, but you're the only man I've ever met who has made me feel both safe and in danger at the same time."

He thought about her putting such trust in him and sat up. "I had best find somewhere else to sleep."

She put an arm on his. "What will the Defleurs think?"

"I don't give a damn what they think. I only care what you think of me at this point."

She paused, and despite the darkness, he knew she was staring at him. Then she sat up and put her arms around him.

"I think you should stay with me."

Malcolm closed his eyes. He was being sorely tested. On the other hand, he wanted to marry her, so he was already shedding his rakish ways. That should count for something.

"Serena, I think we should—"

She planted a kiss on his mouth, and his arms went around her almost of their own volition. Embracing this warm woman, there was no way he could leave her side now.

"I know we will be separated soon," she said, nibbling her way to his earlobe. She seemed as clever at love-making as every other thing he admired about her. "Let's pretend this night is all we have."

Malcolm was certain no female had ever offered him that before, except for the ones he'd paid. The rest inevitably hoped for a promise of marriage, even when he told them ahead of time that wasn't in the cards.

Pulling away, he drew her shift over her head and then quickly yanked off his shirt before pressing her back onto the sheets.

"If you're sure," he said.

She nodded.

"Wait," he said, jumping up to draw open the curtains and let the moonlight stream in. He'd been desperate for weeks to see her bare beauty, and it had been worth waiting for. As the white light touched her skin, she appeared radiant. Perhaps she was a goddess after all. *If not Pandora, then Venus!*

Bending low, he kissed her, intending to take it slowly. To that end, after ravaging her mouth, he trailed kisses down her neck and between her breasts, stopping to satisfy his urgent need to lavish attention on each of her beautiful hills.

As he did, she gasped and moaned, every little sound spurring him on and heating his blood.

When he swirled his tongue around each of her pert nipples before plucking at them gently with his teeth, she arched against him, and then he began his journey down to her essence.

Licking her flat stomach, dipping his tongue into her navel, feeling her hands grip his hair, he eventually made it to the apex of her thighs, and went right past. He nibbled the soft skin of her left thigh, stopping only to blow a warm breath upon her gingery curls, which he could see were dampening for him.

When he kissed the inside of her knee, she made a sound of pure exasperation.

"Is this really how it's done because it seems more like torment than pleasure?"

He smiled against her skin and continued. After he worshipped her slender ankle and made his way up her other leg, she was fisting the sheets. And as he approached her mound again, she started to move sideways, putting the part of her most needing his attention directly into his path.

He certainly wouldn't disappoint a lady. Settling between her thighs, he gently parted the soft folds and touched his tongue to her bud, making her jump slightly, before he began to stroke it in earnest. Serena sighed and relaxed into the sensation until he flicked his tongue across her nubbin and her body tensed again.

She was already close, and Malcolm was determined to let her find her satisfaction before he did anything that might cause her a whit of pain.

To that end, he continued a steady rhythm with his tongue while she gasped and then expelled her breath, alternately moaning and falling silent. Finally, she raised her hips, straining against his mouth, as he increased the pressure and the speed of his caresses.

A husky exclamation burst from her lips as she found her release. Then she stilled.

"Oh my!" she said, her eyes still closed. "That was even better than the first time. But what about you?"

What about him? He felt like a stallion at its first stud as he rose over her and nudged her legs farther apart. Taking note of her languid state, he pressed his staff to her entrance, and her eyes popped open.

Instead of seeing fright in her green gaze, however, she appeared blatantly curious, trying to look down between their bodies. He nudged inside of her, pleased to find her slick with her own satisfied desire, but hopeful he could raise her level of passion for a second time.

Slowly, he pushed forward, feeling his cock instantly coated with her honey. Despite going slowly, he had her full attention when he breached her maidenhead, causing her to stiffen slightly.

Hesitating, he asked, "Was it terrible?"

"No," she said. "Was that it?"

"That was the worst," he assured her.

"Then proceed," she encouraged him, and he did.

Soon, seated fully inside her, he dropped a kiss onto her upturned lips, letting his tongue mimic the movements of his shaft for a few delicious strokes. Then pushing himself up, a palm on either side of her, he levered his body so he could look down at her beauty while pleasuring her.

To his delight, she kept her eyes open, looking into his as they danced back and forth, a rolling movement of tantalizing thrusting and withdrawing. He felt the sheen of sweat across his back, and came down onto his forearms so he could trace his tongue across her glorious collarbone.

Closing her eyes, she arched her neck and appeared to be climbing to a climax yet again. Her tight heat sheathed him like a glove, and he felt his own satisfaction barreling toward him with no way to slow it down.

Leaning on one elbow and reaching between them, he caressed the sweet nubbin that held the key to her release.

"Ohh," she cried out. And then her woman's passage clamped around his arousal, squeezing and stroking him until the powerful sensation low in his spine took over. He spent in short, hard thrusts deep inside her.

As a gentleman, he made sure to collapse beside Serena before tucking her body into the curve of his. Both of them exhausted from the long hours on the road and their heart-racing swiving, he felt her fall asleep before he did.

When he awakened, they were still in the same position. Malcolm couldn't recall having slept so well in years. It was past dawn, but still early enough they didn't have to jump up and hurry onto the infernal hard wagon seat for the remainder of their journey.

Against him, her soft, warm body felt like bliss, and he dropped a kiss upon her glorious copper-colored hair. Everything was perfect, although he was fairly certain his right arm was paralyzed from being under her for hours, and his neck was exceedingly stiff.

Other parts of him were growing stiff, too, just from looking down on his lovely lady. And she was *his*, all of her. She'd given herself to him, and he would never give her back.

Malcolm ran a hand gently over the curve of her hip, and she stirred.

"Time to awaken," he said, leaning down to nibble her earlobe.

Stretching, she gazed up at him with sleepy, verdant eyes, and he would swear she had a look of tenderness matching what he felt in his own heart.

"Thank you for last night," he said. "You are perfect."

Her eyes widened. He supposed she hadn't expected him to begin a declaration before coffee or chocolate.

"I know you think we don't know each other very well, but everything I do know about you, Serena Renault, suits me more than any other female I've ever met."

Silence met his words. He was hoping for a reciprocity of similar sentiment at the very least. Instead, she pulled the sheet up, making sure her beautiful breasts were covered.

"I am not a Renault," she confessed. "My father is an English baron, Lord Elmstead."

Speechless for a moment, Malcolm's mind rearranged the facts. She was British by birth. Her father was a member of the gentry. He'd just deflowered a baron's daughter.

Rolling onto his back, he considered it a moment before realizing it changed nothing. He'd already intended to marry her. All that was left was the asking. He turned to her.

"Is Serena your real first name?"

She nodded.

"Will you marry me, Miss Serena Elmstead?"

Shocked silence, and then an avid denial, "Absolutely not!"

Malcolm sat up in bed, taking the sheet with him as he looked down at her in astonishment. Her cheeks were flushed beautifully as if they'd only just exerted themselves in the grand art of tupping, and her hair was in a charming disarray upon the pillow.

What's more, in the daylight, finally he could satisfy his curiosity—her nipples were peachy rather than pink.

But her green eyes were glittering with some emotion. It looked like fury, but there could be no cause.

"Whyever not?" He asked the first jealous notion that came into his head. "Is your heart engaged elsewhere?" In which case, he would be quite sorry, for she held his firmly in her possession. He might even have to engage in an honorable duel.

"How can you ask me that," she demanded, "after what we did last night?"

He settled back beside her. "Then how can you turn me down, especially after what we did last night?"

"This *is* a terrible time to ask for my hand," she protested, flinging off the sheet and counterpane before turning toward the window, presenting him with her back.

Unless he was mistaken, she intended to get up and walk away from the discussion.

"This is the perfect time to ask," he insisted, resting an arm across her, just enough to keep her from slipping out of his reach.

She clamped both hands onto his forearm, plucking at it futilely.

"Obviously, you shouldn't ask me under *these* circumstances," she said. "In the heat of passion."

"We are not in the heat of passion. I'm starting to feel chilly in fact because you tossed off our coverings."

"War is about to break out," she protested, turning back toward him. "We are in the middle of a conflict."

Leaning on his other elbow, he grinned down at her.

"As long as the conflict isn't between us, I see no reason we cannot come to an agreement, a treaty as strong as the one signed in Vienna."

Pursing her lips, she closed her eyes, effectively shutting him out.

Well, that wouldn't stand. Bending low, he took her nipple between his lips, and then he nibbled.

"Oh!" she exclaimed and slapped his shoulder. "You *are* a rogue."

Ignoring her, he enjoyed himself before moving on to her other plump breast. Her nipple pebbled in anticipation before he even touched it.

With her breathing growing heavier once more, Malcolm couldn't deny them a second round of pleasure. Positioning himself between her thighs, which she willingly parted for him, he nudged inside her. As he did, he put his mouth to her ear.

"You *will* be my wife," he promised. "I've decided."

He heard her growl—an actual feral sound emanated from her throat, even as she kept her eyes firmly shut.

In another moment, however, she arched under him and opened her gorgeous rosy lips as he thrust and withdrew and thrust again.

When she was panting and he was close to climaxing, Malcolm reached between their bodies and stroked her, pushing her over the edge.

Her cry sent him over with her, and soon, they were back where they started, with him sprawled on top of her, feeling as if he'd just run from one side of Hyde Park to the other, and her looking satisfied as a cat after catching a fat mouse.

"Will you marry me, Miss Elmstead?"

CHAPTER TWENTY-THREE

Serena wished he would stop ruining the luxurious aftermath of such wondrous sensations with that same wretched question.

"I cannot breathe," she lied so he would roll off of her, although she instantly missed his warmth and his comforting weight.

"I know why you are asking," she told him, scooting away from him before he could trap her again under his muscular arm.

"And why is that?"

"Because even though you have most certainly behaved like a rake, now that you know I am a baron's daughter, you feel it is your duty to marry me."

Surprisingly, he laughed, even as she got out of bed and grabbed for her chemise to cover herself.

"That's ridiculous," Malcolm said. "That's precisely the opposite of what a rake would do. In fact, that's practically the definition of a rake, ruining a young lady and then callously walking away."

She drew on her stockings. "Ah, but you are an English nobleman through and through. Just like my father. If I were merely anyone's daughter, then you would do nothing more than thank me and forget me. Or maybe you would wonder when we could be alone again as you did the last time we behaved badly in your garret. Instead, since my father is a baron, you want to marry me. Maybe for my fortune."

"Do you have one?" he asked, his tone nothing but amused as he got out of bed and began to dress.

"I suppose," she confessed, as she adjusted the laces of her stays, not too tightly since her gown was loose. She considered what her mother had said about her dowry making her more desirable than even some of the viscounts' and earls' daughters. "I believe I do."

"Since I didn't know that," Malcolm reminded her, "I can hardly be after you for your money, can I? Besides, didn't your father marry your mother, a vintner's daughter? Why don't you think I have good intentions toward a vintner's granddaughter?"

From the confines of the inside of her gown which she'd yanked over her head, now struggling to find the arm holes, she said, "But my father wasn't a rake."

She could hear him laughing, and then, after a moment, she felt his hand slip through the hole to grab hers and draw it out. Then she pushed her other arm out and tugged her gown into place.

"Not that I wish to disparage my future father-in-law," Malcolm said, "but you have no way of knowing what happened between your father and mother when he came to Paris as a young officer, as was probably the case. I assume you were born on the right side of the blanket, but did your time in the oven begin *after* your parents' nuptials or before?"

Lacing up her ankle boots, she ignored his impertinent question, although she knew the answer from her grand-mère.

Pépère's stern face came into her thoughts. "My grandparents will be heartbroken if an Englishman steals me away as my father did my mother."

"Unlikely. I surmise you were never planning on staying here forever. And you're going home to England anyway."

And then he asked the question she knew would follow?

"Why have you lived here so long anyway?"

Having just spent the night in his arms and given her innocence over to Malcolm—and rather easily, too—she was reluctant to tell him the reason for her exile. It would be hard protesting her innocence to a charge of societal misconduct when she'd behaved so wantonly in his arms.

"I misbehaved," she said cautiously, reaching for her spencer.

"During a London Season, I would warrant."

She turned on him. "How did you know?"

"You're not the first young lady to do so. But I know better than anyone you still had your virtue intact, so you couldn't have done anything terribly bad."

"Just a few foolish moments out of sight of a chaperone and one particularly ill-timed walk in Vauxhall with a man who tried to take liberties," she said. "My father banished me from my home for a supposed transgression that didn't even end in a satisfying kiss."

Malcolm's eyebrows rose, and then he swallowed. "Lord Elmstead is a stern fellow, I take it. I shall have to watch myself around him after we marry."

Rolling her eyes, Serena slipped her bonnet atop her head, and then thought better of it and yanked it off again. She drew a comb from her traveling bag and worked to untangle the snarls before she braided her hair and put it up in a bun. With water from the washstand, she smoothed any loose locks. Then she smacked her bonnet on, feeling presentable.

Inside, however, she felt wretched. On the one hand, she had wanted to give herself to this particular man, who had watched her comb her hair with thoughtful eyes before he'd quickly dressed. And she hadn't been disappointed in her choice, eternally grateful she hadn't thrown her virtue away before Vauxhall or since.

In fact, their coupling had been beyond anything she'd imagined. Malcolm had been so gentle and caring—and experienced and skilled!

Yet knowing how rakes behaved, if she married a true libertine, she would be a lonely, abandoned wife, and she couldn't bear it.

"We are *not* marrying."

"You might be carrying my child."

She sat down heavily on the bed. *Wasn't the man supposed to take care of that type of thing to prevent it happening?*

"Are you speaking in jest?"

"Of course not. That's how these things work." He didn't look the least bothered.

In his breeches and shirt, his vest, jacket, and cravat in place, he crouched in front of her, placing a large hand on each of her knees.

"You didn't know?"

"Not exactly, no." She noticed his bemused expression. "Don't you dare laugh at me, Monsieur Branley!"

"That's *Lord* Branley, actually, but to you, always, Malcolm." Raising a hand, he traced his finger along her chin, and the tender touch caused tears to prick her eyes.

"Why did you do it? Why did you ruin me?" she asked.

Shaking his head, he stood up, drawing her to her feet.

"I have been considered a rake since my university days, and I have never minded the title or thought myself unfairly labeled. But in this case, I must gainsay you. I have not ruined you. To put it bluntly, I didn't care whether I planted my seed in your womb"—Serena felt her cheeks grow warm at his words—"because I intended to marry you, a Parisian vintner's granddaughter of unknown parentage. I've had the notion in my head for a while now, which is why I came racing after you from Paris. I assumed you felt the same way."

She caught her breath when he drew her close, wrapping his arms around her.

"Felt how?" she asked.

With no smile now, Malcolm looked entirely serious.

"Utterly in love," he confessed. "Am I alone in that sentiment?"

A veritable flood of relief washed through her. Unable to stop the warm tears down her cheeks, she let them fall.

"Dammit!" he said, releasing her. "I *was* wrong."

Running his fingers through his hair, he started to pace. Then he stopped. "It doesn't matter. I will still marry you if you'll let me. I'll make you a good husband, I swear. I have decided to put my days as a despicable rake behind me. Eventually, you may grow to love me. I'm not all bad, I assure you. I—"

"Stop," Serena said, silencing his rambling which she realized was from nervousness. Delightfully, this experienced man had been anxious, too, worrying over whether she cared for him. "You're *not* wrong, nor are you alone in *that* sentiment. I'm simply so overwhelmed right now."

He remained quiet, his arms by his sides, looking unsure. She immediately switched to English.

"I love you, Lord Branley."

His face broke out in a radiant smile. Then he laughed and answered in his native tongue.

"I was so used to it, I forgot we didn't need to speak in French."

"Let's hope your English is better than your French," she teased. "I would like to hear some of your stories again without the strange instances of cows' udders and fence posts and pineapples where they don't belong."

"Am I that bad?" he asked, pulling her to him.

"If I were you, I wouldn't try to do anything silly like be an English spy in France."

They grinned at each other like children.

"I'm so glad you're coming on the boat with me," she said.

He nodded. "I don't ever want to let you out of my sight."

⟡

"HELL!" MALCOLM SWORE, MAKING Serena jump. Ahead of them was a barricade.

Already anxious, she was growing more uneasy by the moment. The trip to Saint-Malo from Saint-Rémy had been smooth enough until they were about two miles from the port. Uniformed men were everywhere. In the gathering dusk, the lights of their torches created an eerie scene.

"Why are there so many soldiers?" she'd asked a man going in the opposite direction. After all, there was unlikely to be any fighting with enemy forces in the small coastal village.

The answer had been unwelcome. As long as the British were part of the Seventh Coalition, the emperor didn't want them having the benefit of French wine. Apparently, even the smugglers' vessels were now in danger of being stopped and their contraband reclaimed for Bonaparte's empire. Only the captains who could pay off the guards were able to leave.

And of course, every wagon heading toward the coast would be searched, too.

"That should not matter," Serena said. "We aren't smugglers. We shall pretend to be a married couple, and you must play a mute again."

"I don't think this is going to be as easy as it was a few weeks ago, my sweet.," Malcolm said. "The soldiers aren't going to like seeing a couple leaving France. Naturally, they'll assume we're royalists. And I have no baggage to speak of, a saddle bag with very little, while you have two trunks full of clothing and belongings. Any way you look at us, we are either suspicious or the enemy or traitors."

"What do you propose we do?" She hated the tightness in her chest and the persistent fear she'd been living with since that awful day at the Palais des Tuileries.

"How attached are you to the contents of your trunks?" He drew the wagon over to the side of the dirt road.

Shocked at the notion of suddenly losing all her possessions, she wanted to cry.

"If I'd only known," she wailed, "I would have left my things at the Defleurs' home."

"If we'd known, we would have left your things at your family's winery," he reminded her. "We should dump your trunks in the woods and continue on as if we aren't going anywhere except to look at the sea."

"I suppose, if we must." It made her ill to think of the things she had brought from Mémère to give to her mother, not to mention baubles and bits that had been in the Elmstead family for years, which she'd brought with her from England to make her room in Paris feel more like home. And she had a few precious books, too.

"But I shall need to keep the letter for the ship's captain."

"Indeed," Malcolm agreed. "Are you wearing a busk?"

Startled at his knowledge of women's underthings, she nodded.

"Remove it, coil the letter with the bank notes your grandfather gave you to pay the captain, and tuck it all into the space."

She didn't mind him watching as she pulled the long, wooden dowel out from the front of her stays. She would forsake her posture for the importance of the documents. Yet even her beloved busk had been a gift from her mother, carved with two linked hearts and her name. Serena had used it ever since the first time she'd worn the proper stays of a woman.

Handing it to Malcolm because she couldn't bear to toss it into the woods, she watched him slip it into the pocket of his coat. Then he unloaded her trunks, hiding them behind a tree, although she couldn't imagine why. Surely someone would find them and take her things before the war was over.

Feeling entirely dejected, she tried to shore her spirits up with thoughts of home. They continued on toward the blockade, not far from the docks of Saint-Malo. When two Imperial soldiers stood in the middle of the road, they halted the wagon.

"My husband is mute," she said as soon as one addressed Malcolm. "We just came to sit and look at the water."

"This late?" one of the soldiers asked. "In another half hour, you'll hardly be able to see anything."

Serena sent him a sly smile. "It is romantic, monsieur. Don't you think?" She even gave a husky laugh in case he was in any doubt.

But the other soldier was unimpressed by her act. "This isn't the time to be sightseeing," he said. "We are about to go to war."

"Again!" chimed in the other man, sounding none too pleased.

"Is there some reason we cannot go to the sea in our own country?" she asked.

The man turned to Malcolm, looking at him more closely. "Get out of the carriage."

Without hesitating, Malcolm complied, demonstrating he fully understood the language. "Hop on one foot," the soldier added.

Malcolm hesitated, and Serena held her breath, hoping he understood.

He hopped on his right foot twice and stopped.

"What madness is this?" she asked, sounding as insulted as she was scared.

"We're just making sure none of the English stragglers," the man hesitated so he could spit on the ground, "are trying to escape our grasp."

"This far south?" Serena asked. "News from Paris," she added, hoping to impress these men, "is that the English fled weeks ago. They left by way of Le Havre or up north as far as Calais."

"*Bon!*" said the soldier.

"*Vive l'Empereur,*" the first man cheered.

Serena wasn't sure if she was supposed to respond in kind. Instead, she said what was in her heart.

"We are *all* French. Surely, that's what's important," she insisted, then wished she'd stayed quiet when the soldier moved closer to her side of the wagon, pointed his musket at her, and told her to get down from the seat.

CHAPTER TWENTY-FOUR

"Seeing Malcolm bristle, hoping he didn't go for his weapon, Serena quickly did as she was told.

"Are you a royalist, mademoiselle?" the Imperial soldier demanded.

"On the contrary," she said, deciding she must lie believably, or she would never see her parents and brothers again. "My grandparents own the Renault winery in Saint-George-sur-Loire. We are well aware of how much our emperor has done for the vintners in Paris."

After a few seconds, he said, "Very well, you may continue to the docks and enjoy the view."

Malcolm started to climb back on the wagon.

"No," the soldier said. "You must leave the wagon here."

"Whyever for?" Serena asked.

"So you cannot pick up anything or anyone from the ships. For all we know, they're smuggling in English spies as we speak."

Glancing at Malcolm, who nodded, she said, "But who will tend our horse, or make sure our wagon doesn't get stolen?"

They'd intended to leave Malcolm's horse at the stables next to the dock for some other lucky traveler to purchase upon disembarking from a ship.

"I doubt it will need tending for an hour," the soldier said. "And that's all the time we'll give you before you must return."

"As for being stolen, we won't let that happen," the first soldier added. "We'll even take a rest in the back to protect it."

The man who spoke laughed at his own words. The other one watched them silently as Malcolm held out his hand to Serena. They walked away toward the ship and safety.

"NON, ABSOLUMENT, NON!" CAPTAIN Lafère was adamant. "I will not take *him*," he said, gesturing to Malcolm while speaking to Serena.

The captain snapped the letter in his hand for emphasis. "Only you, just as Henri requested. That's all I have room for anyway, and you had better jump on board quickly, mademoiselle, or I'll fill up the space."

"I won't go without him," she declared.

"That is up to you." The man pinned her with a hard stare, and Malcolm knew she wouldn't win this battle.

His gut told him from the moment they'd encountered the blockade this wasn't going to work out the way they'd hoped. It would have been too easy, and the good lord knew he didn't deserve an easy time of it.

"But we have money enough, don't we?" Serena turned to him.

"We do have money, Captain," Malcolm agreed, giving it another try even while sensing that wasn't the issue.

Sure enough, the man shook his head.

"I don't have the space. I have crates and barrels, and room for one old friend's granddaughter. That's all."

Serena turned to him, a panicky look in her eyes.

"What do we do?"

Malcolm wished with all his heart he could fix this to her satisfaction. But the most important thing was getting her to safety, not what his heart wanted.

Grabbing her arm, he took her a few steps away for privacy.

"You will get on the ship as your grandfather wanted and return to England." Malcolm hadn't expected the turn of events, but he hadn't discounted it either. Still, he hated to see the sudden flash of fear in her eyes. She didn't look like the fearless Parisian girl he'd first encountered in the Palais-Royal, and he needed that girl to return so he could send her on her way.

If Serena started to cry or seemed like a wilting flower, he would be hard pressed to send her off alone. But her staying in France was no longer an option.

"Come now, Miss Elmstead. You are the bravest woman I know. This is nothing but a short trip across the Channel." The ship looked sound, albeit smaller than he'd expected, and instead of being moored at one of the large wooden docks, it was off to the side, behind trees, with access only via two planks of wood.

Serena touched his hand and made a sound of frustration. "It's not a silly boat voyage I'm worried about," she said. "What about you? It is no longer safe here."

Malcolm blinked with astonishment to discover she wasn't concerned about traveling alone after all. Having someone worry about him was a strange occurrence, and while he appreciated it, he didn't want her to think about anything except herself at that moment.

Besides, it had never been safe for him in France, but he wouldn't mention that.

"I'll return to Paris as planned and finish what I started."

"You mustn't—" she began.

"Serena," he stopped her. "I've been successfully looking after myself for many years, even with my dreadful accent. Please don't fret."

When she bit her lip, he couldn't help himself. He drew her into his embrace.

"Hurry along, mademoiselle," called out the captain. "We must leave before the last light."

Malcolm didn't want to say anything to her that might not come true if he were injured or captured. But he couldn't let her go without some hope.

"I'll come after you."

Her eyes lit up. "Do you promise?"

Malcolm hated to promise something that wasn't entirely in his control, but for her he would.

"I promise. And this is the first vow I've ever made to a woman, so you'd best hold it in your heart."

"I will," she agreed, sounding calmer.

"*Now*, mademoiselle!" called the captain. "Or never."

Claiming her lips for a last kiss, Malcolm fervently hoped it wouldn't be too long before he was doing so again. She started to put her hands behind his neck, but he couldn't let her miss her passage.

Grabbing her hands, he pressed his mouth harder against hers, and then he pushed her away. Turning her quickly, he sent her in the direction of Captain Lafère's ship with his palm between her shoulder blades.

"Go," he ordered. And she did.

His heart swelled with admiration as she picked her way over the rocks to the gangplank and boarded the ship with nothing but her cloak and her pistol strapped to her ankle.

"Look after her," he said to the captain, who nodded. "For Henri Renault," the man said.

Malcolm hoped she didn't turn around lest he change his mind and snatch her back. Then, staring after her, he hoped to God she turned so he could look upon her sweet face again.

When she was onboard, she did.

He raised a hand, and she did the same, and then the ship slipped its mooring and departed into the twilight.

Breathing a sigh of relief, he turned his steps the way they'd come. All he had to do was sneak up on two armed Imperial soldiers and retrieve his horse.

CHAPTER TWENTY-FIVE

Serena sought to avoid the concerned looks of her mother or the curious ones from her father, so she made an effort to smile, be congenial, and settle into her old life. Her brothers at sixteen and nineteen were as lively and boisterous as ever, and she was glad they were both on a brief break, the elder one, Frances, from Oxford, and the younger, Will, from the boarding school at Winchester. The three of them chatted, laughed, rode horses, and played cards as usual.

In her journal, Serena expressed her gratitude. She was home, which was delightful. She was alive, which was a blessing. And she was thankful there was no talk of going to London any time soon.

The notion of a ball without Malcolm, with any other man's hands upon her, was intolerable. If it came to it and her parents pushed her, she would decline most emphatically.

The thought of a life without her English spy, frankly, left her bereft, but there was nothing she could do except wait. He had vowed to come after her, but the weeks had slipped into months. Word from the Continent was that another great battle would ensue, and hopefully, it would be the final skirmish, one way or the other.

But where was Malcolm?

When she had her monthly flow, she knew she ought to feel relief, at least where her parents were concerned. There would be no disappointed looks over her lack of morals, no shaking of their heads about how she'd failed to mature, and no dire, drawn-out diatribe over her ruined future.

However, deep inside, she could admit to a feeling of disappointment. While it would have made her life terribly difficult, she would have adored Malcolm's babe bouncing on her knee, even if he never came back to her.

Her eyes filled with tears, and she dashed them away.

Foolish thoughts for a foolish woman, she chided herself. She wouldn't have enjoyed motherhood out of wedlock, nor being ostracized, shunned by civil society, and maybe even sent into exile again by her parents.

Although, to her delight, her father seemed to have softened. He expressed sincere happiness in having her home and went almost to the point of apologizing for sending her away somewhat rashly. Serena now understood he'd done it over apprehension for her future, not to punish her. As for her mother, Hélène hardly left her side.

Today, they sat on the sofa in her mother's salon. English sunlight, which she thought wasn't quite as bright as French, streamed in, leaving a checkerboard pattern on the floor in front of them.

Serena was showing her mother a stitch her grand-mère had taught her.

"I'd forgotten Maman's clever handiwork," Hélène said, her head close to her daughter's so she could see what she was doing on the hoop-stretched, linen canvas.

Serena caught the beloved jasmine scent of her mother's skin and hair, breathed deeply, and was glad once again to be home. Swiftly, she kissed Hélène's cheek and continued to push the needle in and draw it out of the small holes.

A flurry of noise downstairs indicated someone had arrived. In an instant, Serena's heart was beating fast. Setting aside the needlepoint, she rose to her feet.

"Shall we go see what's going on," she said. "Perhaps we have visitors."

Her mother stood and smoothed her skirt, a lovely pale hand going to her hair to make sure it was still tidy. To Serena, she looked to be the perfect baroness, and it was hard to imagine her mother working in the Halle aux Vins or breaking with tradition and falling for a young British officer.

But love sprang up without warning, sometimes in the strangest places. Following her mother, Serena hoped her nightly prayers had come true. She wanted to descend the staircase and see the smiling, handsome visage of—

Her grandparents!

"Papa! Maman!" her mother cried, racing down the stairs and beginning a quick-paced flurry of French. She'd turned from an elegant baroness into an excited daughter in seconds.

"I'm so happy to see you. Why are you here? It doesn't matter. I'm thrilled. But are you both well? Is everything fine? What about the winery? How is Paris?" Hélène was encircled by her parents' arms, held in a tight embrace.

Will and Frances, who must have met their grandparents' carriage were also speaking French, circling the group of three like young lions.

Baron Elmstead entered the front hall, too. Seeing her father standing to the side watching his wife's happiness, Serena joined him while her grandparents both speaking at once answered all their daughter's questions.

"Do you wish me to translate, Father?"

"Don't be cheeky," Edward Elmstead said, but he smiled at her. "I can understand most of it. I take it Napoleon has been vanquished again. Hopefully for good this time."

"Where is Waterloo?" Serena asked, overhearing news of the final battle.

"In Belgium, about ten miles south of Brussels. I suppose it will be famous forever," her father mused. "Hélène," he called to his wife over the noise, "invite your parents into the drawing room, unless they want to go upstairs and change or rest first."

Serena knew better than to think her grandparents would want to rest. With a parent on either arm, her mother escorted them into the blue drawing room, her sons following.

"Bring coffee and some sort of biscuits or cake," Lord Elmstead said to their butler standing by. "And if we're not out of there in an hour, bring brandy."

"Yes, my lord." Mr. Tewles strode off to the back of the house. Then her father took her by the arm, and they trailed in behind the Renault side of the family.

"It sounds as if they're here for an extended visit," Serena said. "Isn't this fun?"

"Mm," her father answered noncommittally.

There had always been a little coolness between him and his wife's parents. Since that heartfelt discussion with her grand-mère, Serena thought she knew why. Her father had swept into Paris as a dashing officer, stolen a young woman's heart, and whisked her off to faraway England. Of course, her grandparents had taken the loss of their only child to another country quite hard.

As Serena entered the drawing room, her grand-mère held out her arms. *"Ma chère fille,* you look well."

She kissed Mémère's cheeks and had just put her arm around her when she suddenly heard Malcolm's name fall from her grand-père's lips.

"Monsieur Branley accompanied us over La Manche— the Channel, as you call it—and made sure we weren't detained in Portsmouth."

"Branley?" Serena's father repeated.

"Malcolm Branley," her grand-père said. "A viscount's son."

"Lord Branley!" her father said. "I don't know him personally, but I know of him. Not an officer, but firmly in service to the Prince Regent and Prime Minister Jenkinson. Also not surprising he would be in France at such a time."

"Your daughter knows him," Serena's grand-mère said, and suddenly, all eyes turned to her.

"I . . . I, that is," she began. *What was wrong with her?* It wasn't as if they all knew she'd given herself to him, both heart and body. "I ran into him in Paris. Actually, he ran into me," she babbled. "Literally, sent me onto the pavement. And then we met a few other times."

"But the ball," Mémère reminded her. "And then the Louvre."

Serena sighed. "Lord Branley and I went to a celebratory ball after the emperor—"

"No longer," her grand-père declared.

"After Bonaparte returned," Serena continued. "We danced at the Jardin du Luxembourg." She hoped her cheeks didn't pinken, but she couldn't help thinking of the Medici Fountain and the darkened grotto. "Then there was a masquerade at the Louvre," she added.

"Why didn't you tell us?" her mother asked. "I so love both the gardens and the museum."

Serena merely shrugged, hoping her grand-mère wouldn't mention how she'd been being dragged off to the Tuileries, nor her—

"Then there was her grand escape," her grand-père said cheerfully. "Your daughter was extraordinarily brave, don't you think?"

Hélène and Edward Elmstead gasped at the same time.

"Grand escape!" exclaimed Will excitedly, while Frances merely grinned.

However, her father frowned. "We don't think anything about her bravery because we have heard nothing of an escape." His tone was serious, and he glared at her.

"Don't look like that, Edward," Mémère said softly. "Your daughter is safe with you. That's what matters."

After a pause, he nodded. "Then tell us, Serena, from whom did you escape and why?"

She sent her grandparents a look of dismay. When she'd arrived home, she hadn't announced how she'd fled the Palais des Tuileries and then gone into hiding at the vineyard. Naturally, she'd said nothing about shooting anyone. Thus, her family simply imagined she'd come home as they'd requested, albeit a little earlier than expected.

She inhaled a deep breath. "I was discovered to be helping the Seventh Coalition," she said, her voice dropping.

"You were a spy!" Her father sounded horrified.

"A spy!" Frances exclaimed with admiration. And Will gave a little cheer.

"She was a hero!" Pépère declared.

"Papa," Serena's mother admonished her father, "neither of you should have involved her."

"I didn't mind," Serena said, wanting to defend her grandparents. "I just kept my ears and eyes open."

"I knew I would need brandy," her father said, sending his glance heavenward for a moment. Then he fixed her with another stare. "And what of Lord Branley?"

The instant memory of his naked body atop hers as they made love caused her knees to weaken, and she sat next to her grandparents.

"Lord Branley was also keeping his ears and eyes open. When things became a little heated," Serena added, choosing her words carefully, "he helped me get away from the Imperial Guards and onto a boat returning to England. Grand-père arranged it, just as you requested."

"That's why you came without your things," her mother guessed.

Serena nodded. She had told them there hadn't been room on the ship for her trunks, which wasn't a lie.

"I thought Lord Branley was coming with me." She didn't mean to trail off with a sad tone, but that was exactly what happened.

Everyone fell silent, and her father's expression became suspicious. She knew he was about to ask her more questions about Malcolm, and quickly she recalled her grandparents' words.

"You said Lord Branley helped you as well. Were you in danger?"

Her grand-mère exchanged a glance with her husband.

"Best to let the dust settle after this type of thing," she said, referring to the entire magnitude of exchanging a king for an emperor and back again, all in one hundred days. Her grand-père gave a typically gallic shrug of agreement.

Then instead of speaking about any personal threat, Pépère leaned back and crossed his arms. "While we are here, Jacques and Michel will look after things in Paris, and the staff at the vineyard shall continue on as usual."

"And Madame Lucie sends her love," her grand-mère added, as if they'd merely come away from home on an ordinary visit. "We brought your trunks, Serena."

She startled, remembering how she'd last seen them behind a tree on the road to Saint-Malo.

"How is that possible?" She didn't want to say more, since her parents had been shocked enough for one day.

Her grand-mère smiled. "Monsieur Branley brought us your trunks in our old harvest wagon, all the way to Paris."

Serena shook her head. How thoughtful of him—*and how dangerous!* He must have had to steal the wagon so as not to explain to the Imperial soldiers about her disappearance.

"We're so happy you're here," Hélène said to her parents. "Aren't we, Edward?"

Serena eyed her father, who was forced to agree or risk sleeping in one of the guest rooms.

"Of course," he said. "How long will you stay?"

Oh, dear! Serena hid her smile behind her hand. That sounded less than inviting. Her mother must have thought the very same thing, for she leaned forward toward her parents.

"What my husband means is you may stay as long as you like, and he only wants to know so he can order enough wine for our cellars."

"And that brandy you mentioned," her grand-père said with a twinkle in his eye "*French* brandy I hope, because the English can't make any worth drinking."

"Agreed," Serena's father said, sounding resigned. Perhaps he realized he might as well accept his in-laws and make the most of having a deliriously happy wife.

Later, in private, Serena cornered her grand-mère in the upstairs salon.

"Lord Branley brought you all the way to England, Mémère, and then what?"

Those piercing green eyes, the mirror of her own, saw the truth.

"He left us in Portsmouth with a carriage, mounted a fast horse, and said he had to fulfill his duty by going directly to London."

That was clearly the responsible thing for him to have done. *And yet, would it have been so terrible for him to come see her first?*

Serena twisted her hands in her skirt. He had made a promise in those last moments together to see her again as soon as he was able. It seemed to her he'd been perfectly able and yet had chosen not to.

"I'm sorry, my dear," her grand-mère said.

"Oh, no. Do not be sorry. I'm thrilled you are here safe with us and that he, too, has returned safely to England. What more could I ask for?"

"Perhaps you were expecting him to behave as your father did with your mother?"

Serena startled, at first thinking her grand-mère meant the amorous congress in which she'd willingly engaged with Malcolm. *More than once!* Such behavior might have got her parents into trouble, except her father had done the honorable thing. And that was what Mémère obviously referred to—Malcolm asking for her hand and making an honest woman of her.

Yet he was a rake! He'd admitted it. Moreover, upon returning home, with uncommon leisure time compared to her life in Paris, Serena had perused the old newspapers her parents received thrice weekly from London. Sure enough, in the dusty pile, from the months prior to Malcolm being sent to Paris, his name was linked with many young ladies of the *bon ton*, sometimes not very kindly either.

"Did he mention me?" she ventured to ask.

Her grand-mère smiled. "Of course he did. Monsieur Branley wished me to tell you he hopes you are well."

"That's all?" Tears pricked Serena's eyes. *What had she expected? A message of undying love!*

"No, he also told me something I didn't understand, but he said you would. Monsieur Branley said you must remember what he told you in the flower room."

Serena blinked. *The flower room?* Maybe her grand-mère had not heard the words correctly. Or more likely, Malcolm hadn't said them properly.

"Thank you," she said, hugging the older lady. "Despite Father's gruffness, we are all pleased you're here."

To her surprise, Mémère laughed. "Oh, we don't take any notice of Edward's behavior. We were very hard on him when we first met him, despite the love dancing in your mother's eyes. We thought he couldn't possibly be a real titled English aristocrat, nor that he would actually act honorably toward your mother. It still sticks in your grand-père's throat the way your father took what he wanted and damn the consequences. Yet Edward intended to marry your mother all along."

Then she shrugged. "Unfortunately, your father thinks we disapprove simply because he's English, a *rosbif,* as we say."

Serena couldn't help chuckling at how her very French grand-mere used "roast beef" as an insult.

"But that's silly, of course," Mémère added. "We love *certain* English people." She wrapped her arms around Serena.

MALCOLM FELT AS THOUGH he were moving through treacle. Once back upon British soil, he'd had to cool his heels for a week, waiting to speak with the Prince Regent. His Royal Highness was feeling poorly, probably due to an excess of food and drink.

During the time Malcolm had waited with ever-growing impatience, Randall had also returned, and thus, when Prinny was up to the task of a visit from his special servants, they would see him together.

"I don't understand why you need me here at all," Malcolm groused as he paced the antechamber at Carlton House, while three valets put the regent together in the next room.

"Because you were invaluable as always. What's more, if you intend to stop this line of lark, although I can't for the life of me figure out why you'd want to stop, then you need to tell our regent yourself."

"You could tell him for me," Malcolm suggested, eyeing the door to freedom. "You could say I was incompetent and get me out of the service even more quickly."

Randall laughed. "That wouldn't do at all. With the information from those maps, you really did come through, you know. Take credit. Bow out if you must, but go out on top, and for God's sake, man, get some favors out of the bugger."

"Favors?" Malcolm frowned, as the double doors finally opened to the Prince Regent's bedchamber in which His Royal Highness liked to conduct business.

"Such as a special license to marry. I'm sure Prinny would put in a good word with the archbishop. Otherwise, you'll have to keep that pretty Parisian miss waiting another three weeks."

They took a few steps in. "She's English, I keep telling you, not Parisian," Malcolm reminded Randall.

"Who?" asked Prinny, coming into view. "Tell me all about her, I command it!"

CHAPTER TWENTY-SIX

Malcolm urged his coachman to greater speed, then realized the childishness of it. It had been over two months since he'd laid eyes upon Serena. He could wait another couple of hours.

"Like hell!" Rapping his cane on the coach roof, he was satisfied when it drew to a halt.

Putting the furry fiend, as he'd come to think of his traveling companion, onto the seat beside him, he lowered the window.

"Unhitch one of the horses, Malty. I intend to ride the rest of the way."

"Yes, my lord."

In a few minutes, having ruined the symmetry of his coachman's team, much to the man's annoyance, Malcolm had a saddled horse beneath him and a wriggling furry pup perched in a saddle bag between his legs. He'd fully intended to leave the ridiculous, sentimental, soppy gift behind in the safe interior of his coach, but the fiend put up such a howling fuss as soon as Malcolm closed the door on it, he'd had no choice but to bring it along.

Besides, he had the nasty suspicion the pup would take vengeance upon him by way of soiling his traveling coach and probably chewing the squabs until it was all a disgusting, tattered mess.

They would make good time, and he would be seeing Serena in an hour. Even if his horse went lame, he would run the rest of the way with the fiend under his arm, should the need occur.

⁓

"ANOTHER GUEST, MY LORD," Mr. Tewles informed Lord Elmstead late in the afternoon, the butler's tone one of extreme imposition.

Serena grinned at the way the man said it, as if her grandparents were not merely two but an entire party of twelve who'd been behaving raucously over the past two weeks. True, her grand-père had commandeered the wine cellar, going so far as to suggest tossing out some vintages he considered inferior.

"Les déchets," he deemed an entire wrack, and Serena had translated for him.

"Those are *swill*, Father."

"Swill!" exclaimed Lord Elmstead.

"Swill?" echoed the butler, who had a hand in keeping the very best wines in stock.

"Oui," said her grand-père.

They were not thrown out, however, simply put aside.

And then her grand-mère had tossed down her napkin one day after dinner and declared, *"Nous mangeons comme des bébés."*

"Father," Serena told him, unable to contain her smile, "Mémère says we are eating like—"

"Babies, yes, I understand. Your grandmother finds our food to be too bland."

After that, Mémère took over the dinner menu, demonstrating to their cook how to make renowned Chef

Carême's famous sauces—*espagnole, velouté,* and *béchamel,* each beloved in France.

"Too much of these rich sauces," Serena's father complained, "and I shall start bursting my waistcoat buttons."

Thus, it was somewhat understandable when the butler appeared in the doorway of the upstairs salon late one afternoon, using a tone of exasperation with his announcement.

"Another guest?" her mother repeated, looking up from her needlepoint.

Serena's father and grand-père had made peace over many glasses of brandy and were now playing an excruciatingly slow game of chess. They both paused.

"Yes, my lady," Mr. Tewles said. "Lord Branley is downstairs. Shall I bring him up?"

Serena heard her mother make some reply, but she was already on her feet and flying from the room. Down the main stairs, she raced, not caring how unseemly it was, but she paused when Malcolm wasn't in the large foyer. The drawing room door was ajar, and she ran in, hearing a bark as she crossed the threshold.

"Close the door," were his first words to her, "or I can't put this pain in the arse down."

Doing as Malcolm said, hardly sparing a glance for the brown and white squirming bundle in his arms, she launched herself at him. He released the pup and wrapped her in his arms before claiming her lips under his.

Without another word, she slid her hands up until she could clasp them in his soft hair. As his firm lips moved over hers, she kept repeating to herself, "He's here. He's here. He's here."

After a moment, Malcolm drew back, looking down at her with those rich brown eyes that melted her heart and touched her soul.

"Are you saying something?"

She thought she'd been speaking entirely in her head. In any case, she ignored the question, and Malcolm resumed his breath-taking kiss. In the next instant, she felt his fingers mimic hers, raking into her hair and tilting her head just so.

When their mouths were perfectly melded, his tongue touched her lips and she parted them. As he started the sweet plunder, she sagged against his chest. She was finally in his arms, at last touching him again, and she didn't want to ever let him go!

The warmth of their passion rushed through her, particularly—*oddly!*—across her feet. Until she realized, her feet were actually becoming wet.

Snapping open her eyes, she reared back a step and looked down to where the dog had peed upon her favorite green slippers. At the same time, the drawing room door opened and her entire family came streaming in.

"What in blue blazes?" demanded her father, and Serena was infinitely glad for the pup's terrible manners, which had prevented her father seeing her mouth fused to Malcolm's.

"Father, Mother, this is Lord Branley."

The pup barked.

"And his dog," she added.

"Actually, he's *your* dog," Malcolm corrected. "A gift. It's a boy."

Serena nearly squealed because she knew what it meant.

"You brought me a dog," she said, her voice betraying her excitement. "So permanent! A dog ties a man down."

"Indeed," Malcolm agreed. "It means a man must stay put."

They grinned at each other, each recalling their conversation that seemed to have taken place ages ago in a carriage ride across Paris.

"It has peed all over the Persian rug," her father declared.

"It's adorable," her mother said, scooping the pup into her arms. "Besides, it's just a baby. Serena shall train him. So good to meet you at last, Lord Branley."

"And you as well, Lady Elmstead. I can see where your daughter gets her beauty."

"You did not just say that," Serena's father fumed, crossing his arms.

"Why, yes, Lord Elmstead," Malcolm said, sounding perfectly respectful. "It's an honor to meet you, sir. And why wouldn't I say that? It is patently true."

"Because he said the very same to *my* parents," Serena's mother said, before giving a girlish giggle. The dog in her arms barked again. "You are off to a good start, sir."

After Malcolm greeted her grandparents, Serena watched him tug on his cravat, suddenly appearing serious.

"May I have a word alone with your daughter?" he asked. "And then a private meeting with you, Lord Elmstead?"

Feeling a bubble of happiness, Serena shook her head. "It's not necessary for us to meet privately. My answer is yes. Absolutely."

Malcolm frowned. "You are supposed to let me ask."

"The point of asking is to know my thoughts ahead of asking my father. Now, you know my thoughts and can go straight to the business end of it."

Serena stroked the dog's head where it wriggled in her mother's arms. He was a beautiful pup, with floppy ears, the softest fuzzy baby fur that promised to become silken, and an adorable tail that curled slightly. And all over he was white and brown and even black. His best feature, she decided, when she held his muzzle still so she could really look at his face, were his dark brown eyes with the blackest outline around each, like a Parisian courtesan!

"Let's leave the gentlemen to it, shall we?" Hélène said.

"And Pépère must stay, too, of course," Serena added.

With that, she took her dog from her mother before sending Malcolm another glance. *He's here! He's here!* she sang silently. Then she followed her mother and Mémère, letting the butler close the door upon the three men. If her brothers hadn't already returned to their respective schools, she had no doubt they would be in the drawing room, too.

"I must go change my slippers," she said, despite feeling as if she could float up the stairs on wings of joy.

The other women trailed behind.

"Regarding Lord Branley," her mother said, "I think you have a little tale to tell us, yes?"

AS IT TURNED OUT the men got along very well, having spent as much time discussing Wellington's victory as Serena's nuptial agreement.

"All of a kind," her mother declared Lord Branley, her father, and her husband after dinner. Leaving the men to smoke cigars, the ladies retired to the drawing room for aged ratafia of the finest brandy. Naturally, the pup, who alternated between bursts of running around and long periods of exhausted sleep, went with them.

Since they'd already had a decadently rich flummery with almonds and raspberries at the table, they now settled for a plate of butter biscuits, which Serena found very compatible when dipped in her ratafia.

"Stop that," her mother ordered. "What manners!"

"Try it," Serena said. "Both of you."

The sugary baked treats melted on her tongue with a burst of the cherry-infused brandy. The other ladies rolled their eyes but tried it, soon declaring the combination delicious.

Everything was going smoothly at last. Serena's marriage contract had been worked out in a very short time, with a generous dowry bestowed upon her. It would be doled out as an allowance, since Malcolm said he didn't need it for their household.

"We are three fortunate women," her grand-mère said, "despite how the two of you counted on your hearts winning over rakes who could as easily have left you stranded."

Serena and her mother stared at one another, then smiled. *How wonderful to have beaten the odds!*

"How did you meet Pépère?" she asked Adèle.

"The old-fashioned way. My parents made an arrangement with Henri's parents."

The notion of a forced engagement seemed terrifying, but Serena knew it had been commonplace.

"Of course, we met secretly to make sure we were suitable," Mémère added off-handedly. "Otherwise, by mutual agreement, one of us would have done something to cause the wedding's cancellation."

Serena's mother burst out laughing. Then she asked, "Such as what exactly?"

Adèle shrugged, blushing a little. "He would have been found publicly in the embrace of someone else. Or I would," she said with a mischievous gleam in her eye. "As the fates would have it, we liked each other on sight, and his embrace interested me more than any other."

Serena admired her grandparents' plan of escape had they not suited one another.

The door opened, and the men strolled in, each taking a seat beside the woman he loved.

"That was the quickest cigar you have ever smoked," Hélène said to her husband.

"It's Branley's fault," Serena's father declared. "He couldn't wait to rejoin the company of our daughter."

"How sweet." This from her grand-mère, who continued to dunk her biscuits, receiving amused glances from Pépère until she stuck one in his mouth.

"I hope never to be out of her company for very long," Malcolm said. "No more trips to France or Belgium or Russia for me."

Her grand-père coughed.

"Not that there's anything wrong with France," Malcolm hurriedly added. "I meant no more *assignments* to the Continent. Most assuredly, we'll visit. Yearly, if it suits you. Or more often whenever possible."

Serena put her hand over his to shut him up before he agreed they should move back to Paris permanently.

"Any regrets about giving your resignation to the Crown?" her father asked his future son-in-law.

"None whatsoever." Malcolm glanced fondly at Serena, then he spoiled the romantic moment by adding, "Better to be henpecked by a wife than shot at by a soldier."

Luckily, the notion of bossing him around amused her enough not to be insulted, but the other men laughed a little too hard.

"Actually, I do have a regret, come to think of it."

Malcolm's words surprised her, and she leaned forward. The anticipation from herself and her loved ones was palpable. *What could this successful man with a distinguished career, a fortune, an upcoming title, and now a fiancée possibly regret?*

"In my years of service, I never managed to meet the renowned Fox. Some think maybe he doesn't really exist but rather is a composite of more than one Parisian *intelligencier*, a group of spies in one. Regardless, I would like to have known such a character, if he existed."

First Serena's mother, then her father, and then her grand-père began to laugh.

"Why is that so funny?" Malcolm demanded.

Serena glanced at the other members of her family, until Mémère nodded.

"You did meet the Fox, as you call the famous spy," Serena said. "I promise you."

Malcolm cocked his head, and then he looked around the room. She could see it was dawning on him, and yet when he turned to her, he asked, "You?"

The room exploded in laughter again.

"Well, her hair *is* red like a fox," Malcolm explained, his face flushing to match at his ridiculous guess. "But I know she is too young. Still, she was so helpful in Paris, I just thought for a minute . . . ," he trailed off.

Now Serena's cheeks heated as well, not from embarrassment but from happiness at her fiancé's compliment.

Then he looked around. "Lady Elmstead would have been too young as well when she left France."

"And she has always been on the fairer side of blonde," said Edward, looking adoringly at his wife.

Malcolm looked at her grandparents. "Of course! The Fox, *le Renard*—and you are Monsieur Renault."

"I am," agreed Pépère, "but I am *not* the Fox."

"Then—?" Malcolm broke off and stared at Adèle Renault.

After a gracious nod of her head, Serena's grand-mère said, "In this case, monsieur, it is *la Renarde*."

"My wife was just as red as her granddaughter," said Henri. "Before she blossomed into this lovely, silver-headed queen. But she is still our famed *Renarde*."

"I am truly honored to be told the family secret," Malcolm said.

"You *are* family now," Serena's mother declared.

"Almost," her grand-père said. "If you don't fulfill the marriage contract, we will hunt you down and slay you. If you ever give away the identity of my wife, I will slay you myself, and it won't be pleasant."

Malcolm coughed. "You mean there are pleasant ways to slay someone."

Henri Renault said nothing until he sipped his wife's ratafia and made a face at its sweetness.

"You would be surprised, Monsieur Branley," he said. "You would be surprised."

MALCOLM WAS, IN FACT surprised by everything that evening, by eating quintessential French cuisine in the utterly British household and especially by being allowed to spend time alone with his fiancée, out on the back terrace, overlooking Lady Elmstead's lovely rose gardens.

"Naturally, they trust you," Serena said, leaning against the stone railing, her new pup at her side. "Or at least they trust you're smart enough not to risk their wrath."

"Especially not the Fox's. Why didn't you tell me I was running all over Paris and the Loire Valley with the Fox's granddaughter?"

"You didn't ask," she teased.

"I can't believe I'm here at last," he told her.

"I wasn't sure you would come," she confessed.

Malcolm drew back, staring at her with consternation.

"I promised you I would."

"I know, but I thought maybe you'd said that merely to get me onto the boat."

"Yes, perhaps," he agreed, "but only because I had no way of knowing I would make it back from France. When I did, I gave your grandmother the message to remind you of my love."

Serena shook her head. "Mémère said only something about remembering a flower room."

He grinned, feeling so light and happy, and entirely sure of his future. "I told her to remind you of what I'd said in our room at the Defleur's house."

"*Oh!* Not the *salle des fleurs.*" Then she grinned. "I love you, too, but when we visit France again, why don't you pretend to be the mute baker."

Laughing hard, Malcolm drew her close. Although two generations of her family were indoors, mere yards away, he decided to take the risk.

Holding her face in his hands, breathing in the familiar floral scent of her skin, he slowly pressed his mouth to her.

After many minutes, he lifted his head. "I can't believe anyone would object to that," he said, before brushing his lips across the soft skin of her neck. "Not even the Fox."

Then he kissed her again, and this time, he slid his tongue into her mouth. He felt her shiver in his arms, and his own body answered with a surge of heat to his loins.

Would she make him wait until their wedding night? If he could figure out a way to get her alone, he would gladly risk her family's wrath, as she'd put it.

When he drew back a second time, she smiled up at him. "They might object to that," she said.

"That last kiss? Because we stroked our tongues?"

"No, I meant your improperly wicked thoughts. That wouldn't be at all acceptable." She sighed, and he held her more tightly, letting his hands roam down to squeeze her round bottom. She gasped.

"How do you know what I was thinking?" he asked, squeezing her soft flesh again.

"I can feel it," she told him, tilting her hips forward. "And I am every bit as aroused."

He groaned. "How will we manage the long wait?"

"I am the granddaughter of the Fox," she said. "Our rooms are on the same floor."

"And I can pick a lock, my lady," he offered.

"You wouldn't have to, my lord. I sleep with the door unlocked," she said, then added, "and my pistol under my pillow."

"*Hm,* I think you can dispense with that custom. At least for tonight."

"And when we're married?" She stood on tiptoe and, after tugging on his cravat to bring him closer, returned the kiss to his neck.

"When we're married, I shall protect you, but I'll also lock our bedroom door."

"I will probably still keep my weapon," she said, then touched her tongue to his skin, making him shiver.

"Then I will remember your prowess with the pistol and behave in such a perfect husbandly fashion you shall never think of drawing it upon me."

"Fair enough. Yet tonight, I shall come to your room. I know which boards creek and what time my father retires. Also, if we're discovered, he probably won't challenge you to a duel if I confess how I stole into your chamber, unable to help myself."

"Good thinking," he agreed, already counting the minutes until she arrived in his bedchamber despite having hours to go before they retired. "And are you?"

"Am I?" she questioned, then pressed her lips to his.

He nibbled on her lower lip for a few moments before he looked her in the eyes.

"Are you unable to help yourself? For I swear, I am entirely under your spell. I love you, Serena, and I shall attempt to make you happy for the rest of my days."

In answer, she drew his head down to hers, ready to kiss him soundly once again, when she felt a wet warmth across her feet.

EPILOGUE

1815, Berkshire, England

Rémy, as Serena had named her dog, still ran around her legs but no longer relieved himself on her feet, which was a great improvement in his manners. In fact, he had been thoroughly house-trained in the three weeks they'd stayed with her parents while the banns were read on successive Sundays before their wedding. He was now a very good boy.

Serena had wanted to name him James, but when Malcolm found out she loved the name, he suggested she save it for their first son, and thus she chose the place where they'd first consummated their love.

Her new husband seemed entirely pleased to be a wedded man, and in the two weeks since their marriage, he showed utter contentment at being settled down and becoming a *former* rake. In his own way, he'd also become house-trained, and she considered him to be a very good boy, too.

Currently, Malcolm was outside making sure everything was ready for their upcoming trip to London. He was determined to introduce her properly to Mayfair society, and to show her off at the Covent Garden Theatre and

Astley's Amphitheatre. And of course, he would stroll with her through Vauxhall, showing her off as Lady Branley, and the next Viscountess St. John.

"We'll make sure you don't have any twigs in your hair," he'd said when she'd told him the tale of her previous disgrace. "On second thought, I can't promise I won't press you against a tree for a kiss, but no one shall say a word since we're married."

She laughed. They laughed a lot, which she adored. And Rémy's antics made them laugh even harder. After their wedding day, they'd traveled from her parents' home in Wiltshire to his parents' country seat in Berkshire so she could spend time with her new mother and father-in-law, as well as Malcolm's siblings, all of whom had come to the wedding. His sister who'd welcomed Serena warmly, asked a hundred questions a minute about Paris.

Finally, Serena had promised to take the girl over someday soon, causing Malcolm's eyebrows to raise.

"When everything has calmed down," she assured him. "It will be a joyful visit. We can go back to all the places we visited together."

"Except the catacombs," he teased.

"Exactly," she agreed.

"Did I tell you the Prussians looted the Louvre before order was restored?" he asked.

She shook her head, recalling how wonderful that day had been before the soldiers took her away. "You are more magnificent than Apollo Belvedere," she vowed, enjoying the way her husband blushed. One day, they would walk the Louvre again.

Yet today, they were off to London, considered the greatest city in the world, although Serena would always hold Paris most dear in her heart as the place they'd met and fallen in love. *Poor Napoleon.* She couldn't help feeling sorry for the emperor. How he would miss his city now that he was exiled again, this time to the island of Saint Helena. She hoped they made madeleines for him.

"Are you ready?" Malcolm asked.

She had on her traveling clothes, her trunks were packed, her lady's maid was packed but not in a trunk, and she'd hugged her new extended family goodbye. Even Rémy had just done his doggy duty upon demand after a quick walk in Lady St. John's garden.

"I'm ready," she said, linking her arm through his as they wandered out toward their spacious four-horse carriage. "I must confess, it's a nice change to be traveling with you while not running from someone."

Rémy suddenly came barking up from behind with a stick in his mouth.

"I guess he's bringing something of his own," Serena mused, bending down to pick him up, although he was now a good nineteen pounds or so. "What is this?" she exclaimed.

"What is it?" Malcolm asked, taking the dog from her. In truth, they actually shared Rémy like a beloved infant, taking turns holding and brushing him, and almost always fighting over whose lap he would stretch across in the evenings.

Serena tugged at the familiar piece of wood in the dog's mouth. He resisted.

"It's my busk," she said in amazement. "How on earth is that possible?" She'd removed it in Saint-Malo to have room for the letter down the front of her stays. She kept tugging, but Remy refused to give it up.

Malcolm was laughing. "Reach in my pocket. Cook gave me suet biscuits she baked for him. I swear, he's going to be the most spoiled dog in England. I'm sure he'll trade you one for your busk."

Her husband was correct. In a moment, Serena was staring at the straight dowel of wood her mother had once given her, now with a few tooth marks but otherwise none the worse for wear.

"But how did he get it?" She stared at Malcolm.

"I'd entirely forgotten about it," he confessed. "After you left with that grumpy captain, I was going to try simply to get my horse away from the guards. But then, knowing I was going to ask for your hand, I wanted to do better and retrieve your trunks, which meant I needed the wagon."

"That was very kind of you," she said, "yet also dangerous. Perhaps idiotic, in fact." At seeing his crestfallen face, she added, "But I am most grateful. You know that. I've thanked you in a dozen ways, haven't I?" They smiled at one another. "In fact," she continued, "you are the best husband in the world, and I was thrilled to have my things back. Go on with your story."

"I wouldn't shoot those men in cold blood, although they didn't know that. I snuck up behind them when they were standing close, sharing the same flask. I stuck your busk in the back of one and my pistol in the back of the other, and told them not to turn around because *we* had guns trained on both of them. They thought they could each feel a barrel in the back. I made them get on their knees and said if they let us take the wagon, we wouldn't shoot them."

"That was well done of you," she said, "but how did Rémy get my busk?"

"I just told that story to dazzle you with my skills, wife, and all you care about is the dog."

Turning, he placed, Rémy on the floor of the carriage where he could chew more easily on his suet treat.

"With my heart racing like thundering horses," Malcolm continued, "I jumped into the wagon and went back for your trunks, and truthfully, I forgot all about your busk in the pocket of my overcoat."

She blinked. "And so?" she prompted.

He looked down, and Serena followed his gaze. Sliding his hand into the pocket, he held it up to show her how it was entirely chewed open with his fingers poking through the lining.

"I guess Rémy's not so well-behaved as I thought," Serena said.

They laughed. Then he held out his other hand and assisted her up the small iron steps into the carriage.

When Malcolm's hand brushed her bottom as he released her and then stroked her ankle before she took her seat, she realized he wasn't so well-behaved either. It was going to be a pleasurable journey to London with her incorrigible rake of a husband.

Finis

ABOUT THE AUTHOR

USA Today bestselling author Sydney Jane Baily writes historical romance set in Victorian England, late 19th-century America, the Middle Ages, the Georgian era, and the Regency period. She believes in happily-ever-after stories with engaging characters and attention to period detail.

Born and raised in California, she has traveled the world, spending a lot of exceedingly happy time in the U.K. where her extended family resides, eating fish and chips, drinking shandies, and snacking on Maltesers and Cadbury bars. Sydney currently lives in New England with her family—human, canine, and feline.

You can learn more about her books, read her blog, sign up for her newsletter (and get a free book), and contact her via her website at SydneyJaneBaily.com. She loves to hear from her readers.